THE KILLING
AT NGO THO

GENE D. MOORE

PYRAMID BOOKS NEW YORK

THE KILLING AT NGO THO

A PYRAMID BOOK
Published by arrangement with W. W. Norton & Company, Inc.

W. W. Norton edition published May, 1967
Pyramid edition published May, 1968

Library of Congress Catalog Card Number: 67-12445

PYRAMID BOOKS are published by Pyramid Publications, Inc.,
444 Madison Avenue, New York, New York 10022, U.S.A.

TO HARRY SCURR,
WHO MADE THIS BOOK POSSIBLE

1

HE WAS ALONE, and he was lost for damn sure, and the patrol had somehow moved away and out of contact. The thought of calling to Major Phan-Tien Huc was idiotic, and with his immediate and automatic rejection of anything that would give away their position, came anxiety verging on panic.

Somewhere in the distance he could hear firing, and his panic increased—some son of a bitch had countermanded his absolute edict against any aircraft, chopper, fixed wing, VIP transport, or anything at all, over the objective area for any goddam purpose whatsoever for seven full days. One hundred and sixty-eight hours without fail, and stated to every pilot in the 128th Aviation Company in support of the province, in terms that could not be misunderstood, the day before he and the patrol had quietly slipped into the jungle.

If he ever got out of this someone's hide would be on the wall, because sure as hell that firing could only be an anti-aircraft weapon of some type, although it was damned strange that it was so hard to identify. The rhythm was like nothing he had heard before—smooth, then faltering, then with a different interval between rounds. Then, faintly, he could hear a voice, surely not a Vietnamese, calling his name.

He came awake, vaguely fumbling his way upward from

the depths. Disoriented for the moment, he gazed without recognition around the clean and well-furnished room, noting with amazement the softness of the bed, the crisp and clean sheets. This was wrong, wrong, wrong, he lived in an unscreened thatched hut with Minh and Huc, and he slept in a hammock he had made out of closely spaced cross sections of bamboo, laced together with commo wire.

The voice came again. "Scott, you bastard, open the door before we break it in." Only his brother Boyd Leonard, Brigadier General Boyd Leonard, Chief of Staff, Ryukus Command, had that hoarse, penetrating voice.

In a single movement he was out of the bed, through the door of the bedroom, snatching a crumpled towel to wrap around his waist, and at the door. He hesitated one short moment before releasing the bolt. This was going to be one hell of a hard thing to explain to his older brother; and he wondered how in the devil anyone knew of his arrival here in Okinawa late last night.

Boyd came through the door as if he were charging the Navy line, leaving time for only a glimpse of a group waiting behind him, including at least two Oki houseboys bearing breakfast trays, before clamping a roughly tender headlock on him.

"How come you sneak in here without letting me know, boy? How come?" he growled, giving one last twist before releasing him and holding him at arm's length. "And what the devil are you doing here at all? I thought you were the U.S. Army's answer to all problems in Viet Nam, and that the fate of the nation hung on your every word."

Keen gray eyes, eyes from which Scott had never been able to conceal the slightest transgression, were searching his face, and he could see Boyd's joy of reunion fade into concern. Scott knew he must look like death warmed over—God knew he felt like it, now that the first excitement of awakening to Boyd's voice was fading. The sawgrass cuts and scratches on his face and arms and hands, and the leech bites overlaying them, some healing, some infected, and all painted with both iodine and merthiolate in Kei's most thorough manner, must look shocking against his yellowed coloring, and the bandage she had fashioned to cover the long shallow cut along his left ribs was far larger and bulkier than was required. Forestalling the questions that he could see coming in rapid fire order, he said, "Boyd, you're the most welcome sight I've seen for a long, long time. I didn't call you last night because it was so damned late and

I figured an older man like you really needed his rest. I thought I could wait until this morning to surprise you, which leads to how in hell you managed to find out that I was even on your crummy little island?"

"I get a list each morning of who is scheduled to come, who came, and who is leaving or has left during the past twenty-four hours. I need it—we have so damned many carpetbaggers coming through here. This morning there you were, as having arrived courtesy of some unscheduled TAC aircraft last night. . . . Look behind you."

Still clutching his towel Scott turned to the group standing just outside the doorway.

"Hello, little brother-in-law—part-time, that is. It's been a long, long, time, almost five years," said Allan Patterson, stocky, dark, and with his family handsomeness and compact grace of movement. His handshake was firm and warm and true friendship was in his eyes. As he saw the questioning look in Scott's eyes, he continued, "Yes, I know all about it, or at least as much as my beautiful young sister cared to tell me. The way I figure is that your troubles with my darling sister Cindy are your troubles, not mine. You married her, not me, and we were friends long before you came to be a relative. I hope you'll be a friend long after, if it comes to that."

This is all coming damned fast, thought Scott. Two nights ago, or a lifetime ago—it all seemed so remote now, he and Major Huc and Minh and the rest of Trink's task force had been on their stealthy approach through the swamp—and now here was Boyd, whom he had hoped to evade, and Allan whom he had never expected to see.

"Thanks, Allan," he stammered, wanting to say so much—how he valued the friendship offered, and how he had dreaded meeting with AP news' most celebrated correspondent these last few years. In his awkwardness he was grateful for Boyd's interruption.

"Allan came in a couple of days ago. Getting the background on our support mission before diving into Saigon and fanning out in all directions for one of his coverages in depth of the whole screwed-up mess, bringing clarity out of confusion for the benefit of the great American public." There was the slightest edge of sarcasm in his voice. Or maybe it was envy, there had always been a strange mixture of respect and contempt in Boyd's attitude toward Allan. The respect of one good mind for another, coupled with the impatience of a man of direct, decisive action for the bystander. "Maybe you can take him back with you when you leave, and keep him on the straight and narrow."

Back my ass, thought Scott. I'm a soldier out of a job for sure, and I may be a soldier headed for a court-martial, just as the grinding, cramping, tearing vice of his bowels tore him asunder.

"Goddam," he gritted, "be with you in a minute," and barely made it to the bathroom. Straining, convulsing, in a spasmodic liquid flow, he emptied himself, vaguely appreciative of the clean tile-lined bathroom. Again and again the spasm gripped him, until weak and spent, he arose, flushed the reddish, stinking mess behind him, and stepped into the shower.

The water hit him in a lukewarm flood, soothing if not invigorating, and he began to regain his awareness. It's goddam hard to think of anything else in the world when that hits you, he thought. Not sex, not duty, not anything, except maybe the fear of getting your frigging ass shot off. Remembering how he had squatted, Vietnamese style, with his pants around his ankles and carefully pulled from the line of fire during the movement inland from the river, and thinking of how even after he had taken such precautions he had ended up hours later, after the killing, with both pants legs full of the frothy, bloody mess, and not knowing or remembering when or where it happened. He scrubbed his entire body. Slowly, carefully, ruthlessly ripping the scabs of each laceration to let in the cleansing lather.

The long cut running laterally along his ribs looked fairly good after he had removed the bandage, and was without the angry redness of all the other of his wounds. Kei would have been proud, he thought tenderly. She had tried so hard—it was a shame that she had no real training except what little the special forces sergeants had been able to give her. Maybe someday he could help her—and with this thought came the full realization of how little he could help anyone now. After the good General Simon Wesley had finished with him there would be nothing left except the bitter formality of the submission of his application for retirement.

"Scott, are you okay?" Boyd's voice came over the roar of the shower.

"Fine, I'll be right out," he answered, reluctantly cutting off the shower and stepping out onto the tile. As he gingerly patted himself dry, he tried to face the problem of Boyd.

Last night he had had it all planned; stay holed up here until near sailing time, get aboard early, go to the cabin and stay out of sight until after sailing, and under no circumstances get Boyd involved. It had all seemed so simple. Of course, he couldn't have anticipated Boyd's routine check of all arrivals and departures, although he might have known the thorough bastard would set up something like that. If anyone ever got on top of a job and rode it, it was Boyd. He always knew everything that went on in his own back yard.

He wondered what time it was, and how many hours were left before sailing, and whether he could fend off Boyd's questions long enough—but even as he thought of this he realized how futile such an attempt would be. Boyd would have the whole story out of him, no matter what fine resolutions he might make. He might just as well face up to it and give the whole thing from the beginning, in proper sequence. Allan was a different problem. Allan didn't exactly pry, really didn't ask many questions. He got more by a properly timed skeptical look, a noncommittal grunt, or a frank statement of disbelief, than anyone else with a barrage of cross-examination. Boyd and Scott had both watched him work over some generals in times past, those who thought they were real tigers, and had seen how Allan reduced their generalizations and semi-evasions to the bare bones of the true situation. A keen mind lay in waiting behind his quiet manner. One thing could be relied upon with Allan, though—if he gave his word on a matter, no story would ever be written nor would there be the slightest leak to any other correspondent. Also, never had Allan written anything, good or bad, in praise or censure, concerning either a close friend or a relative.

Dry now, and peering into the fogged mirror, Scott carefully looked at himself for the first time in days. His thick, once jet-black hair, now liberally flecked with gray throughout and almost solid gray at the temples, was cropped so short as to form a skull cap, and looked no different than it had for years, except that here and there lumps caused by the swelling of insect bites, leeches, cuts, and bruises gave him an odd lack of symmetry. His face, with its heavy black brows, finely molded nose, wide and sensitive mouth, and firm jaw, also reflected hard usage. Cuts, bites, and abrasions, some infected, some healed or healing gave him a look, he thought, of some senile teen-ager with jack bumps. "You're a mighty poor-looking specimen, and to hell with it," he half muttered as he opened the

2

BOYD WAS SEATED on the rumpled bed, distastefully surveying the mass of rumpled clothes that had been jammed into the duffle bag.

"For Christ's sake, is this all you've got with you?" he growled, poking at the pile and coming up with a wrinkled pair of shorts that seemed to be fairly clean. "And who in hell taught you how to pack a duffle bag? I've seen raw-assed recruits do better than this."

"That's all there is. I didn't have time to pick up the footlockers I've got in Saigon. And for your information, you nit-picking old woman, I didn't pack that bag," said Scott, taking the shorts and gingerly slipping them on. "I had some high-priced help."

"What's that mean?" asked Boyd quickly. "There's something mighty goddam funny going on, and I think about half of it is the screwy way you're acting. If you're a medic evac, which you damned well should be from the looks of you, why in hell weren't you manifested that way? Don't you think it's about time you said a word or two?"

"Easy, easy, Boydie Boy," Scott dredged up from his memory the affectionate phrase of their mother and almost the tone and lilt of her voice. Ignoring Boyd's unspoken surprise, he jerked open the bedroom door. "Where's all that breakfast I saw carted in here?"

Three plates of ham and eggs, three cups, and a large pot

of coffee were laid out on the low coffee table. Allan sat composed and waiting on the couch. As Scott came through the door, Allan reached for the coffee pot and began pouring. Without raising his eyes, and in a quiet and almost casual tone he asked, "When was the last time a medic checked you over, Scott? At the risk of hurting your tender feelings, you are looking even uglier than usual."

Gingerly sinking to the floor and crossing his legs in gook lotus style, Scott took his first tentative sip of coffee. Slowly and carefully, he thought. He'd be damned if he was going to be sick today. Just be careful and don't present your stomach with any sudden problems in the form of a mass of food. Sneak up on it a little bite at a time.

Boyd, following him into the room and seating himself on Scott's right, directly across from Allan, joined in, "Answer the man, goddam it," he said, "and you might also shed a little light on how you got in such condition in the first place, and as to why in hell you've honored us with such a well-planned visit." Sourly he let his eyes travel from Scott's face, down his chest. and to his folded legs. "Although the answer doesn't really make one hell of a lot of difference." And with a sudden decisive motion he laid his fork down, pushed back his chair, and went to the telephone, dialing with precise but hurried speed.

Scott watched him, speculating, but knowing the symptoms. He was just about to be taken charge of. He just hoped Boyd wouldn't be too disappointed and hard to handle when it came time to leave for his sailing, because leave he was going to, come hell or high water. Sailing on that ship today meant more than just obeying orders. Like some wounded animal, he needed a place to hide, a lair to lie in and lick his wounds, and perhaps when he felt some better, he might write his own report on what had happened. General Wesley was so frigging sure of himself, had accepted the evidence of his own eyes with such eagerness, and had cut short all explanations, so blindly, that it would be a real pleasure to make the old bastard admit that he had gone ape without reason. Just a private admission between the two of them, man to man. He would be quite satisfied with that, Scott thought, as he half listened to Boyd's conversation, and slowly and cautiously took a few more sips of his now cooling coffee.

The conversation was terse and to the point. A medic colonel was informed to get his ass on the way with supplies sufficient to treat everything from multiple abrasions to bubonic plague and, no, the patient could not come to the hospital.

Boyd hung up abruptly, and came back to his chair. Raising his cup, he uttered a single word, an unmistakable command, before drinking. "Talk," he said.

Slowly and carefully Scott began. "Of course I owe you both some explanation. But before I give it I'm going to have your word, Boyd, that you will stay out of it. And I mean completely out in every sense of the word. And you, Allan, are going to treat this as privileged information, forgotten for any purpose whatsoever as soon as you walk out of this room. Agreed?"

"Absolutely," Allan answered quickly, even as Boyd began his protest.

"Goddam it, Scott, I refuse to have my hands tied before I even know what I'm going to hear. There may be something on which I would be compelled to act, and I'll make no stupid agreement which in any way restricts me in doing what I know should be done."

"Crap," said Scott, meeting Boyd's angry and puzzled eyes, "what I tell you now is between the two of us, and you either hear it that way or you hear nothing. And just so you don't waste a hell of a lot of time in bringing yourself around to accepting this, you should know that I'm sailing this afternoon on the *Buckner,* and that nothing is going to stop that. And really, if you won't agree to my terms, you can shove it. If I had any real choice, I'd tell you or anyone else nothing, which is what I've been instructed to do. If you ever find out about this officially, you're free to act within the bounds of your own conscience, but until you do, what I tell you stays inside your rocklike head. Understood?"

Slowly, with reluctance, because Boyd Leonard was not the man to accept terms from anyone on any subject, Boyd's eyes lowered. "Have it your way."

"First I'd like to show you an official document that comes but rarely to a soldier, and thank God for that." Rising, with only a small flinching as the flexing of his muscles twitched small wounds into painful awareness, he went to his battered dispatch case on the corner table and pulled out the papers inside. Separating the many copies, he handed one to Boyd and one to Allan and resumed his seat. He needed no copy for himself. He had watched General Wesley write the indictment and the freshly inked orders were stamped in his memory. Omitting all the letterhead and official gobbledygook, the guts were a model of military writing.

1. Having been relieved as senior military advisor, Ngo Tho Province and IX Corps, Army of the Republic of Viet Nam, for reasons of grossly immoral conduct, occurring on June 10, 1962, Colonel Scott B. Leonard, 0-36820, U.S. Army, will proceed Oakland Army Terminal, Oakland, California, via Okinawa, and utilizing surface, repeat surface, transportation, there to await further assignment orders.

2. Colonel Leonard is directed not to establish contact with friends, relatives, fellow officers, or others during the course of his delay in Okinawa, except such legal counsel as he may see fit and necessary.

"Grossly immoral conduct," shouted Boyd, and repeated, "Grossly immoral conduct? What in hell did you do? Lay some ranking Vietnamese wife, publicly fornicate with a covey of whores, or screw a male Viet Cong. What in hell is gross enough for Simon Wesley to put this in writing and in your orders before he's even had time enough to conduct a proper investigation of whatever the hell you did. By the date of this, your grossly immoral conduct only happened yesterday." Boyd's indignation and voice mounted steadily, until he was almost sputtering as he yelled, "I've never heard of such a goddam thing."

Scott glanced at Allan, who sat quietly with a quizzical smile on his face.

"For Christ's sake, let's not go into orbit, Boyd," Scott said with irritation. "General Wesley thought he really didn't need any investigation, since he was personally on the scene."

"But goddam it," he began, "You're acting like you're accepting this, and that you are . . ."

"Knock it off, Boyd," Scott said curtly, "I'm not acting like anything except a man who has to be on a boat at fifteen hundred hours this afternoon, and who hasn't got a lot of time to waste. If you want to hear what happened, be quiet and listen. The way I read those orders I'm free enough to give you the story since I didn't contact you. You came to me. But for Christ's sake let me get on with it." Glancing at his watch, he continued with urgency, "My God, it's already eight fifteen."

Not really subdued, but accepting, Boyd sank back in his chair and sipped his coffee, never taking his eyes from Scott's face. Allan who had not moved throughout this outburst, nor changed the expression of his face, sat in poised expectancy.

"I'll tell it my way, from the beginning, and if you don't understand, stop me, but don't waste what little time we've got on details."

3

WHEN SCOTT LEONARD stepped off the Pan Am charter into the stifling wet heat of the Vietnamese night, he knew what he had come to, and what he had come for. A man made his own career, and made it the hard way, he thought; he was one of the few who had asked for this assignment. Asked hell, he smiled to himself, he had exerted every pressure he could think of on Opie Bergsdorf in the colonels' assignment branch of the Office of Personnel Operations to get him here. And not just here to Saigon in the headquarters of the Commander of U.S. Forces Viet Nam, COMUSMACV. He was to be the senior U.S. Advisor to the IX Vietnamese Corps, Ngo Tho Province, and well aware as he was of the many slips that could occur, the many dead-end jobs in MACV Headquarters to which he could be assigned, he was prepared to go all the way to insure that he did not end up in some staff job in Saigon. With a quiet confidence bordering on arrogance he knew his capabilities and potential, and he did not intend to waste his time pushing papers across some desk. This new job was nothing more or less than the jobs he had done as a major and lieutenant-colonel in two different tours in Korea as advisor to the ROK Army, and he knew with pride that he had done well. This place was different only in terms of climate and the nature and tactics of the enemy, and he knew his ability to adjust to these variables. Long ago, during his basic training as an infantryman—my God how long ago was 1941—he had first realized the absolute futility of dwelling on transient physical discomfort, and the degradation of a man's dignity that came from preoccupation with his own personal comfort and welfare.

"Colonel Leonard?" A young captain addressed him at the foot of the gangway. "I'm Captain Thompson, General Wesley's aide." His salute was right out of the manual. Neat, sharp, and nervous, thought Scott, like every aide General Wesley had ever had. Evidently the old bastard hadn't changed much over the years.

"If you would please follow me, sir," Captain Thompson continued, as Scott returned his salute, and slowly turned toward the terminal. Suppressing the almost overwhelming urge to stride out at a normal pace, Scott followed along as sedately as possible. After all, a full colonel was only one rank below general and everyone knew how decrepit they were, he rationalized with disbelief, and besides this young soldier has probably had some real bad experiences in his time with cranky old farts who really can't make a normal rate of speed. And working for Wesley was enough of a traumatic experience without anyone else adding to the burden.

Than Son Nhut, Saigon's airport, was distinguished by nothing except the absolutely freezing blast of the air conditioner in the VIP lounge, a well-isolated section of the main terminal, where he was led by the constantly clucking Captain Thompson. Was the Colonel in good health, had the flight seemed long, was the Colonel tired, and as they entered the lounge, would the Colonel be good enough to give him his baggage checks, and would the Colonel perhaps like a beer while his baggage was obtained. In something less than good humor over all this idle chatter and concern with his welfare, Scott accepted the beer. Bami Bami was the label—Thirty-three in Vietnamese, graciously explained the Captain—and it tasted like all French beer everywhere, thought Scott as he gulped it down.

The journey into Saigon from Than Son Nhut was an exercise in futility insofar as gaining any understanding of the layout of the city was concerned. Thompson was completely at a loss on questions as to the locations of telephone exchanges, power stations, bridges, main power lines, or radio stations. So Scott gradually stopped all effort and relaxed into a quiet verging on somnolence. To hell with it, let General Wesley train his aide to observe those things, which are the proper concern of a soldier in a foreign land, and let General Hankins, Commander, COMUSMACV, worry about the security of Saigon.

As the darkness of the suburbs between Than Son Nhut and Saigon faded, Scott was amazed at the bright and seemingly carefree life of the city. Pedicabs vied with diminutive Renault taxicabs and with bicycles in a constant pattern of hazard in front of the staff car, and as they approached the true center of the city the streets appeared to be literally packed with people moving purposelessly in all directions—the men in undistinguished adaptations of western dress, the women in that loveliest of national costumes, the *auo-dai*. Like vari-colored butterflies they floated, each slender and small, in silken trousers and flowing over-blouse and over-skirt.

The Brink Hotel. Scott rejected it with resentment the instant his car stopped in front of the gate, guarded by two small but magnificently trim Vietnamese. This is again the enclave type of mind, he thought, as Captain Thompson hurriedly alighted to help him out of the car. A little bit of America created right here in Saigon, and he felt he could almost predict what he would find inside. Surely a bar, with the usual collection of regulars, the social semi-alcoholics who required company for their drinking, with a sprinkling of local whores who had achieved a semblance of respectability through a steady shack with some particular officer. Each room with its air conditioner, the windows sealed tight against all but filtered air, and furnished with locally made western-style furniture. And throughout the building a sense of exclusion of all without, of being an island of things familiar, in the sea of Viet Nam.

Someday, he mused, as Captain Thompson scurried around his baggage, assembling houseboys, and needlessly directing their efforts in unloading his two footlockers, the duffle bag, and the disreputable old Air Force B4 bag he had used for so many years, and his similarly well-used dispatch case—someday he would be in the saddle when one of the advisory groups went into a new country and would be able to start it right. Establish only an absolute minimum of Headquarters and staff, and run all the rest out of the cities and hotels to stay with the troops. Live with them, eat with them, and become one of them. Learn the language and be more than just an ineffectual observer.

Knowing that, in fact, he was not likely to ever be in a position to change much of anything, he followed Captain

Thompson into the antiquated elevator. His room was as he had expected, somewhat more dreary perhaps, with the air conditioner running at full blast.

"Sir, you have two appointments tomorrow morning," Captain Thompson announced nervously. "First, with General Wesley, Chief of MAAG, at nine-thirty, and later with General Hankins, COMUSMACV, at ten. Breakfast will be in the top floor dining room starting at six, and I'll pick you up at nine. I know it's pretty late now, but can I get you anything before you retire?"

"Nothing at all, thank you, Captain," said Scott gently, realizing that he had been something less than cordial, and that his attitude must have contributed considerably to Captain Thompson's nervousness. "I'll see you in the morning."

In spite of the crudely lettered sign attached to the air conditioner, which warned against even so much as touching any of the controls, Scott shut it off and slept the sleep of utter exhaustion until his built-in alarm, which had never failed him, woke him at the usual hour of five. Thinking to hell with it, that he had nothing to do before nine, he slept on until eight. Showered, shaved, and in a clean uniform that had retained its sharp state-side press in his B4 bag, he breakfasted on black coffee and half a papaya, served in the now deserted dining room by an alert and smiling Vietnamese houseboy, and at nine precisely descended in the rickety elevator. The heat was almost a physical blow as he stepped from the air-conditioned comfort of the building, and Scott felt the sweat begin to dampen his entire body. Better get used to it, he thought, you've got a long time of this ahead.

Captain Thompson's relief was so apparent as to be pathetic. When Simon Wesley said nine o'clock, it seemed that Captain Thompson had the responsibility for getting the body there on time, no matter what the rank of the visitor. As they drove out the gate, past the smartly saluting guards, down a short side street and then into the swarming traffic of a main thoroughfare, Scott gazed with interest at streets and the ever-moving mass of Vietnamese and the liberal sprinkling of European types—some U.S. forces in various Army and Air Force uniforms, some obviously U.S. civilians, and many unidentifiable by dress or manner—and thought with uneasiness over his coming interviews.

General Simon Wesley was not a stranger. Scott had known him since Wesley had been a Lieutenant Colonel in Italy on the Anzio beachhead, and he had not changed

22

throughout subsequent meetings over the years. A combat soldier's soldier, he would appreciate Scott's desire for a job in the field, but it just might be that he would need someone on his staff here in Saigon and if that were the situation it would be a rough go. Simon Wesley had never been known to pay the slightest attention to the personal desires of any of his subordinates, and only the barest possible attention to those of his superiors. Verging on egomania, he was utterly ruthless when crossed or when neglect of duty was involved, and an implacable enemy once one had incurred his dislike. But his virtues were many, and well outweighed his faults. He was completely loyal to those of his command who had earned his faith, thought that God had created no finer thing on earth or in heaven than a good soldier, and was utterly fearless. In battle, in the face of civilian criticism of the military, in any endeavor, once he had committed himself he went all the way, and like his friend Patton, he had often seemed completely out of step with times of peace.

General Wesley he could probably handle, thought Scott. But General Hankins was a different kind of a problem. He did not know him personally and he was sure that it was not ordinary procedure for a four-star general to interview every colonel who passed through Saigon for advisory duty upcountry. The best that he could hope for was that maybe Wesley, who he was sure liked him personally, had arranged this as a special courtesy.

The staff car swung through a gate heavily manned by Vietnamese guards and into a compound, evidently once spacious but now with the courtyard jammed with temporary wooden buildings. "MAAG Headquarters," announced Captain Thompson who had sat quietly beside Scott throughout the ride, and hastily scrambled out and held the door for Scott. "If you'll just follow me, sir," he continued, mounting the long flight of stone steps leading to the doorway of the only permanent building and holding to his sedate, for-older-gentlemen pace.

The sergeant in General Wesley's outer office was evidently expecting him, and without breaking stride Scott was ushered into the General's office. Air conditioning again, he noted. He wondered if the medics had ever made a comparison of the health of those who existed in the ambient temperature and those subjected to the recurring shock of the change from damp heat to damp chill of air conditioning.

General Simon Wesley sat at his wide desk, returning

Scott's salute with a half salute, half wave. Small and slender, almost bald now, but with a smooth and unlined face distinguished by a hawk-like beak of a nose and the most glittering and penetrating of black eyes, he looked as fit as always. Coming around his desk, he warmly grasped Scott's hand, leading him to a chair alongside the desk.

"Sit down! Scott, it's good to see you again." His voice always came as a surprise, high and thin, and really not in keeping with his reputation as a real bona fide, ass-chewing, combat-ready tiger. Looking closely at Scott as he returned to his seat he asked, "How'd they ever manage to get you here. It can't be that anyone in his right mind would ask for anything like this assignment?"

"I asked," replied Scott briefly, returning Wesley's smile. "Not that I'm claiming to any special sanity, but I figured that this is the only war we've got, and that I should get out here and into it before it was all over."

"You needn't have rushed," Wesley replied, with a marked tone of bitterness in his voice. "From the way things are going we're going to have this place as a training ground for quite some time. Not that it's worth a damn for us. These goddam Viets won't understand a damned thing we tell them, and when they do understand won't do what they are told. I just can't see how in hell their minds work. Even when on rare occasion we know exactly where there is a concentration of lousy Viet Cong and we tell them exactly what to do here in Saigon, by the time it filters down through what is laughingly known as their chain of command, it's screwed up beyond all recognition. Nine times out of ten not a damned thing is done, and the odds are that on that rare tenth time when they do do something, it's done in such a completely loused up manner that nothing good comes of it. Just a simple thing, like precaution against ambush, which they fall into time after time, seems to be beyond them. I've only got four more months here, and I can tell you that this is the first job I've ever had in my life that I look forward to leaving. I only hope that before I go I don't lose what little control I've got left and give one of these no-good bastardly Viets a fat lip or a good boot in the balls."

Scott sat in amazement. To hear the top man in the advisory side of the U.S. command display such petulance and spite was incredible, and all the more so when clearly in his memory was an address given to his class at the Command

and General Staff College at Fort Leavenworth by this same man—many years ago, in the bitter days of the fighting in Greece, when General Simon Wesley had been one of the first of those soldiers to be called upon to give advice to a foreign army in combat. Then freshly returned from his tour in Greece, his advice to that class of future Army commanders had been on the necessity for the diplomatic soft sell, and the necessity of never appearing to direct or to talk down to a foreign officer, or to appear to force or order them to do anything. Never offend national pride, and if at all possible lead them to believe that they thought of all good things themselves.

Scott's amazement must have shown on his face, despite his conscious effort to remain expressionless. Thankfully, Wesley could not read his mind, and put his own interpretation on the meaning of Scott's expression.

"You'll find out soon enough," he continued in a deadly calmness, which was even more emphatic than rage would have been. "That bastard you're going to be associated with is one of the worst of the lot. Arrogant, supercilious, and plain goddam stupid. I'd of had his ass out of there long ago but he is in solid with at least half of the junta, and there isn't a thing that I can do to get him fired. Brigadier General Huang Huu-Lac—you ever heard of him?"

"Never," answered Scott. "I guess I'll get to read his dossier shortly though, and by the time I get with him I should have a good idea of the way he operates."

"Operates? That bastard hasn't operated yet. All he does is sit there in his own little kingdom, where his word is law, and screw himself silly, what time he's sober enough to get a hard on."

Captain Thompson announced his presence at the open office door with a faint tap and an apologetic cough. "We should leave now, sir, if we are to be on time for your appointment with General Hankins."

"Yeah, I guess so," grumped General Wesley, glancing at his watch. "What does old Hank Hankins want to see you about, Scott, I didn't know you had ever served with him?"

"I'm damned if I know," answered Scott with surprise, "I thought that you had arranged all this. I've never even met him before."

"Not guilty. All I know is that one of his aides called Captain Thompson and asked that we both report to him this morning." Leading the way out of the office and down

25

the long flight of steps to the waiting staff car, he paused before entering, "Maybe your big brother Boyd had some hand in setting this up."

During the short ride to the remodeled apartment building that housed MACV Headquarters and the procession through various offices—the successive echelons required before being ushered into the presence of General Hankins—Scott had little time to speculate as to just what the hell was going on. Even so, as he tried to keep some semblance of sense in his replies to General Wesley's rambling dissertation on the sad state of affairs in both the way the U.S. forces and the Vietnamese were running the war, he had an acute sense of foreboding.

General Hankins, a giant of a man with a leonine head of silver hair, a broad and serene brow, and ice-blue, direct eyes, gravely acknowledged General Wesley's introduction of Scott, and without preamble began.

"You have been recommended to me as an excellent replacement for the chief of our U.S. Forces Plans Branch, and have been specifically asked for by Major General Short, who will arrive next month and who will be in charge of all plans. Since I generally don't like to change an officer's assignment without at least talking it over, I wanted to meet you this morning."

He would have gone on, but Scott, knowing that this above all things was not what he had come all this way for, interrupted. "I am appreciative sir, but I would prefer to be in the field. I feel . . ."

"Shut up, Scott," barked General Wesley. "Sir," he addressed General Hankins, "I'd like to discuss this with you in private."

General Hankins, his normally pale complexion slowly flushing to a quite startling crimson with a glint of anger in his eyes, gazed steadily at Scott for a long moment, and then gave the briefest of nods to General Wesley.

"Wait for me outside, Colonel," General Wesley continued, and as Scott saluted sharply, turned, and opened the door, he heard the General go on in a voice almost choked with rage. "Hank, this is the third time someone on your staff has tried to pull this shit, and . . ." The door closed behind him.

Scott sat quietly for an endless fifteen minutes, willing himself to relax, twice refusing the offer of coffee from the Air Force major who occupied the office, before General

Wesley emerged, his face grim, and said grittingly, "Come on, let's get your ass out of here before they kidnap you."

Once in the car, as Scott began to speak, Wesley harshly, almost viciously, said, "Don't ask any goddam stupid frigging questions. Those sonsabitches are always trying to pull something like this, and they have always won before. This time we'll do things a little differently. All you need to know is that the rest of this day will be taken up by briefings on what you're getting into and that my chopper will take you upcountry at five hundred hours tomorrow morning. That suit you?"

"Yes, sir." Scott decided that silence took precedence over any expression of gratitude. The silence continued during the short ride back to the MAAG compound, although it was evident that General Wesley was near the bursting point. His face was flushed and heavy, his breath gasping, and he sat in almost catatonic rigidity except for the trembling of his hands. As the car stopped again at the foot of the stairway and Captain Thompson scrambled from the front seat to open his door, the General uncoiled like a spring, pushed the door open violently, and went up the steps at a dead run. "Thompson, see that he gets the full treatment today, and see that he leaves on time in the morning," he shouted from halfway up the steps.

4

CAPTAIN THOMPSON watched General Wesley anxiously, and after he had disappeared through the doorway he continued to stand, perplexed and disapprovingly shaking his head. "I've never known him to act like this," he said. "The surgeon has warned him time after time against moving so damned fast, or taking anything so seriously." Turning to Scott, he continued in real concern, "I'm worried about him, I have been for a long time, but today is the worst that I've seen him. If he lets himself get that mad many more times, he's going to be seriously sick."

Looking at this grim young man, whose only concern was genuine worry over the health of a man, who at best treated him with curt formality, and more often with studied rudeness or barely controlled rage, Scott felt the familiar warmth of one good soldier for another. Captain Thompson had such a single-minded sense of duty that he probably never once gave thought to whether or not General Wesley treated him ill or well, thought Scott. So completely unlike many aides he had known, who assumed their General's rank as their own, and wore it with insufferable arrogance.

"Captain Thompson, suppose you just point me in the direction I'm to go and tell me who I'm supposed to see first, and then you go check on General Wesley. You can join me later."

Quickly, and with a real note of relief and gratitude in his voice, Captain Thompson said, "Either Colonel Buckmeister, the G3, or Colonel Dodds, G2, whichever one is available, since our Chief of Staff, Colonel Fuller, is in the hospital with dysentery. They are both in that building over there." He pointed to an unpainted wooden building with long overhanging eaves and open screened sides. "I'll get the others lined up just as soon as I make a quick check on General Wesley. We haven't got much time, sir. What you're going to get today usually takes three or four days for a newly assigned officer."

He was off up the stairs, taking two or three of the shallow steps at each stride in haste that was a far cry from his sedate pace when escorting older officers, thought Scott, as he called softly after him, "Be careful." He could well imagine that General Wesley would be more than a little irritated if he had any idea that his aide was mothering him.

Entering the building through the screened door with its firmly affixed sign warning against entry by other than authorized persons, Scott found himself in a long hallway with rooms to right and left formed by movable half partitions. The first sign on the right announced the office of the G3, and as he paused in the doorway a tired and worn Colonel, gray and older than he would have expected, but with an alert intelligent look in his bloodshot eyes, briefly glanced up from the mass of papers on his desk. "Check in two doors down the hall," he began, and then actually seeing Scott for the first time, "Excuse me, Colonel, I'm Colonel Buckmeister, the G3. Can I help you?"

"Scott Leonard. I'm scheduled for IX Corps and I've just had the word from General Wesley. I'm to get myself read in on the situation today and leave here first thing in the morning, and from what I hear that's rushing the schedule a little bit."

"It's damned unheard of, and it's also damned near impossible. We usually take at least three days, and in a case like yours, where the situation is quite a bit more complicated than usual, we usually take a little longer. Mind telling me what the rush is? The man you are to replace is still up there so there needn't be such a hurry. We're not all that uncovered."

Long ago, Scott had learned the dangers of relaying the differences between senior officers. But now he had no choice. Unless Buckmeister understood what had happened earlier this morning he would not understand the urgency.

30

And Scott knew he would be much better prepared if he had the complete cooperation of Buckmeister.

"You may or may not hear of this from General Wesley. Probably you won't," said Scott, holding Buckmeister's eyes steadily, "but I think you're entitled to know, and it's damned important to me to have your cooperation in getting as much of the full treatment as is possible in the time we have. The truth is that some sonofabitch fixed me up with a job on the MACV staff, and I told General Hankins that I didn't want it. Then, with me out of the room, General Wesley evidently told General Hankins that he wasn't exactly happy over MACV short-stopping officers assigned to advisory duty for desk jobs here in Saigon. When we left MACV headquarters our boy was in a fine frothing rage, and his last words to me a few minutes ago were to get briefed today and to get out of Saigon tomorrow at five hundred hours on his own personal chopper."

"You turned down a job working with General Hankins, and for a lousy job out in the boondocks? You must be out of your mind, or else you know something I don't," said Buckmeister in amazement, and with a trace of irritation in his voice.

"I did just exactly that," answered Scott, "and if thinking that a soldier's job is best done where the soldiers are doing something more than wearing out their asses on a chair behind a desk is wrong, then I guess I'm out of my mind." Thinking to hell with this sonofabitch, if he won't cooperate I'll do it the hard way and drag what I want out of him, he continued, "Now let's get on with you telling me the things I should know, or have you got some other idea of just how you're going to comply with General Wesley's orders?"

"Take it easy, Colonel," said Buckmeister stiffly, "I meant nothing personal, and I'll see that you get what you need in a real cram course. Just one moment while I get things organized and we'll go across to the war room." Stepping over to the paper-thin half-partition he gave two short raps on the wall. Immediately there was the sound of a chair being pushed hastily away from a desk and a young major appeared in the doorway.

Somebody has damned big ears, thought Scott, and then sensing the stillness that had settled over the whole building and that there was no privacy in such a place as this, he realized that his exchange with Buckmeister must have been heard by a great number of people. He also realized as he turned his gaze from the new arrival in the doorway and

31

briefly locked eyes with Buckmeister, that he had made an enemy. That's the story of your life, he thought, in town only a few hours and you've managed to offend a very influential man, for which you will probably be very sorry in time to come. Not that the sonofabitch was exactly nice to me.

"Colonel Leonard, this is Major Roth," Buckmeister said curtly. "Major, I want you to get the word to the rest of the staff that the top priority job for today is the briefing of Colonel Leonard. We'll have it in the usual order, G2 followed by G3 Plans, and then G3 Operations and Training, then G4 and G1 and the rest. You know the routine—get the best briefers available throughout the staff and get the G2 on his way to the war room on the double."

With a brief duck of head in acknowledgment, the Major was on his way. "Would you please follow me, Colonel," asked Buckmeister. Without looking back he strode out of his office door, down the hall, out the door, and turned left into a similar building adjacent. Here however there were no movable partitions or office cubicles, and the entire front part of the building housed a well-equipped war room. Map boards with the usual acetate overlays and their blur of red and blue grease-penciled markings covered the far wall and the wall to the right of the entrance. Several men were busily converting written data from reports into map symbology.

As he followed Colonel Buckmeister forward into the room, his eyes busily scanning the numerous maps that covered each of the Vietnamese Corps, Scott was aware of the door again slamming behind him and he was suddenly grasped by the arm and swung around into the sweaty embrace of an obese giant of a man. Big Zeke, Colonel Ezekiel Dodds. At least he had one friend in court.

"Scott, you old bastard," rumbled Zeke in his deep and cracked bass voice, "It's worth the whole goddam tour over here just to see you again. You know, it's been almost ten years, just after you and Cindy were married, and we were all stationed at Benning. You going to join us here?"

Scott stood gazing with affection at the red-faced sweating giant before him, fatter than ever after these years, and with his hair grayed to the point of whiteness. This man once saved my life, he thought, remembering a hedgerow and a stone wall in Normandy where he had lain wounded in both legs and slowly bleeding to death and pinned down by murderous small arms and machine-gun fire, and how

Zeke had suddenly bounded over the wall and picked him up and literally thrown him over the top to safety. And how Zeke had followed him back so quickly that they landed almost simultaneously, and had growled a single remark, "Fucking Krauts can't shoot worth a damn when they can't hit a thing as big as me." Then quickly fixing tourniquets on both of Scott's legs he was off along the wall, and fifteen minutes later had gathered up a small squad of stragglers and led them in an attack that overran the Krauts. This Zeke was a man, and let no one be deceived by his appearance. Inside that almost shapeless blob was an incredibly agile strength.

"Zeke, I'm so very glad to see you, I can't tell . . ." Scott began, only to be cut off by Buckmeister saying with great sarcasm, "Colonel Leonard has just declined any duty back here in civilization and has insisted on going where the soldiers are. And let's get on with it, we haven't much time. Zeke, the name of this game is to get Colonel Leonard read in on the entire picture well enough to move out to take over as IX Corps advisor at first light tomorrow. You two can have your old buddy talk in what time is left, but for now let's get moving. Colonel Leonard, Colonel Dodds is our G2. Give him the works Zeke—terrain, weather, political organization, personalities, everything." Turning he strode down the aisle to the front row of folding chairs.

Seeing the puzzled look in Zeke's eyes, and the beginning of a protest, Scott said quickly, "Let it ride, Zeke—I'll explain later," and followed Buckmeister to the front of the room. What piss poor luck, he thought. If I'd had sense enough to associate the name Dodds with Zeke, I could have gone to him first and avoided any run-in with Buckmeister. As it is, now there's going to be nothing but trouble between me and this bastard. Taking his seat alongside Buckmeister, as Zeke continued on toward the large one-over-twenty-five-thousand map with the caption of IX Corps above it, he realized that outside of the three of them and two map posters at work on the far side of the room, the room was vacant.

"Will we wait for the rest of the staff, Colonel?" he asked.

"We will not. The briefers will come in on schedule and leave when they are finished," answered Buckmeister curtly. "These people have better things to do than waste their time sitting here listening to each other."

I might just as well go all the way with this troop, thought

Scott. He may not think that I'm lovable when we're all done, but he's damned well going to know that I'm not going to be pushed around. Quietly he said, "Let's not do it that way today, Colonel. When I have a logistics question brought to my mind during a G3 portion of this little session I don't want time wasted while someone scurries around trying to find the man who has the answer. I want the answer right then, and we can't have that with a series of people with very special knowledge moving in and out of here. Let's do it all together and at one time."

"Colonel Leonard, we have been giving these briefings to a great number of people for a long, long time . . ." Buckmeister fairly bristled with outrage, when Scott broke in, "Save it, we're just wasting time. I don't give a damn how you've managed these things in the past. This one is for me and me alone, and that's the way I want it. Besides it might be very educational for your staff to hear a little bit about what the command as a whole is doing." Steadily, and letting his own eyes reflect the dislike he saw in Buckmeister's, he held the man's gaze until finally Buckmeister turned and called to one of the map-posters, who had by now all but ceased any pretense at work, "Sergeant Dempsey, please pass the word for the staff . . ." He broke off as he heard the entry door open. Captain Thompson came hurriedly into the room, and Buckmeister continued, "Never mind, Sergeant. Captain Thompson will you have the briefing staff in here as quickly as possible. Colonel Leonard, this will take at least twenty minutes. I'll return when all are assembled." Abruptly he made for the doorway, almost treading on the heels of Captain Thompson, who in quick understanding was well on his way on his errand.

Scott turned to Zeke, who had stood with an entirely expressionless face during his conversation with Buckmeister. "Well, there's nothing like a little stupidity to make life worth living, is there?" he asked.

"What in hell have you done to get Buckmeister so pissed off?" Zeke asked. "He's usually fairly peaceful."

"Screw him," said Scott. "I'm usually fairly peaceful, too, and this clown started the donnybrook. This must be my morning for inciting everyone I meet to riot. In a short hour and a half I've done real, real well." Quickly he went over the entire morning with Zeke—the meeting with General Wesley, their meeting together with General Hankins, the private session between the two Generals that had followed, Wesley's apoplectic rage afterward and his instructions to

Scott, and finally his bad-luck encounter with Buckmeister. Zeke was hugely amused when Scott described his involuntary response to the offer of a MACV staff job, and even more when Scott told of Wesley's reaction to this recruitment effort.

"Those two hardheaded old bastards have a go around over something every so often and I guess they were just about due again. Basically, from what I've seen and heard, I think they respect each other all to hell, but they are two such different types that it's almost impossible for them not to clash. Wesley has been in damned poor health lately and that has added to the problem. I'd guess that he wasn't able to get a clear-cut agreement out of Hankins to forget about your being assigned to MACV, and so he thinks getting you out of town is the best way to solve the problem. He knows damned well Hankins won't call you back once you're actually on the ground and on the job, since this would make us look bad to the Viets. He's also counting on the fact that Hankins knows all about our processing routine here and probably thinks he has three or four days to mull this around before he really decides to do something. Odds are, Hankins will decide to let it ride and never mention it again, but I'd sure like to be there if he should decide to call for you and Wesley has to explain that you just don't happen to be in town. That little session would be a classic."

"What's with this man Buckmeister?" Scott asked. "There was no reason in the world for him to sound off the way he did the goddam minute I told him I had turned down a job here in Saigon."

"Scott, you probably couldn't have hit on a better thing to get him against you if you had tried. You see, he once had V Corps, came here just like you have, although he fought the assignment all the way from Fort Benning, where he was in some training assignment, until he arrived here. I hadn't gotten here yet, but from what I hear, he couldn't squirm his way into a job here at the time, so they shipped his ass on up to V Corps. I guess he screwed up by the numbers during the short time, maybe three months, that he was there. Had all the Viets hating his guts almost on first sight. Giving orders right, left, and center. Patrol here and patrol there, and all the while never leaving his compound except on rare occasion to visit the Viet Corps Commander on some grievance or other, and all the time half scared out of his ass, afraid that the Congs were going to assassinate him. About the time he had really gotten bad,

35

the old G3 here was evacuated due to complications in his health caused by the heat and cheap booze and strange pussy, and General Wesley brought Buckmeister back down here. You know, it still bothers him more than he'll ever admit that the Cong have never taken him off their death list, but just transferred the action from the V Corps branch to the Saigon office. Hell, we're all on that list—in fact right now someone back at the Brink or the Rex or wherever you're staying has probably gone over your baggage for identification and your name will shortly appear on the list, first here in Saigon and later at Ngo Tho when they find out you have been moved. It doesn't bother most people. You acquire a collection of these little sheets they put out and have them translated, showing that someone really cares about you. It's a sort of a status symbol for all the rest of us. But not for him—it really makes him nervous."

"Christ, has the man no pride? Everyone gets a little nervous at times, but what kind of a man lets it become common knowledge that he's bugged?"

"Well, Scott, let me tell you one thing for sure. You've made Buckmeister back down twice now, and if I'm any judge of character you'd better never turn your back to him. When I said a minute ago that he was usually a fairly peaceful man I didn't mean that he wasn't an unmitigated sonofabitch when he's aroused."

"So, what can he do to bother me?" asked Scott, smiling. "Once I get out of town there isn't one hell of a lot—except wait for me to make a mistake up there and then try to hang my hide on the wall. Which will never happen because I'm not going to make any mistakes serious enough for that."

"Don't you believe it," warned Zeke. "You just don't understand the way we operate here. First you've got the problem that Buckmeister has the idea we should control things all over the damned country from here in Saigon, and that he has sold old Wesley on this concept. Incidentally, did the good General give speech number one on the overall nogoodness of the Vietnamese?" With Scott's nod he continued. "It's a frigging shame. The old boy should have retired a long time ago but I guess he just keeps hanging on in hopes of a third star. His health is bad and I think it's affecting his judgment or else he would never have bought Buckmeister as his G3 or any of his screwball ideas. Anyway, he has, and every day we publish a daily operations order for each of our senior advisors, telling them exactly what operations are to be accomplished during the next forty-eight hours. I mean each patrol, each ambush, each clearing and holding operation or sweep or village search. This goes out by radio teletype and is for U.S. eyes only. Our Corps advisors are supposed to lay these operations on with the Vietnamese, and each advisor submits a daily operations report on his accomplishments for the day. At the same time that this is going down through our chain of command, every day General Wesley chooses a few of the more important and spectacular little goodies of the day and tries a selling job on his opposite number in the Ministry of Defense. The odd thing about this whole senseless merry-go-round is that the source data for all our plans and directives are basically the intelligence reports that our people are submitting to us, plus some little bit we get from the Air Force and MACV headquarters. All we are doing is telling our people what to do on the basis of them telling us that something has happened, but I can't seem to get the point across to anyone. For instance, we get a completely unfounded report that some number of Congs were sighted near some damned village, so quick as a flash we order the village searched and held."

"Well, it does make for work here in Saigon, and you know that there's nothing more likely to end up in trouble than an idle soldier," said Scott, amused at Zeke's vehemence. "So how does this affect me, except that I am going to have a lot more paper work than I had thought, what with daily reports and all. Don't tell me anyone out in the field pays one hell of a lot of attention to all this."

"Of course they do. These are orders we're sending out. Orders, goddam it, not suggestions, and you can't imagine the detailed explanations as to why something wasn't done that are required each day. I'm not saying Buckmeister can really hurt you in any way unless you really goof up, but he can sure as hell make your life miserable. Am I getting through to you, finally?"

"You are, Zeke, you are at long last," said Scott, and was silent for a moment. "You say all this is radio traffic. Don't you have a daily courier flight?"

"To some of the Corps, but not to you. You have the distinction of being one of the few province capitals which is relatively unvisited due to the widespread prevalence of little brown men with sharpshooter medals covering all the best chopper approaches, and the landing strip there isn't completed for fixed wing of any size yet. Of course we fly in the area all the time, but usually only on an actual mission

37

and with Air Force planes firing suppressive missions first. That is one reason why you are taking off so early in the morning. You'll leave here while it is still dark and get there at first light or a little after, about one hour and fifteen minutes flight time. One nice thing about it is that you won't be plagued by a steady stream of visitors like Jim Gould is up at Da Nang. You're just not going to be in a tourist-visited country, boy."

"Thank God some small advantages do accrue," said Scott, with a plan already in his mind as to just how he could escape from any untoward interference from Buckmeister for at least short periods of time.

"Of course there is one quite unique way to escape all this, Scott," said Zeke slowly, and with distaste in his voice, "and that is the way the man you're going to replace tomorrow does it. Tom Meir has a gimmick which seems to bring real joy to Buckmeister's heart. It's real simple—ignore all orders and simply report on the general bastardry of the Vietnamese commanders. Old Tom never even mentions the specifics of what he has been told to do, he just gives a report on the escapades of General Huang Huu-Lac, of how drunk he was the night before, and how many women he laid, and that he was so hung over that it was not possible to even talk to him, let alone pass on the day's orders to him."

"My God, is the man really that bad?" asked Scott. "Wesley mentioned that he had tried to have Huu-Lac relieved, but I didn't think that he could really seriously have reason to suggest this to the Viets."

Zeke sat studying Scott for a long moment, glanced at his watch, and said, "The whole thundering herd will be roaring in here in a moment and I haven't time to tell you the whole story, but just bear in mind that there ain't a goddam word of truth in a single report we've received from Tom Meir, even though Tom would swear on his life that they are completely factual." Hurriedly, as he again looked at his watch, he continued, "I don't know how long this briefing is going to take—it may well last far into the night—but if we get separated I want you to be sure and see me, all alone, before you leave in the morning. I'll meet you at the field just before you take off if we can't get together later in the day or this evening, but remember that you need at least a half hour with me before you leave." Zeke's air of total seriousness was broken by his final remark just as the door opened and the procession began. "Of course, I don't really believe you're ever going to get out of Saigon. By now

Buckmeister has called up some old asshole buddy at MACV and Hankins is probably well aware of the foul conspiracy afoot to smuggle you out of town."

Captain Thompson led the troupe through the door, and at a nod of permission from Zeke, stationed himself on Scott's left and began the introductions. There were five officers—three lieutenant colonels, and two majors.

Colonel George Loveless, G3 Plans, was thin to the point of emaciation, but with a grip that belied his apparent frailty. Blonde, blue-eyed, and with a bony handsomeness, he was reserved but correct in his greeting of, "Welcome aboard, Colonel Leonard. Let's hope we can fill you in adequately in the short time that we have."

"That bastard Buckmeister," Scott raged inwardly, as he shook hands and responded with what he hoped was a good imitation of warmth and friendliness. He has undoubtedly spread the word with vengeance that this is a crash action to get me out of town, and probably explained the reason why there is such urgency to every one of these fine young gentlemen. Zeke's prediction concerning Buckmeister's probable call to MACV Scott now accepted as a *fait accompli*.

Colonel George Bradford, G3 Operations and Training, radiated a guarded friendliness and his handshake was warm and firm. "Glad to meet you, Colonel Leonard," he said with sincerity. "I've worked with several of your former officers—Greg Smith, Brad White, and Jim Davis—so I feel I almost know you." This was a man Scott could warm to, one who was not afraid to make his own judgments.

Major Gurney Bellows, the G1 briefer, small, dark, with an acne-scarred face and a hard and damp grip, mumbled a brief "How do you do", and Major Dewey Lancaster, G4, a hulking, rawboned man—at least six-six, thought Scott —red-haired, and densely freckled, was almost apathetic in his limp hand and simple "Colonel Leonard," spoken in a wispy voice in acknowledgment of the introduction.

Lieutenant Colonel Albright, the Signal Officer, bringing up the rear of the little procession, was a cat of a different cut. Where Bradford had been friendly but had in some degree held back, Albright was the personification of exuberant friendliness. Young, stocky, blond and curly-headed, with an open-faced handsomeness that fairly reeked of cocky self-confidence, he seized Scott's hand as if it were a prize. "Colonel Leonard, sir, I'm certainly glad to meet you," he said in a marked southern accent. "You'll find that you've got the best commo set-up of any of our commands and you'll want for nothing. Since you're the most isolated we've got to treat you the best, and we surely have."

Scott liked him on sight. "You're the first Signal Officer I've ever met who bragged of his communications," he said. "Usually they are desperately explaining why something isn't working and blaming the bastard at the other end of the circuit."

"I can't do that, Colonel—my young brother Joe is your commo officer up there. Besides, while this isn't quite stateside or Bell Telephone standards, we've got a real working system. Of course, in your case all voice commo is radio, push to talk, and you'll probably use that only once in a while, but we've got solid radio teletype circuits into you and a raft of spare equipment all warmed up and ready to go on the air in case of failure."

One of these days you and I will have a long and private talk, young man, Scott thought, just as Colonel Buckmeister came into the room and walked forward to his seat in the silence that fell upon his entry. He still carried some signs of his recent rage, but the suspicion of a grim smirk shadowed his face. You bastard, thought Scott, you miserable bastard, you really tried, didn't you. What a low scummy trick, but I'll see you in hell before you'll get any goddam satisfaction out of me. We'll just let it ride and hope to Christ that either the man you passed it to in MACV has got better sense than to stir up trouble, or that if he is the same kind of shit you are and does go to Hankins, the old man himself will see behind it and refuse to do anything.

"Let's get this over with," Buckmeister said in a surprisingly quiet and even voice. "G2 will give you his pitch first."

Zeke stepped to the map and Scott closed his mind to all but the sound of Zeke's voice and the sight of the map. It was a total focusing that had come only through long training and the knowledge that lives, his own and others, hung on his understanding and recording every single item of information given him. No taking of notes, no glossing over of some items as not important, no wandering of attention, but total rapport with the voice and the sight of the map, and complete recording, indelible recording, of all things said.

Ngo Tho Province lies close against the Col Mung Bada mountains on its western border. It is intermittently broken in the south by the valley of the Mekong, and, for some fifty miles faces Cambodia to the west, and, along the ridge of the watershed borders Laos on the north. The French mapped the area in the late thirties, but did not include minor routes, and the dense foliage has made our aerial photography useless in defining them. The region is largely unpopulated except by some few bands of hill tribes. The Viet Cong are in almost full control of the entire range of the northern hills, and passage is made northward into Sy Ghan only rarely by ARVN forces, and then only in heavily armed convoy.

The southern boundary of Ngo Tho Province is formed by the Se Reo Kri River, which makes a wide and sweeping bend beginning just inside the Cambodian border and enters Viet Nam flowing almost due west, continuing along the southern border of the province, and eventually swinging south to join the Mekong some two hundred miles to the south. Unlike much of Viet Nam and Cambodia, the area is not solely dependent on the monsoons for moisture. The innumerable north-south streams provide for a full stand of water in the paddies all year long and in times past this single province furnished fully one quarter of the rice for Saigon and the coastal cities. This, of course, defines the Viet Cong objective in Ngo Tho quite simply. Either discourage the production of rice, or after having confiscated all required for their needs and for the needs of other of their forces operating in adjacent provinces, insure that as little as possible reaches the Vietnamese economy.

To accomplish this they have assembled a considerable force that intimidates the peasants in the outlying areas and carries on an incessant campaign of terror and destruction in the defended and more populous areas. Fourteen fortified villages have been constructed in the most productive regions and appear to be a success with the people, and ARVN troops deployed in the most critical areas have established a degree of security. However, the attacks have steadily increased in frequency and in the size of the Viet Cong units involved until this year's harvest is expected to be less than half that of preceding years.

An appreciation of the population is essential to an understanding of the military and political problems of Ngo Tho. In addition to some few Viets and a more numerous sprinkling of Khmers, there are Champas, Meos, Thais, and a number of others all generally lumped under the term Montagnards, although each tribe is a distinct ethnic group, avoiding all but the barest contact with other tribes and leading a poverty-stricken and nomadic existence. This separation of peoples is a basic problem of the province. It is important to note the general lack of national identity. Only the urban Vietnamese in Saigon and the larger cities have a sense of nationality. The average Viet thinks of himself as belonging to his family and then to his village and rarely identifies further to even the nearest large city or the province, let alone to the nation. Even more than the Viets in this purely local identification do the other ethnic groups cling to their old ways and loyalties. Illiterate and knowing only the forest and the land, they move from place to place, unaware of province or national boundaries. Government to all these peoples—Viets, Khmers, and the hill tribes alike—invokes only the image of the tax collector or the police, and where there is not open hostility there is evasion or apathy. This, of course, is the problem we face, the U.S. and the Vietnamese—the communication of an understanding of the aims and purpose of the government and the creation of loyalty to the cause, the defeat of the Viet Cong. And at the same time the salesmen for the other side are trying to win that same allegiance, with one significant advantage. Where persuasion is not effective they can influence the decision by acts of terrorism designed to demonstrate that we are ineffective, cannot control the land and cannot win the struggle.

Ngo Tho Province is commanded by Brigadier General Huang Huu-Lac, who is both the civil chief of the province and the Commanding General of the Army of the Republic of Viet Nam (ARVN) IX Corps. His force consists of the 12th ARVN Division with headquarters in Ghum Kong, the 30th ARVN division with headquarters in Khan Ghe, five separate Ranger Battalions, a river flotilla of seven specially built low-draft U.S. Navy rivercraft, and twenty-eight Self-Defense Force Battalions. This entire force numbers some forty-five thousand men and is the best equipped and most elite in the ARVN. Every member is a volunteer, none are from the Saigon draft, and from all indications morale and *esprit de corps* are high, although there is a general feeling of frustration over not being able to come to grips with the Viet Cong, who are estimated to be at a strength of less than twelve hundred regulars in the whole of the province, with probably an additional three thousand sympathizers available on call in certain localities.

General Huu-Lac is a member of one of the oldest Vietnamese families, one of the mandarin class who have for centuries served as administrators and governmental dignitaries for the old emperors, and since the 1880's for the French. His father was a close personal friend of Vinh-Thuy who became the emperor Bao-Dai, which ironically means "Keeper of Greatness," and was one of the first patrons of Ngh Dinh Diem, being instrumental in securing Diem his first high appointment as Minister of Interior for Bao-Dai in 1932. General Huu-Lac is now some fifty-odd years old, is married to Le Xuan Trink, also from one of the mandarin families, in an evidently compatible and happy marriage that has produced three boys and one daughter. The oldest boy is now almost twenty-one years old, and the daughter, the youngest of the children, is sixteen. All three boys and the girl, as well as Mrs. Huu-Lac, have been in the States near Washington, D.C., for the past two years, the ostensible reason being for schooling.

Personally General Huu-Lac is a polished and well-educated man, speaking both French and English fluently, and professionally he is most competent in every sense of the word. Like many others of the current high command of the ARVN he was once a regular officer in the French Army and saw service in both Italy and Germany during World War II and was highly decorated by the French. It is significant that he is representative of the older officers, the hard core of the Vietnamese Army in this regard. He is one of this élite group—which did not, however, prevent him from fighting against the French with the Viet Minh, and he reputedly was at the fall of Dien Bien Phu.

It is somewhat surprising that Huu-Lac remains in such universally high esteem among the members of the present junta since he was known to be well thought of by Diem, and was, in fact, one of the key officers who backed Diem in his 1955 war with the Binh-Xuyen and Bao-Dai for control of Saigon. However, it is a fact that he has fared well under all the successors of Diem and is presently a favorite in all respects. Knowledgeable Vietnamese are wary of discussing this, of course, since it is not especially safe or profitable to discuss personalities or to speculate on the reasons behind the rise or fall of individuals, but the comment is generally to the effect that Huu-Lac is his own man and is for Viet Nam as a whole rather than favoring any particular political or military faction, and that this is so recognized as to insure his continued usefulness to any regime in power.

Two things can be said against Huu-Lac from our standpoint. The first is that our reports show an ever-increasing anti-U.S. bias, and the second is that he is evidently drinking to excess. One final and unusual item worth noting is that Huu-Lac was promoted to Major General by Diem just before the Big Minh coup but he has never acknowledged this advance in rank and continues to sign himself as a Brigadier, in spite of the fact that from the Ministry of Defense on down and all outside of his own province address him as a Major General.

Colonel Nguyen Kim is Chief of Staff for General Huu-Lac. He has much the same background, both family and professional, but where Huu-Lac is a reasonably devout Catholic, Kim is a Buddhist. He has an unknown number of wives and a correspondingly unknown number of children. He is a true *bon vivant* in the highest tradition of the French and was in open conflict with Madame Nhu during her puritanical drive for the austere life during Diem's last days, and was saved from a fate of God knows what several times only by Huu-Lac's personal intervention. The two have been friends for years both here and in France and work in absolute harmony.

This same situation is true of the relationship between Huu-Lac and his two Division commanders, Major General Tran Thuy commanding the 12th Division at Ghum Kong and Major General Le Hue who has the 30th Division at Khan Ghe. Unlike the situation in many of the Corps where there is constant back-stabbing and by-passing of commanders in an attempt to gain favor with the junta in Saigon, all Huu-Lac's subordinates appear to be completely loyal to him, and the Saigon crowd seem to understand and respect this so that all orders and directives go to Huu-Lac and not to his Division and Battalion commanders. That is not to say that all is as smooth and orderly as can be, since he is still subject to the usual rash of conflicting civil and military directives and to the start-stop-go interference that is normal.

Throughout the morning, the entire afternoon, and until well after eight in the evening, it continued. After Zeke came the others, each with the minutia of his area of responsibility. The plans to gain control of the province, which Scott accepted with great reservation after his conversation with Zeke, the status of current operations, the logistic problem, the personnel shortages, both U.S. and ARVN, communications, everything a Corps advisor should know, or at least everything available to Wesley's staff. Through it all Buckmeister was in full participation, fielding Scott's questions himself when required, sending out for required data, prompting briefers to expand on items he considered important, and so fully in command of the details of his job that Scott's dislike gave way to a reluctant admiration for the man's professional competence. Finally the end came, the last question was asked and answered and the room cleared except for Buckmeister, Zeke, and Scott. As Scott slowly and almost numb with fatigue, folded the single small slip of his notes, gazing dully at the map, and placed them in his shirt pocket, Buckmeister asked curtly, "Are you quite satisfied, Colonel Leonard?"

Scott turned slowly and met Buckmeister's eyes. You're a real enthusiastic hater, aren't you? he thought as he saw the naked dislike reflected in the man's gaze. In spite of Buckmeister's painfully correct manner during the entire briefing, it was evident that his dislike for Scott had not abated in the slightest. So be it, you bastard, he thought, and aloud he said, "Your boys did a real fine job, Colonel. Just the way I wanted it. The next time you have them all together again please pass on my appreciation and my compliments on a truly professional job. I'll be sure to mention this to General Wesley the next time I see him and say some kind words in praise of your efforts in conducting this little exercise." Purposely he let a tone of patronage cover his final remark. I don't want any bastard just disliking me, I want him to hate me if we can't be friends, and the harder he hates the better, because sure as hell he is going to try to hang me and the madder he is the better the chance that in his eagerness he'll step on his dick.

The effect on Buckmeister was all he desired, but although his eyes glistened with rage, in a visible effort he controlled himself. Rising to his feet, and with an almost snarled, "Goodnight," he stomped to the door and disappeared into the darkness.

"Man, you do ride them rough, don't you?" Zeke said in a mockingly amazed voice. "You've got about as much tact and diplomacy as a meat ax."

"It takes years of study and practice," answered Scott, grinning. "The fact is that no matter how I acted now it wouldn't change his feeling toward me one bit. So screw him, and where in hell in your little village can a man find a cold double double martini?"

"That's the easiest question you've asked all day," answered Zeke. "You are in the Paris of the Orient, my boy, and you can get anything you want, from opium to ass. You name it, we got it. For a price, of course—hardly anything is for free—although it just so happens that I know a couple of young Vietnamese ladies if you want to make an evening of it."

Fatigue was beginning to settle over Scott like a filmy net that made each movement a horrible effort and dulled his sense of time and awareness. The past three days, leaving Travis Air Base just outside of San Francisco, one day in Hawaii getting a routine orientation at CINCPAC, and yesterday flying from Hawaii into Saigon, had cost him much sleep, and the humid and oppressive heat wasn't helping. "Let me have a rain check, Zeke," he said. "The way I feel now I couldn't do either one of your young ladies or myself any good. Besides, you're supposed to have something important to tell me before I leave."

"My God, Scott, you are getting old, old, old. I can remember when you were a real tiger who would never let a little thing like the loss of a few hours sack time or a hard day stop you from a night on the town, especially a strange town with all to offer that this one has," Zeke said in mock seriousness, and then becoming truly intense he continued. "You're right, this is not the night for getting laid. You and I have got to have a talk. Let's get out of here."

Leaving the briefing room to the care of the sentry on duty just outside the door, they crossed the compound to a small foreign-made sedan parked in the shadows.

"Get in, and save your witty remarks—I've heard about every variation on the subject of me and this car," said Zeke.

"You stopped me just in time," joked Scott. "I was just going to ask if you were the poor relative around here that they couldn't provide you with a decent-sized car and a driver, and to wonder how you ever got that lard ass of yours into this thing."

"I don't want any goddam driver, Viet or U.S., listening to my conversations, and some of the places I go I don't want advertised by driving a stateside automobile. This way I'm not so conspicuous, and just so you won't worry, I've got overload springs on my side."

Scott smiled in the darkness at the thought of the gigantic figure of Zeke ever being inconspicuous among the small Vietnamese, as he asked, "Where are we off to?"

"The Frenchman's. One each Monsieur Gaston, who runs as fine a restaurant as you'll ever find, and who will supply you with anything else your little heart desires. For me he provides, among other things, the most accurate and reliable information on various subjects of interest. Such as who is shacking with who. Very few of our brave troops here in Saigon get laid without old Zeke knowing about it, sometimes even before it happens. And Gaston and I manage to keep track of all the drunks pretty well too."

"Is that how you get your kicks these days?" asked Scott good humoredly. "I think they call someone who likes to watch a *voyeur*, but what in God's name do they call someone who gets a bang out of hearing about it?"

"I get my kicks, as you so nicely phrase it, the same way I always have, in the saddle," answered Zeke, and in a fair imitation of the patronizing tone Scott had so recently used with Buckmeister, continued, "And your snide remarks only prove the full extent of your ignorance and your abysmal stupidity. You probably think all the Viet Cong are out in the boondocks, sneaking up on the Viets and our fine unaware U.S. soldiers. You may even think that all Viet Congs are male. It just ain't so, Colonel, this town is full of them and some of their best agents are women, and it's my business to know when our people are getting seriously involved with a woman. And I mean *any* woman, until we've checked her out and she has been certified as untainted by any Viet Cong sympathy. We're not at all concerned with anyone who goes for a one night stand, drunk or sober, but when anyone starts getting really serious about a particular girl, we start checking both of them out. The same thing holds true for anyone who starts lapping up too much booze, especially if he combines it with a loud mouth, and Scott, believe me we've got more student alcoholics than you can imagine. Remember I told you that Buckmeister's predecessor was moved out of here for some rather unusual reasons. The G2 before I inherited the job was responsible for his sudden departure."

As they talked Zeke took the car out of the compound and through the cluster of guards at the gate in a screeching flourish, and raced at an insane speed through the swarming streets. Bicycles, pedicabs, tiny Renault taxis, and pedestrians seemed to part miraculously in front of the car at the last possible instant as Zeke wound in and out of the traffic. The streets grew steadily brighter and more crowded and finally they entered an unusually wide avenue, almost a market place, lined with flower stalls that were a blazing rainbow of color, and Zeke slammed to a stop at the curb,

5

THE HEAT OF DAY still remained, and the loss of the small breeze the movement of the car had provided made it even more noticeable as they crossed the broad sidewalk dotted with tables. Almost all these were filled with round eyes Scott noticed, and as they entered the restaurant proper there was the same prevalence of Caucasians, with the only Vietnamese being the male waiters and a sprinkling of bar girls dressed in skintight western-style dresses. The room was surprisingly small, with tables to the left and straight ahead and a bar on the right, and it was jam-packed. Even the bar was completely occupied, and as they hesitated in the doorway Scott raised his voice over the din of voices, "It looks like there is no room in the inn tonight. You know of another place?"

Zeke grinned. "You think old Zeke would eat in here with the peasants? Follow me, son, and we will dine in the style to which I've become accustomed." Moving with surprising speed considering his bulk and the closeness of the tables, he went straight down the length of the room. Scott followed him, wishing for the air-conditioning that he normally found so unnecessary, down the length of the room and through a curtained doorway, and turning to the right, up a short and narrow flight of steps. Zeke opened the door at the top to release a flow of cool air and strode into the room with Scott close on his heels.

The room contained a single table, covered with a snow-white cloth, and six chairs. Seated at the table was a truly startling man. He had an immense head, completely bald and fish-belly white, and the most protruberant eyeballs Scott had ever seen. His head was the head of a fat man, but his shoulders and arms and chest were thin almost to the point of frailty, and his hands, which cupped a beautiful crystal brandy snifter, were more like claws than hands. Seated next to him, so close that her lush breast pressed against his elbow, was a startlingly beautiful Vietnamese girl, who with only a brief glance at Scott and Zeke, returned her attention to her companion. Their entrance had evidently interrupted a serious and intense conversation, which the girl was reluctant to abandon. She gently grasped one of the talon-like hands and murmured something in a supplicating tone of voice. His eyes on Zeke, and with a single harsh word to the girl, the man arose, a smile increasing the grotesqueness of his face.

"Zeke, *mon ami*, welcome, welcome," he said, coming around the table and extending his hand, which was immediately lost in Zeke's giant paw. "My house is your house, for both you and your friend."

"René, this is a very old and very good friend of mine, Scott Leonard," said Zeke. Scott shook the proffered hand, dry, smooth, and cool, not unlike a bird claw, and murmured an appropriate "How do you do."

"Scott, René Gaston is both a friend and a professional consultant without peer," and turning to Gaston, he continued, "Much as I'd like for you and Scott to know each other socially, we just don't have the time tonight. I'll fill you in later on some assistance that Scott may require in Ngo Tho, but right now what we need is privacy and food, if you don't mind."

"But of course," Gaston responded, with a look at the girl who stood now at the far side of the table. She immediately came around the table in a sinuous and voluptuous walk, to take his arm. "Our conversation can continue elsewhere," he continued with a sudden leer.

"The room has been swept, hasn't it?" asked Zeke as Gaston opened the door.

"Completely, and only one hour ago by your so efficient man Stone," answered Gaston as he went out the door, his arm around the slender waist of the girl, and carefully closed the door behind him.

"Man, there's one of the all-time champions of catch-as-catch-can, free-style, no-holds-barred, grab-ass lechery," marveled Zeke. "Within his own set of rules, that is, which are fairly complicated and mainly centered around the idea that he never suggests jumping in the sack himself, nor does he ever pay for anything. He's so goddam ugly that it's a matter of pride or something with him, even though none of his sporting partners do it for love. It's always for some purpose, maybe to save a brother or a husband from being conscripted into the ARVN, or save the family fortunes from being taken over by the government, or for any number of reasons, but never for cash-on-the-line money. Just one minute until I get some chow on the way," he broke off abruptly, and opening the door he shouted down the stairway, "Chateaubriande, *avec,*" and immediately slammed the door again without waiting for an acknowledgment.

"Wait until you taste the steaks here," he continued, moving to the sideboard and surveying the array of bottles. "How about a martini to whet the appetite?"

"You really need to ask?" answered Scott. "That's what I need the most, and not one but two, in the same glass at the same time."

"Coming up, made by one of the greatest martini mixers who ever was," said Zeke as he busied himself with the makings. "We can talk here on any subject up to and including Top Secret. I come here often and while I trust Gaston and all the people who work for him, there is always the possibility that one of them has the Congs on his back and might just assist in having this place bugged. So I have an electronic sweep made of the place every day about this time—by Sergeant Stone, who is one of the greatest living experts on finding all the fancy little gadgets that are so easily available these days. Never found anything yet, but that doesn't mean that we've relaxed."

Handing Scott a coldly beaded glass filled to the brim, he sipped from his own appreciatively. "I've got a lot of things you should know that I wouldn't tell just any chowderhead that came down the pike, and which I would deny knowing like hell if any of those clowns like Buckmeister taxed me with it. I figure though, that you and I have been friends for many long years and I can trust you not only not to repeat anything I tell you, but not to let anyone suspect that you are anything but a replacement fresh from the mainland who doesn't know a single thing except what he has been told in official briefings. Also, and entirely aside from friendship, you are following a real sick act in Ngo Tho and you need every advantage if you are to restore any degree of prestige to our effort there." Looking at Scott steadily for a moment, he smiled, "Not that I worry about you, and in a way you're lucky since anything you do is bound to be an improvement over what Tom Meir has been doing."

"What's he been up to that is so bad?" Holding his drink to the light appreciatively, Scott sipped and then gulped thirstily.

"It's not so much what he has been up to or what he has done that is bad, it is more a matter of the type person he is. Deacon Tom, he is known as by his old buddies, of which he ain't got many, and he is a real wrong type to have any sort of assignment which requires any adjustment to a new way of living. He can't eat anything but U.S. stateside food, cooked in a U.S. stateside manner, and he equates a liking for anything else with moral degeneration rather than peculiarity of taste, appetite, or custom. He thinks that polygamy—and some of these non-Catholic Vietnamese have three or four quite legal, wives—is absolutely horrible and agin the will of God. He loathes the demon rum and people who are slaves to it, meaning anyone who has as little as one martini," said Zeke, refilling Scott's glass. "And while it's bad enough to have such convictions, he compounds the felony by looking down his sanctimonious nose at everyone, Viet and U.S., who differs from his ideas of what is right and proper, and he does it in such an obvious manner that it took the Viets no time flat to catch on to the fact that he wasn't really with them. You know, it seems to me that it should be real simple for Department of the Army to set up some damned near fool-proof system for screening his type out and insuring that they are not assigned to any duty with other than our own troops. And I mean real simple, not something that would take a team of headshrinkers a great research effort to come up with. Such as before assigning a man to a country, serve him a meal of the native food and if he shows any sign of flinching or asks any childish questions like "what's that"—automatically disqualify him. You know, I sometimes think there are more goddam perversions about food than there are with sex, and if you don't believe me just think about all the absolutely documented cases among our POW's in Korea where some finicky mother's boy laid on his pitiful ass and died rather than eat rice with worms in it. Of course any man has preferences as to what he likes and what he isn't just crazy about, but when it's a matter of offending

52

someone else, especially someone whose good will is important to both you and your country, a man ought to be able to eat anything, and even fake enthusiasm. Hell, you were an advisor in Korea—did you eat their *kim-chi* with them?"

"You better believe I did, and I even got to the point where I liked the fresh stuff, although some of the real vintage, one- and two-year-old stuff was a little powerful. One good thing though, each time I had to go back to I Corps or Eighth Army to discuss something or get a decision out of them, I had a real short conversation. All I had to do was breathe a little in their faces and they wilted real fine and agreed to almost anything just to have me out of their office and get the air cleared."

Scott thought for a moment. "Of course, I'm with you all the way on the problem of getting the right types assigned to this kind of work. We've both seen too damned many officers who were fine with our own troops but turned out to be a complete wash-out when they had to deal with foreigners. Someday the two of us ought to sit down and make up your test."

"Yeah, and ain't it a shame that you and I aren't right up there at the top making all the important decisions and applying our brilliant minds to the correction of all the evils of the system, old buddy," jibed Zeke wryly, and then returning to seriousness he continued. "As I said, old Deacon Tom fairly drips godliness and good clean living and pure thoughts, and has no hesitancy in making his views known. This is bad enough in his relationships with the Viets, let alone his junior officers who have got to conform, at least on the surface, to his blue-nosed ideas, but what has really blown things for him is that he isn't all that good. For all his extolling of morality, he has a pretty significant weakness which the Viets have discovered through a subtle series of tests, and now that they know he is something of a hypocrite they are treating him in a really shabby manner. Shabby, that is, if it weren't also so goddam funny."

"I'll beg you if you wish, but don't take so damned much pleasure in drawing this out," said Scott. "You know I'm a little tired after the last few days, and I'm sure it would offend you all to hell if I were to drop off into a nap while you were prolonging your story." The two martinis were at work soothing his taut and strained nerves, and as he extended his glass for a refill he thought that actually, considering everything, he had never felt better.

"Not if I know you—you won't go to sleep as long as

there is some little nugget of information to be gleaned on Ngo Tho," answered Zeke, "but just to come right out with it, old Deacon Tom has a sex problem. Like he'd screw a snake if someone would hold its head. And the Viets had provided him with several willing young women, which Tom in his stupidity thinks is all a secret between old Tom and the young ladies. How he can believe that he can slip around and get a little, in an area where he is one of the few round-eyes, without everyone in the country knowing about it amazes me, but sure enough, he really thinks that this is all private business. He's got quite a surprise coming tomorrow when he departs, personally arranged by General Huu-Lac."

There was a gentle rap on the door.

"That will be two of the finest steaks you've ever had," said Zeke, rising, going to the door, and opening it wide. A smiling Vietnamese, short even by their standards, and completely dwarfed by Zeke's gigantic body, stood with a tray balanced at shoulder height in each hand. Behind him somewhat down the stairway, stood another, and the head and shoulders of a third waiter were just visible further down the steps.

"Come in Minh," said Zeke with warmth. "This is my friend Scott Leonard, who is to be trusted as you would trust me."

As Zeke stood aside, the Vietnamese came into the room swiftly and smoothly deposited the covered trays on the table. Standing aside, he stood erect and at ease, watching intently as his two companions arranged the exquisitely fragile china and the massive silverware, and deposited the bread, an immense bowl of crisp salad, and a silver wine bucket with coldly beaded sides and two napkin-wrapped bottles protruding from the top. The two waiters completed their work with a final flourish, uncovering the trays and setting before both Scott and Zeke, who had returned to his seat, a magnificent steak surrounded by mushroom caps and small browned potatoes. With a single word to his companions, who quickly left the room, Minh stepped forward and carefully removed one of the wine bottles from the bucket and with precise skill inserted the corkscrew and drew the cork.

The first mouthful of steak was as marvelous as the aroma had promised, and Scott savored it as he chewed slowly.

"This drinking on an empty stomach sure makes the

54

stomach emptier," said Zeke around a mouthful of his steak. "Normally we do this in some style, and René considers me a first-class barbarian those times like tonight when I'm in a hurry and have everything on the table at once. But whether slow and easy, a course at a time, or like now, it will be a long time before you find a place like this. Agreed?"

"Agreed," said Scott, carefully cutting a second bite of the tender steak as Minh poured the wine, a rich red against the white of the tablecloth. "Try it," Zeke said, "I don't know where or how our host acquires this stuff but it's the greatest."

Scott sipped appreciatively and as he raised his eyes his gaze met that of Minh. Grave and unsmiling, and in perfect unaccented English Minh asked, "It's a hell of a lot better than some of that dago red you get stateside, isn't it?"

Surprise almost caused Scott to drop his glass and Zeke broke into a huge guffaw. "You look a little shook, Scott. Didn't you understand the man? He asked you a question."

"I guess I am a little surprised," said Scott. "I suppose I expected an accent or something."

"What you really mean, Colonel," said Minh, "is that you didn't expect a rice paddy coolie to even speak your language, except for a little pidgin. Don't apologize, that's the way I want it and I really work hard to keep my cover. Not a damned soul in this place except René, Vietnamese or otherwise. has any idea that I know anything other than my own language, and outside of Zeke, a couple of your generals, and my superiors in the War Ministry, not a soul in Saigon knows a damned thing about me."

"Minh is just now between assignments," explained Zeke, "and don't ask me what the last one was, or the one before that, or what the next one will be, because friends though we are, there are some things I'm just not authorized to know. But while he is waiting for whatever he is waiting for he works here as a cover, and incidentally picks up more in the way of information from our mouthy buddies than you'd ever think possible. You know the types I mean, security-conscious as hell in the office, don't let anyone see anything except on a need-to-know basis and lock the safes up tight at night before they go home, and then come in here and talk shop all during dinner and a session at the bar, and they just know it is safe because the goddam waiter can't even understand enough English to take their order."

"It's quite true," said Minh, sitting down at the table and

pouring himself a glass of wine, "but what the hell, there's no difference in soldiers no matter what army they are in, and everyone has the same security problem. What's the old saying to the effect that when they're out in the field all they talk about is screwing and drinking, and when they're back in civilization they can spend a whole night in a whorehouse doing nothing but telling war stories."

Scott was amazed as he watched Minh, casually slouched in his chair across the table, first sipping and then gulping down his glass of wine. When he entered the room he had been the model of a self-effacing waiter. Even when Zeke had introduced Scott and made his statement that Scott could be trusted, there had not been the slightest change or in fact any indication that Minh had heard and understood. Now he was completely at ease as an equal, with no trace of his waiter mannerisms. And his command of English was perfect.

Zeke was obviously appreciating Scott's puzzlement. "Don't strip a gear in trying to figure this out, Scott. Let me introduce Colonel Minh Vinh Lac, Army of the Republic of Viet Nam, assigned in some mysterious manner to the Intelligence Division of the Ministry of Defense, and with duties which are none of our business except insofar as they sometimes permit him to give us a hand. Minh and I are old friends, we were in the same class together in Command and General Staff at Leavenworth, and we became somewhat closer friends during a small incident while we were traveling in convoy out to San Francisco after the course was finished."

"Small incident, hell—this big bastard saved my life, and don't let him tell you I'm exaggerating," interrupted Minh.

"You should have been there, Scott," Zeke said, "it was fun, although some bums managed to hurt Minh pretty badly. Of course, it took six of them to do it."

"I'd like to have seen it," agreed Scott.

"They would have killed me if it hadn't been for Zeke," said Minh simply. "I owe my life to him."

"Knock it off, Minh," said Zeke with embarrassment, "You'd have done the same for me."

"I would have tried," said Minh, "but I could never do what you did." Turning to Scott he continued. "These hoods weren't just the average man on the street. They were tough and they were mean, and I doubt that anyone in the world except Zeke could have cleaned the whole crowd of them."

"That's enough of this crap," said Zeke with even more embarrassment. "We're not here to talk about how tough I am. I want Minh to give you a little more of his background Scott and then I've got one or two items about what you're going into in Ngo Tho, and then you need some sleep. You look just about beat."

As they talked Scott finished his steak and potatoes and a small portion of the salad. And the food together with the martinis and the several glasses of wine combined to make him feel at peace with the world and pleasantly drowsy, so that while he looked forward to sleep he felt no urgency.

"Don't worry about me, Zeke," he said. "Minh, where did you pick up such a command of our language—surely not in the nine or ten months that it takes to get through Command and Staff School."

"Hell no, I practically grew up in the States," answered Minh. "My father was a professor of economics at the University in Hanoi, and he had several tours of study at various universities in the U.S. Every time he took me along, and since he was a great believer in your public school system I went to school wherever we happened to be—Chicago, Washington, D.C., New York, Los Angeles. All through grade school and my first and third years of high school. I practically grew up with English as my language, although you can be sure that my father never let me forget that I was Vietnamese, and while the other kids had homework, I had a double portion—my school work and my Vietnamese study. My father was a scholar in the best sense of the word," he said with obvious affection and pride, "and while I was expected to get good grades in my school studies, it was absolutely required that I be a model of perfection in the Vietnamese subjects he loaded on me. We last returned from the States in 1951, and by 1953 my father and my two brothers were dead."

There was absolute stillness in the room as Minh's last words seemed to linger on in the air. Minh sat quietly, his eyes vacantly staring, as he continued in an even and detached tone of voice. "They were all killed by Ho Chi Minh, as surely as if he had pulled the trigger—my father, my brothers and their wives and children. He would have killed my uncle and me if he could have caught us, and all because my father was a professor of economics and had studied in your country. If he had been a professor of languages or an engineer, or almost anything else, they all might have lived." Raising his eyes to Scott's he continued with an almost wild intensity. "Only my uncle, my father's younger brother, and I escaped, here to Saigon. Out of all of them, only the two of us." Smiling a smile that was almost a snarl, he continued. "Zeke says he doesn't know what I do for my country. He knows well enough—although as he says, not many do. I kill communists. Individually or in groups, here or in Hanoi, or Phom Pei or Hong Kong, or any place I'm told to go. I kill communists to avenge my family and I'll continue to kill them until I have either killed them all or they have finally finished me."

Scott sat quietly and in silence, looking at Minh and knowing that he need not say anything in routine condolence. Minh dropped his eyes to his wine glass and taking it up finished the dregs. Quiet again, he said, "I'm glad to have met you, Scott, and I hope that we will run into each other again soon, but I must go now. I know the area in Ngo Tho like a book and General Huu-Lac like a brother, so if you ever run onto anything that looks like real action there, get word to me and I'll come running." Rising he extended a hand that felt to Scott like a small hard rock, and slapping Zeke on the shoulder, Minh went out the door. As he quietly closed the door behind him, the air of quiet, respectful attentiveness of the perfect waiter seemed to settle like a mantle around him.

"There goes a man who is very much a man," said Zeke. "Regardless of his size, he's one boy I'd always be glad to have on my side, and I don't think that I'd sleep well at night if I ever thought that he was after me."

"He is pretty goddamned impressive," agreed Scott. "Even though it has been quite some time ago he seems to still feel very badly about his father."

"You're right, and I don't think that his feeling for revenge has lessened one small bit even after all these years. I've heard a story, which I'm inclined to believe as gospel, that when he and his uncle, who is a major general in intelligence, came south they went first to Hue and requested an appointment with Bishop Ngo Dinh Thuc. You know the one I mean. He was Diem's brother, and the ranking cleric in the Catholic Church in Vietnam. This was in 1954, during the time that all the Catholics were coming south out of Hanoi and the bishop was a pretty busy man, so it took almost a week before he could get around to seeing them. When he could fit them in he was somewhat surprised to find that they did not want to talk to him in his office or his home, but insisted on meeting him in the cathedral. They were there first, waiting for him down in front near the altar, and the uncle made a short statement to the effect that they both had a solemn duty to avenge their family, that the Commandments forbade killing, that they could not remain Christians and break the Commandments, and so until such time as their revenge had been accomplished they both were renouncing their Christian religion. They both then knelt and said a farewell prayer and walked out. Evidently they now kill with a completely clear conscience."

"My God, I don't think that I've ever heard of anything quite like that," said Scott. "Although I can appreciate the logic, and I can also appreciate that any man with such a truly fine sense of honor is a man I'd be proud to have as a friend."

"I am proud that he is my friend, and I'm sure that he liked you. But enough of that little tiger—let me tell you some more about Tom Meir and General Huu-Lac and then we'll call it a day."

"Fire away," said Scott. "I guess that I can stay awake a little while longer."

"Remember that I told you that Meir was reporting Huu-Lac to be a fornicating drunk, and that it really wasn't true. Well, these reports all started because Huu-Lac was getting damned tired of Tom Meir coming to see him each day with a long list of things Headquarters here in Saigon thought the General should do. One day when old Tom called around with his usual line of horseshit, the Chief of Staff, Colonel Nguyen Kim, gave Tom a spur-of-the-moment story about how Huu-Lac really wasn't fit for duty that day because he had been so really smashed the night before. I don't think that at the time anyone thought that Meir would report this to Saigon, but little did they know Tom, and I guess he could hardly wait until he wrote it up and dispatched it. Of course our reports are supposed to be for U.S. eyes only, but something like that was too good to keep and some way or other the radio operator had no sooner finished sending it out before Colonel Kim had the thing, word for word. He and Huu-Lac thought this was both hugely funny and a perfect solution to the problem of Meir's daily visits, so they fell into a routine of Kim giving Meir a story each morning, complete with the details of just how much Huu-Lac drank, how drunk he was, and how many women he laid, which Meir dutifully reported back to Buckmeister. This has been going on for over two months, and the only bad thing about the whole screwed-up routine is that Buckmeister gets General Wesley all charged up and he goes storming over to ARVN Headquarters of the Ministry and tells them what a mess they've got in Ngo Tho, which makes him look a little ridiculous since every Vietnamese in any position of responsibility knows the whole story. I know that I should tell Wesley the facts, and believe me I've been on the verge of getting him and Buckmeister off alone and laying it on the line, even though it would really hurt me with the Vietnamese and they might never trust me in anything like this again. But Wesley has been in such bad health lately that I've been reluctant to get him all stirred up, and you can bet he'd have nothing short of apoplexy if he had any idea that he had been so badly misinformed by one of his key advisors. And when he really understood that this had been deliberately connived by Huu-Lac and Nguyen Kim and that his actions to get Huu-Lac relieved of command had made him look stupid in the eyes of the Vietnamese, I'm really afraid of what might happen."

"I can see your point," agreed Scott, "although I hope to hell I never run such a screwed-up operation that one of my staff has any reluctance in telling me anything as serious as this."

"Don't we all hope the same thing," said Zeke. "Anyway, Scott, I thought you should know all this for two reasons. First, you'd begin to wonder if you weren't being pretty lax in the performance of your duties if you knew your predecessor had been reporting a situation of which you could find no trace, and second, while I expect that you and Huu-Lac will get along real well and that he expects anyone to be an improvement over Meir, he just might not welcome you with open arms, and he and Kim might decide it was a good idea to continue their little fraud for a while just to test you."

"You can't know how I appreciate all this, Zeke," said Scott warmly. "I suppose I'm about the luckiest bastard over here to have met you today, and I'm damned sure that there are few U.S. types in the country who ever suspect the things you know. And you're damned fortunate to have a friend like Minh."

"You better believe it. Through him I've met more top-level Viets who have treated me with absolute trust than ever would have been possible otherwise, even if I had spent my whole frigging life here and really understood their customs and spoke the language. There is of course the problem of knowing a number of things that I can't do much about, like this situation with Meir and Huu-Lac. But all I can do is try to maintain a balance between what I could do and what I should do, and whether doing anything at all about a specific situation is worthwhile as weighed against a violation of the trust given me and the possible stoppage of my sources."

"I think you're developing too sensitive a conscience, Zeke. You know damned well that if you were ever faced with a situation where it was a case of our national interest against the Vietnamese you wouldn't wait even part of a second, even if you knew for sure that it would blow every single one of your sources, including Minh. You're confusing your duty with your reluctance to watch any U.S. soldier, especially a general officer make an ass of himself, and you have my personal endorsement, for what it's worth, of the way you're handling the situation. With anyone else it might be possible to tell the Huu-Lac story and count on the man to not raise hell but just quietly ignore the situation. Not Wesley. He'd want the blood of everyone concerned in his blind rage of having been deceived, and entirely aside from his personal health, which is really a secondary consideration, his attempt to make someone suffer would hurt the U.S. effort very seriously."

"I know, I know. I really haven't much choice to do other than I'm doing," replied Zeke with a trace of irritation, not directed at Scott but at the whole situation. "And I have probably exaggerated my concern, but what the hell, you're the only man I've seen in months that I can even discuss the problem with, so you'll just have to excuse me wringing out my soul in front of you."

"You're excused," said Scott smiling with real affection at the fat and ugly giant opposite him. "You're excused, and I'm honored that you'd trust me enough to tell me all this tonight. But you're not done yet, you know. Let's have a last drink and you tell me what astounding surprise Huu-Lac has arranged for our departing Tom Meir."

"Good idea, how about a little brandy?" said Zeke, rising and going to the sideboard and pouring two huge dollops into a pair of crystal snifters. Handing one to Scott, he sniffed deeply at his own, took a small sip, and then a huge gulp. "All likker is made for gulping, not sipping," he said. "Feel that beautiful warm glow sliding down to hit bottom. That Gaston is a jewel beyond price." Taking another generous mouthful, he continued. "As I said, Deacon Tom is a real upstanding Christian except for once in awhile when his hormones back up on him. I guess that he has always been like that, from some of the stories I've had from people who have known him over the years. Not being a headshrinker, I have no idea of how he reconciles his little forays into sin with his standards for other people, and maybe he doesn't excuse himself and really suffers for his transgressions—but however it is, he does transgress. Of course, the Viets made it easy for him and provided him with plenty of opportunity in the way of some specially selected maids to work in the MAAG compound. Old Tom got a sneaky piece from three or four of them, and then finally settled on one named Kei as being the best-quality ass in the group and ran all the rest out of the compound. You've got to admire one thing about him, he is sly and he is quick. He has been knocking this young queen off for months without any of his officers having the slightest suspicion that Deacon Tom is doing anything other than uttering a few well-worded prayers when he retires to his room. From what I'm told he has developed a real tight schedule, and the minute she has progressed in her work to the point of getting around to his room he arrives on the scene, bangs her, and is on his way back to his office almost without breaking stride. You understand Tom is not a lover, in the sense that he wants any conversation or dalliance, which is a good thing in a way, since Miss Kei doesn't speak any English. All Tom wants is the act, and the report is that he hardly even speaks to the girl, although he is quite generous with the pay."

"Real couth, and heavy on the suave," said Scott. "With that description of instant intercourse as background, what is this surprise in store for our Prince Charming?"

"I don't know who among the Viets thought of this, but whoever it was deserves recognition as a brilliant and original thinker. Slightly sadistic maybe, but real original. Everyone knows that love or affection doesn't enter into Tom's mind so that it wouldn't hurt him at all if anything should happen to the girl. But it would hurt him badly if Huu-Lac or one of the Viets were to tax him with the fact that they knew just what had been going on all the time, and had in fact arranged the entire passionate affair. But it would be completely out of the Vietnamese character to do anything so crudely. In a pretty astute evaluation of Tom's character and of what is likely to have the greatest effect on him, they came up with a plan for a little farewell ceremony, consisting of a short speech by Colonel Kim telling Tom how the vigilance of the Viets has resulted in turning up a notorious Viet Cong female agent working right in the MAAG compound and how, while she has confessed freely to being a Viet Cong, she has not yet disclosed her source of information within the MAAG Headquarters. Colonel Kim will be very sympathetic and share in Tom's horror over the situation and will assure him that the Vietnamese questioning will continue until the agent Kei—and this will be the first identification of Tom's girl friend as the spy—has revealed all, and that Tom can be assured that the name of her contact within the compound will eventually be revealed and a full report made. He will also assure Tom that they know they have got the right girl because she has admitted having a U.S. boy friend and has much more money than any Vietnamese girl could ever acquire legally. As proof of the intensity of the Viet effort to get the full truth out of this spy, and knowing that Tom as a true fighter of the Viet Cong would appreciate a memento of the occasion, a sort of a war trophy, they will present him with the breasts of Kei, sliced off in an effort to make her reveal the identity of her lover."

"Christ, that's a little hard on the girl, isn't it? Talk about carrying a joke all the way—surely her sense of humor doesn't extend to a contribution of this sort."

"Hell, you know damned well that by the time Kim gets that far along with his story Tom will be so goddam shook he won't know what he is handed. Actually they will fix up a couple of tits off a brood sow, with the hair clipped off, and that will be near enough for Tom to believe that they are really torturing Kei and that she will eventually break and give his name and all the passionate details of their relationship. Kim will bid Meir a final farewell with the assurance that the tits will make marvelous exhibits when properly tanned and mounted, and will give him an address in Saigon where this can be done overnight and very cheaply, and finally, convey General Huu-Lac's personal promise that a full and detailed report will be given to the U.S. Command."

"That should give Meir something to worry about during his trip back to the States, and for a long time afterward," said Scott. "They must really have an erection for him to stage such an elaborate affair. I suppose I'll be a witness to all this, and I'll play it straight down the line. I'll be both surprised that anyone could infiltrate our security measures and grateful for the Viets having uncovered the young lady, and of course, I'll be most intrigued and amazed by the marvelous trophy and pat Meir's back all the way to the chopper when he leaves."

"That's my boy," said Zeke, tossing off the last of his brandy. "Drink up and let's get out of here and get you into the sack."

Now that sleep was truly a possibility, fatigue again settled on Scott's shoulders like a heavy and unyielding weight, and finishing the last half-inch of his drink, he followed Zeke out of the room and down the stairs and into the heat and noisy din of the main restaurant.

At the street door Zeke paused for a moment, his eyes searching the restaurant and the bar. "I'd hoped we'd see Gaston again before we left but I guess he has been asked properly by now and will be fully occupied until along about noon tomorrow. No, we walk," he interrupted Scott's move toward his Renault at the curb. "The Brink is just around the corner," and guiding Scott's arm, turned him to the right.

The street was packed with people, all in a hurry, so that movement was difficult for the short distance to the corner, and then as they turned, it became quiet and dark with the guard post of the Brink an oasis of light ahead, and the many stories of the building looming against the dark sky.

They walked in silence along the sidewalk and across the street to the gate, the two guards on either side of the closed grill snapping to attention upon their approach and a non-com in the cubicle inside coming forward at the double to unlock and open the gate. "I'll leave you here, Scott," said Zeke, "So good night, and believe me it was real nice to see you again after all these years." He paused for a moment. "Jesus, we've been yakking so damned much I forgot to even ask about Cindy. How is my favorite girl friend?"

In spite of himself Scott could not prevent the reserve in his response or the tinge of bitterness in his voice. "She's just fine, Zeke," he answered. "I'll tell her that we've met again when I write." A fine goddam man you are, he thought, as he had thought in rage and frustration and sadness and shame a thousand times before. As a soldier you can cope with anything and solve any problem, but you can't cope with one hundred and ten pounds of wilful and perverse female and you can't solve the problem of your marriage.

Mistaking his coolness for fatigue Zeke said cheerfully, "Please do that and give her my true love. If I had ever married it would have been someone just like her. Now, off to bed, and either Captain Thompson or I will be here at four hundred hours to get you out of bed and out to Than Son Nhut and on the way to Ngo Tho. I assume that you're still going—if Buckmeister had been successful in having you diverted to MACV you can bet that some bearer of the tidings would have been in contact by now."

"Thanks again for everything, Zeke," said Scott, weary and tired, and depressed at the mention of Cindy.

6

SCOTT AWOKE QUIETLY and completely at three-thirty. Only four and one half hours since he had finally dropped like a stone into the forgetfulness and oblivion of sleep, but he felt completely refreshed. Sleep was just like screwing or drinking or fighting or working, he thought, sleep hard while you sleep, just as you work hard when you work, to get the most out of it.

In twenty minutes he had shaved and dressed, using the fairly presentable uniform he had worn the previous day and only changing his shoes for the jump boots he took from one of his footlockers. Stowing his shaving gear away in the B4 bag, he closed it, carefully guiding the worn zipper in its course, and hoisting the duffel bag onto his right shoulder, he maneuvered the B4 bag and dispatch case with his free arm. Kicking the door shut behind him, he made his way down the hallway to the elevator. The footlockers could wait here in Saigon for a long while, maybe his entire tour.

It was still dark outside as he came through the lobby doorway, and the brightly lit gateway seemed to be even more of an oasis—and also a target, he thought—in the stillness of the early morning. The guard NCO came running to help him, but Scott made it to the iron grilled gate alone and dropped his load, puffing slightly from the exertion. Scott savored the quiet and the freshness of the morning air. It was warm, though not unpleasantly so, and after the heat of the previous day it seemed almost cool.

An undefinable whisper in the distance became the sound of a car driven at high speed, and as Scott walked through the now-opened gate, a staff car squealed its tires around the corner and pulled to a stop in front of the gate. Captain Thompson came out from behind the wheel and around the hood of the car, sharp in fresh short-sleeved tropical worsted, and coming to a heel-clicking stop, saluted briskly.

"Glad to see you again, Colonel," he said warmly and cheerfully. "And if I may say it, you look mighty fresh considering the day you put in yesterday."

"Thank you, Captain," said Scott, responding to the warmth in Thompson's voice, and thinking again as he had thought the previous morning when Thompson had been so truly worried over General Wesley, that this was a fine young officer of whom the Army could well be proud. "Let's stow this gear in your trunk and be on our way." Picking up the duffel bag by the carrying strap, he half lifted, half dragged it the few feet to the rear of the car.

"Is this all you are taking with you, sir?" asked Thompson dubiously, opening the trunk and moving to pick up the B4 bag and the dispatch case.

"This is all there is, except for the two footlockers upstairs, which I'd like you to have picked up and held someplace until I call for them," answered Scott, and seeing that the Captain still looked a little reluctant, continued, "Look, Captain, I'm an old soldier and I've been through this routine before. I know what I really need each and every day, and I know what is just nice to have. The nice-to-have stuff is upstairs and I'll get along without it for awhile, okay?"

"Of course, Colonel," said Thompson. "It's just that most people who come through here on their way upcountry seem to have more gear." Closing the trunk he stopped a moment in indecision. "I have a truck that should be right behind me, which was for your baggage, and if we leave now—" He broke off and then brightened as the sound of a heavier vehicle came to them, and an OD painted pick-up came around the corner.

Scott got into the car as Thompson quickly dismissed the truck. "It's only four now, sir," said Thompson, getting in behind the wheel and starting the motor. "We're well ahead of schedule, thanks to you being up and ready. Colonel Dodds will meet us at the field. He would have been here with me but he had an errand first."

"He needn't have gone to the trouble of seeing me off," said Scott, "But what kind of errand can he have at this hour of the morning?"

"Beats me, sir," answered Thompson. "All he said last night when he told me to pick you up was that he was going to try to get something he thought you would need."

The drive through the silent and deserted streets in the morning coolness was pleasant, and Captain Thompson drove slowly and in silence. Not the nervous silence of the night of Scott's arrival or the journey yesterday morning to General Wesley's office, but rather the silence of one who is at ease. Maybe this young man is beginning to understand that not all senior officers make a life work of chewing ass, and are not all completely dependent upon young officers to carry them around, thought Scott. "How did the General make out yesterday?" he asked.

"Not very well," answered Thompson worriedly. "He went to his quarters right after he left us, and although I checked on him several times during the day he didn't seem to want to see anybody or to do anything except sit and read. Sometimes he didn't even read, he just sat and stared out the window." Thompson was silent for a moment and then continued, "He's really not sick, I guess, in the sense that he's got a bug or anything, but just the same he's not at all in good health and he has changed a lot in the last couple of months. We used to be out in the field all the time, visiting the Corps and Division advisors, and even down to Brigade and Battalion, but lately he just doesn't go anywhere. He says it's a waste of time and that if he is to do anything at all to improve the situation he had to do it here in Saigon by giving some direction to the Viets' effort. I don't really understand it at all."

"It is a problem," said Scott slowly. "But there isn't a hell of a lot you or anyone can do about it. You're doing the best thing that you can do by just sticking to your job and protecting him from as much annoyance as you can."

"That's what I thought," answered Captain Thompson, and then brightening he said, "One good thing about yesterday, though, was that I was free to attend most of your briefing, and it was a real education for me. You really wrung the staff out, and I think that some of them learned things about that province that they had never even suspected before." There was genuine admiration in his voice and he was oblivious of any intent to flatter Scott.

"Thank you, Captain. All it takes is years of experience and a few bad times when you find yourself in a spot where asking a few simple questions beforehand could have saved you one hell of a lot of trouble."

They had long ago left the city proper, and turning off the main road that led to the commercial side of the field, wound through a darkened tent village of U.S. forces and emerged at a far corner of the field where a light showed in a large and open hangar.

"Here we are, Support Group Flight Operations," said Captain Thompson, pulling to a stop in a path of light streaming from an open side door. "Lieutenant Smith should be around, he's the General's pilot, and he should be just about ready to take off."

They went through the open doorway into a scene of surprising activity where fifteen or twenty HU-1A choppers were being serviced by teams of mechanics. A young Lieutenant left the group gathered around the near machine and came forward to salute and report. "Lieutenant Smith, Colonel, I've filled a departure time of 0445 with Base Ops but we can change that to leave earlier if you wish."

"I'm glad to know you, Lieutenant," said Scott, extending his hand. "I think that we had better wait, at least for a short while. I'm expecting Colonel Dodds to show up any minute now." He continued, watching closely for the Lieutenant's reaction, "I hear we have a fairly rough ride ahead of us." Captain Thompson had passed on to the group of men and recruited a detail to load Scott's luggage.

"That's what I hear too," answered Lieutenant Smith carelessly, looking after Captain Thompson, and then realizing that Scott was watching him, he turned to Scott and met his gaze steadily. "But I also hear that it's all a goddam rumor, and that if you fly the flight pattern you are supposed to it's as safe as a church. We'll go up to six thousand feet and hold there until we're about twenty minutes out of Ngo Tho and it's light enough to see the ground and then go down to the deck and run on in. I don't know where all this panic started over this Ngo Tho run but it isn't a damned bit worse than a number of others we've got, and hell, you've got Major Larsen's 128th Trans Company up there, flying all over the area and their losses aren't much worse than anyone else."

"Well, what did get this idea started?" asked Scott. "From the way I heard it there are places where we were going to be like ducks in a shooting gallery."

"I'm damned if I know, other than because we lost a couple of MACV top-level staff officers up in that area due to some real, real lucky ground fire, but don't you believe that shooting gallery story, and just remember that this duck knows how to duck," said Lieutenant Smith with casual confidence.

Thinking that this young man was either damned cocky or badly overconfident he asked, "Are you coming back today after you drop me?"

"My orders are to stay until dusk and then come on back, although I'm supposed to check in before departure in case I'm to lay over and bring Colonel Meir out," answered Lieutenant Smith, and looking past Scott toward the door, "Here's Colonel Dodds now."

Turning toward the doorway Scott saw Zeke coming toward him, still in the same rumpled uniform he had worn last night, and followed by two soldiers, each carrying what could only be a case of liquor. In spite of the relative coolness, Zeke was drenched in sweat and walked like a man who had been in a hurry for so long that he could not now slow down.

"Scott, I come bearing gifts, and gifts of the sort to increase your popularity in your new home," he said, pumping Scott's hand. "Last night after I got in bed I just happened to think that I had heard that both Huu-Lac and Kim were Scotch lovers, so I routed a club officer out of bed and he reluctantly provided me with two cases of Ballantine's."

"Sir, we've about run out of time," interposed Lieutenant Smith. "I'll get this aboard, if you'll come out soon. I'm straight ahead about fifty yards, just beyond the light coming from the door," he continued, pointing out the hangar main door.

"Right, Lieutenant," acknowledged Scott, and to Zeke he said, "Zeke, you needn't have done all this. Christ, what you did last night was above and beyond the call of duty, but acquiring two cases of Scotch in the middle of the night is damned near pure heroism."

"No trouble at all, and I'll bill you for it later," said Zeke. "And now let's get you loaded and on your way."

Leading Scott at a quick pace out the hangar door, he headed for the chopper, a new HU-1B, Scott noted, which was parked in a cleared area with its landing lights ablaze. By the open hatch Captain Thompson and Lieutenant Smith were watching the last of the luggage and the two cases of Scotch being stowed.

"Colonel Leonard, this is Lieutenant Glenn, my co-pilot, and Sergeant Crouse, crew chief," said Smith, introducing the two men who had just secured the load. As Scott shook hands and acknowledged the introductions, he continued, "I'd suggest you ride in the crew chief slot. You can see better and we can talk on the intercom. Have you ever ridden in an HU-1B, sir?"

"Only the A model, Lieutenant," said Scott. "We poor people back stateside haven't a chance at this new stuff."

"Well, even with the A, you know that this is the Cadillac of choppers, and that we've got speed and power to burn. Still, we all wear a little protection, just in case," extending a flac vest to Scott.

Fumbling his way into the vest with Lieutenant Smith's help, Scott turned to Zeke and Captain Thompson. Grasping Zeke's hand he said, "I hope I'll see you up in Ngo Tho soon, Zeke, and again, I can't thank you enough for everything."

"Don't say it," said Zeke. "If there's anything I can't stand it's hand-licking gratitude. You'd have done the same thing for me in the same situation, I know."

Captain Thompson shook Scott's hand vigorously and silently as Scott said, "If you ever need a job, Captain, here or elsewhere, give me a call and I'll do my best for you."

"I'll count on that, Colonel," said Thompson, as Scott turned and climbed aboard, taking the seat slightly behind and between the two pilots and adjusting his headset.

"The switch is here," Lieutenant Glenn's voice came through the intercom as he turned and grasped the control box attached to the headset cord, and Sergeant Crouse quickly adjusted the seat belt and shoulder harness.

Scott turned and waved to Zeke and Thompson, who had withdrawn well away from the path of the rotor blades as Smith wound up the motor.

In moments they were airborne, the landing lights still ablaze, rising smoothly over the low adjacent buildings.

At one thousand feet Smith switched off the lights and his voice came over the intercom. "Like I said Colonel, we'll go to six thousand feet until we're about twenty minutes from Ngo Tho and then hit the deck. Our heading will be three

72

ten for about thirty minutes and then two seventy, and our speed about one-fifty knots. ETA is 0620 hours."

Finding his switch and locating the heading and air speed indicator on the dimly lighted instrument panel, Scott said, "I understand, Lieutenant Smith. Point out any scenic sights that come along."

"There won't be a single one, Colonel," said Smith cheerfully. "When we turn on to our two seventy heading, the Gy Than hills will be out of sight on the north, to the right, and the Se Reo Kri will be on our left, also well out of sight. It's a real dull run at this time of the day."

Scott was silent, and after a short look behind where Saigon was a faint glow on the horizon, settled easily into his seat and relaxed, thinking that one of the first rules to be learned was that when he hasn't got anything else to do a soldier should sleep. Although he felt quite alert and wide awake, he closed his eyes and began a slow and rhythmic breathing, which would provide for almost as much rest as total sleep, although he would not lose awareness of his surroundings.

"We're about twenty minutes out of Ngo Tho, Colonel," Lieutenant Smith's voice came over the intercom. "I'm going to start a fairly fast let-down now, and we'll go the rest of the way in right on the deck. Hope we'll be on them and over them before they have any idea we're even in the area."

The rising sun was now directly behind them, throwing long shadows from each fold of the ground below, each clump of trees, and giving a nightmarish appearance to the unfolding ground. "This is a damned poor time of the day to gain any appreciation of the terrain," said Scott. "Just where in hell is Ngo Tho from here?"

"Dead ahead," answered Lieutenant Smith, dropping the chopper's nose so that the ground, at first imperceptibly and then in a rush, came up to meet them. "Kind of hard to judge distance in this light until you get used to it. I'll hang a little high for a few minutes and then we'll get down to it."

"Your idea of high differs somewhat from mine," said Scott watching the horizon come at them, and when he looked directly down, a dark mass of foliage rushing by below. Five minutes, ten minutes, fifteen minutes of unbroken underbrush, trees, with only an occasional clearing to indicate the work of man, and suddenly Scott realized that it was full daylight. Talk about the dawn coming up like thunder—Kipling had described it real well, thought Scott. There was none of the lingering half light of the temperate and northern zones. It was either dark or light in the tropics.

Suddenly the ground below changed, and became a solid unbroken grassland with only an occasional sparse grove of trees. "Ngo Tho is still dead ahead, just a couple of minutes over the horizon," said Lieutenant Smith, almost, but not quite, relaxing. Ahead the grassland ceased abruptly, to become to an unbroken maze of interlocking rice paddies stretching ahead and to the right and left for as far as the eye could see. And directly ahead in the distance was a cluster of stark white buildings, French Saigon style colonial, surrounded on all sides by native Vietnamese houses. Without circling in the traditional traffic pattern, but going directly in, Smith throttled back as they approached the nearest of the buildings, a two-story white stucco surrounded by a high stucco fence. Near the marked chopped pad, was a small cluster of figures.

"MAAG Compound, Colonel, your home for lo, these many months to come," said Lieutenant Smith, and glancing at his watch, "Two mintues ahead of our ETA, which is not bad if I do say so myself." Smoothly yet quickly he set down, and flipping switches in rapid sequence, cut his motor.

Scott sat quietly for a moment watching the group of some seven or eight officers approach, instinctively ducking their heads even as the rotor blades slowly diminished in speed. In the lead was a short, dark, slender man with an improbable pot gut. Deacon Tom himself, thought Scott, as the man moved closer and he could see the silver eagles of his rank on his collar. I had imagined someone more gaunt and burned by the fires of hell, but this one is equally in character. He opened the door, fumbled for the step with his right foot, and hit the ground, turning just as Meir arrived, hand extended and a wide and joyous smile on his face. "Thank our good Christian Lord for your safe journey, and I assure you that you are most welcome. I especially am glad to see you, as you can well imagine." His voice was surprisingly deep and resonant, and he fairly reeked of friendship and good will. "Just a moment and I'll introduce you to your staff, but first," and turning to Lieutenant Smith who had dismounted and come around the chopper to stand at Scott's side, "Lieutenant Smith can you be ready to take off again in one hour "

"Yessir, but I thought . . ." began Smith, to be cut off by Meir. "Colonel Leonard, I know that it is customary for there to be several days overlap between the incoming and outgoing senior advisors, but I have just had a message from Colonel Buckmeister ordering me to return to Saigon as soon as possible today. I'm truly sorry, but I will have time only to introduce you to these gentlemen and to General Huu-Lac, the commanding General of the ARVN IX Corps and of Ngo Tho Province, and then I must be on my way. The message left no doubt as to the urgency of my return."

In a pig's ass you're sorry, thought Scott, but you couldn't make me any happier if you had tried. Scott had always hated situations where he was forced to go through a period of understudy. However, he said gravely, "I'm very sorry to learn of this. Something must have come up since I last talked to Colonel Buckmeister yesterday evening and I guess I'll just have to make do as best I can." Pushing past Meir to where the others stood, evidently awaiting a summons for introductions, he shoved out his hand to the nearest one of the group, "I'm Scott Leonard," he said. The solidly stocky, gray-haired Lieutenant Colonel grasped his hand warmly, meeting his eyes levelly, but before he could respond Meir said quickly, "This is my, or should I say your, executive officer, Colonel Gerrard," and in quick succession he ran through the rest of the group. Lieutenant Colonel Stowkowski, Plans and Operations, a worried and harassed-looking, young, tall, and blond officer. Lieutenant Colonel Storm, Intelligence, short, fat, and dark. Lieutenant Colonel Swann, a tall heavily built blond with a placid and unworried look in his eye, who functioned as Headquarters Commandant as well as Supply and Maintenance Officer. Lieutenant Colonel Pickering, Personnel, slightly built, with heavy horn-rimmed glasses, a dark and delicately handsome face and a painfully shy and diffident manner. And finally, standing well back as befitting a young Captain in such an illustrious group, Albright, the communications officer. Scott barely had time to acknowledge this flurry of introductions as Meir tugged at his sleeve, urging him toward a gleamingly clean jeep parked near the gate in the high wall of the compound.

"We really must hurry, Colonel Leonard," he urged. "On

the basis of Colonel Buckmeister's message I changed our appointment with General Huu-Lac from this afternoon to seven-thirty this morning." Hastily climbing into the back seat of the jeep, he introduced the driver, a Vietnamese soldier who sat with eyes straightforward and with ramrod stiffness. "This is Sergeant Hoan, your driver. He understands only a few words of English, but he is a good and careful driver, about the best we've got. You know, of course, that all our drivers, guards, cooks, and that sort of support personnel are provided by the ARVN. Let's go, Hoan. General Huu-Lac."

Without so much as a glance at either Meir or Scott or acknowledgment that he understood any of Meir's speech other than the command to go, Sergeant Hoan put the jeep in gear and slowly moved through the gate where the four trim and spotlessly uniformed guards snapped to attention and presented arms, and as slowly entered into the sparse traffic of the street.

"Our headquarters here was once the villa of a French rubber planter, and I think you'll find that your quarters are fairly adequate, although we really don't have quite enough office space," Meir said as the jeep continued to move slowly down the almost deserted street. "We're close enough to General Huu-Lac's headquarters to enable quite close liaison and still maintain our own organizational integrity." They had now approached a busy intersection and Sergeant Hoan stopped, awaiting a break in the stream of traffic. Dilapidated trucks and small sedans, bicycles and pedicabs, and horse- and buffalo-drawn carts filled the wide street solidly, loaded with rice bags, firewood, fresh produce, and all the myriad of cargo typical of an agricultural and marketing center.

Suddenly Hoan shot the jeep forward, miraculously missing a horse cart and slid snugly into the stream of traffic behind a lumbering truck piled high with a collection of cooking utensils.

"Slow, dammit, slow, Sergeant Hoan," nagged Meir in a tone of intense irritation, and then to Scott. "I have tried and tried to instruct our drivers in safety and to educate them to a sensible rate of speed, and Hoan is usually quite well disciplined, but even with him I must keep at it constantly, and I'm sure some of my officers are very lax about this and permit their drivers to be very reckless."

Slowly now, after their spurt into the flow of traffic, they

76

followed the truck while other cars passed them in a darting flow, the drivers alternately braking and accelerating and swinging in and out in the wild melee.

Meir pointed out the places of interest—AID Headquarters, the U.S. Seventh Day Adventist Hospital, the United States Information Service Library, the open-air market in the town's central square. Everywhere Scott noted the presence of smartly uniformed ARVN soldiers on alert as guards of the larger buildings and the numerous short bridges which they crossed, and he noted with approval the similar alertness of the uniformed police, and the fact that they seemed to be completely approachable to the people, with many a long stop while a policeman gave directions to some confused peasant, or halted the dense traffic in both directions to allow the turning of a buffalo-drawn cart.

Sergeant Hoan gradually slowed almost to a halt and then turned into a narrow side street between two-story wooden buildings that abutted directly on the street without the usual sidewalks, and after a short block entered upon a small square bounded to the left and right by a high wall, and directly ahead by a three-story white stone and stucco building with a wide elevated veranda. Every available parking space within the square was taken by ARVN vehicles and there was a mass of confusion as soldiers loaded and vehicles backed and maneuvered to exit through a narrow lane in the left wall.

"What the hell is all this?" he asked in amazement. There must have been at least fifty vehicles and four hundred soldiers massed in the square; a single man with a basket full of grenades perched on the wall or the rooftops could have a field day.

"This is General Huu-Lac's Headquarters," answered Meir.

"It's rather obvious that it's someone's headquarters," said Scott with a trace of sarcasm, "but what I meant is, what is this little exercise in chaos ahead of us?"

"Oh, this is the guard relief, concerned with all the municipal guard posts. Relief takes place every four hours, and this is the fresh detail going on duty now. Go on, Hoan."

Warning himself of the danger of jumping to a hasty conclusion, and trying to believe that this was not as vulnerable a situation as it appeared, Scott held his silence as Hoan maneuvered directly across the square in the now thinning

77

traffic and came to a stop in front of the steps leading upward to the veranda and the front doorway. Jumping out, Scott turned and watched Meir's awkward scramble from the jeep, and then followed a half step behind him as they mounted the short flight of stairs. Just short of the top, Meir stopped and turning to Scott, softly whispered. "I didn't want to say anything in front of Hoan, because while I'm convinced that he doesn't understand English, it is better to be overcautious. But I do hope that Colonel Buckmeister filled you in on Huu-Lac and his drinking. Colonel Kim assured me on the telephone a short while ago that the General was in good condition this morning, but even so I'm not absolutely positive that he will be in shape or in the mood to meet you just now. We'll just have to see, but in any case you will meet his Chief of Staff, Colonel Kim, and he will arrange a later meeting with Huu-Lac if necessary."

"Understood, lead on," said Scott in a neutral tone of voice, thinking God save me from ever exciting the dislike and contempt that this poor benighted, self-important little bastard must have aroused here. Some people have a real talent for displaying their inborn sonofabitchness on every occasion.

Meir continued to the top of the steps and across the wide veranda to where a young Viet officer was waiting in the doorway, standing at rigid attention, and saluting almost violently as Meir came to a stop in front of him. Meir returned his salute and said, "Good Morning, Major Huc." Half turning to Scott he continued, "Colonel Leonard, this is Major Huc, who is an aide to General Huu-Lac."

Again came the almost startlingly violent salute, the eyes directed rigidly straight ahead. Scott returned the salute with casual correctness and extended his hand. "I'm most happy to meet you, Major Huc, and I hope that we'll become well acquainted in the coming months." There was hesitation, almost open reluctance, in Huc's slow relaxation of his position of rigid attention and his meeting of Scott's offered hand, and when his eyes met Scott's there was no attempt to conceal his dislike. He said, "How do you do," with flawless diction and a trace of an English accent, and then, "Will you please follow me. The General is waiting."

This young soldier seems to have a rather king-sized erection for all us poor U.S. soldiers, thought Scott, as he followed Major Huc and Meir up first one and then the second flight of wide and graciously rising stairs. It will take

78

some doing on my part to get any change for the better in his attitude, but a General's aide is worth the effort, and sometimes when anyone is as truly anti as he seems to be they become just as pro once they begin to change.

The interior of the building was beautiful, both in design and in the care that had been lavished upon the gleaming bannister and steps and corridor floors, and on the spotlessly clean white walls. A sparkling cascade of crystal chandelier hung from the top of the stairwell, almost dazzling in the unfiltered daylight from the many-paned windows that marked each landing. Without pausing or looking behind him at the slightly puffing Meir, Major Huc crossed the wide corridor, opened the massive dark door, and standing to one side, ushered both Meir and Scott into an immense anteroom. A single desk stood at the far end of the room, unoccupied now, but evidently belonging to Major Huc, since he picked up a pack of cigarettes as he passed. The walls on three sides of the room were lined with benches. Leading the way to a second and equally massive door, Huc opened it and again stood to one side inside the room, and as Meir and Scott entered, announced in his faultless English, "The Colonels Meir and Leonard."

Although the room was somewhat smaller, the arrangement of the furniture was identical, and behind the desk guarding the far door sat a stocky, broad-faced Viet Colonel with a black and bristling crew-cut. Without haste, and with studied dignity he slowly rose.

"Good morning, gentlemen," he said, his marked accent a distinct contrast to the faultless diction of Major Huc. "I welcome you to Ngo Tho, Colonel Leonard," he continued as he came around the desk, and ignoring Colonel Meir's outstretched hand and his presence entirely, grasped Scott's hand for one quick shake and then quickly and almost forcibly disengaged. "I am Colonel Kim, Chief of Staff to the General Huu-Lac, who will see us shortly, and at a most unusually early hour for an appointment, I think." Turning to Meir he asked coldly, "I assume a great urgency attends your return to Saigon that it is not possible for you to stay for some few more days. There is a most interesting development which would benefit from your presence."

"I'm sorry but I have the most explicit and definite orders to return immediately," answered Meir in an apologetic voice, but still unable to conceal his eagerness. "I have no idea why, but I assume there is some need for consultation

79

in the next few days before I leave for the States." Almost disinterestedly and as an afterthought he asked, "What is the development you're talking about?"

"Later, Colonel Meir, after we have talked with General Huu-Lac," said Kim. Raising his eyes to Major Huc, who had positioned himself at the door to Huu-Lac's office, he gave an almost imperceptible signal and Huc immediately opened the door and entered the room, not quite closing the door behind him. Again speaking to Scott, in a carefully neutral voice, without warmth, but at least without the frigid coolness of his address to Meir, he continued. "We have, of course, a biographical brief on you, Colonel Leonard, submitted some weeks ago when you were first nominated as senior advisor, and we are quite happy to note that you have had considerable combat experience, in North Africa, Italy, France, and Germany, and in Korea, and both staff and command duties. Somewhat a different type of experience than you will have here, but at least useful as background."

Silently Scott nodded. My dear Colonel Kim, he thought, you really can't imagine what a lot of time you're going to waste if you think that talking down to me or patronizing me is going to get under my skin.

All further conversation was ended by Major Huc's announcement from the doorway, "General Huu-Lac will see you now," he said, almost with resentment that his General had so consented.

Colonel Meir was the first into the room, hurrying forward to the unusually tall and slender Vietnamese who stood before a brocade divan, and extending his hand.

Scott paused in the doorway, struck by the beauty of the room and only half-hearing Meir as he protested his regret at leaving and his apologies for requiring an appointment at such an early hour. A long, low divan of orange brocade, stood behind General Huu-Lac, and immediately in front of this was a low, jet-black table, covered with delicate figurines, all of canary-yellow glass. Black, orange, and yellow, were the colors of the room, and the tasteful arrangement of the various low and comfortable chairs and divans and the numerous tables gave an impression both of space and clutter.

Huu-Lac's eyes were on Scott. Allowing the briefest of handshakes with Meir, and a brush-off of "Please do not disturb yourself. It is not important," he moved around Meir to meet Scott. His grip was firm and strong and his direct and penetrating gaze seemed to instantly evaluate Scott's character and personality. Gravely, and without a trace of cordiality, he said, "I welcome you to my province and I sincerely hope that you will find your duties to be rewarding." As Zeke had told him, Scott found his English to be near perfect and almost unaccented.

With equal gravity Scott replied, "I am most happy to be here and to join you in your effort to free your country from those who are your enemies. I only hope that I can be of some small assistance in your fight." While he felt an instinctive liking for this grave and unsmiling man, he recognized that he, Scott, was not to be accepted on trust, and that until he had been examined, tested, and found to be of worth, his conduct must be that of dignity and silence.

Meir interjected impatiently, "I'm sure you will find Colonel Leonard is generally well-versed in his duties, General, and that just as soon as he gets read into the situation and familiar with the country, he will be of great assistance to you and your staff. We haven't much time so far, since Colonel Leonard just arrived a few minutes ago, but before I leave you can be sure that I and my staff will go over the whole situation with him and brief him thoroughly on your problems, as we see them."

"I'm sure you will, Colonel Meir," answered Huu-Lac, without looking away from Scott, and with an irony completely lost on Meir, "And since time is of importance to you today, I'm sure that you will want to get started as soon as is possible." Continuing to Scott he said, "I would be most happy if you would be my guest at dinner tonight. I will have Major Huc pick you up around eight, if that is convenient." For just a moment Scott thought he detected a hint of a smile in Huu-Lac's eyes, and certainly there was at least a slight tinge of warmth in his voice.

"I thank you very much," answered Scott, "and I am sure that eight will be quite convenient."

Quick to seize upon the opportunity to end the interview, Meir began heartily, "General, it has been a real pleasure to serve here with you and I've enjoyed every moment of it, so much so that several times lately I've seriously considered requesting General Wesley to extend my tour with you. Unfortunately, I waited too long to do this, but I do want to assure you of my real regret at leaving and to thank you for all the consideration I've been shown by you and your staff, and to wish you the best of luck in your continuing fight."

"The best of luck to you also, Colonel Meir," interrupted

General Huu-Lac, briefly shaking Meir's hand, his tone barely civil. "At eight," he continued to Scott, and turned toward the massive teak desk in the far corner of the room with an attitude of complete dismissal.

Meir was hurt. It was evident from the astonishment on his face that he had expected an exchange of compliments and mutual regrets over his departure, and that this offhand and almost contemptuous rejection of his little speech was most painful. He stood for a moment dumfounded, until Scott, aware of the movement of Huc and Kim toward the door behind him, stood to one side and motioned for Meir to precede him.

Startled, Meir moved to the door, the childlike look of rejection on his face slowly clearing. Without looking back, Scott followed past Major Huc, who had stationed himself in position to close the door, and into Colonel Kim's office.

Doggedly, not to flout the convention that required all partings to be conducted in a spirit of regret and mutual admiration, Meir began again. "Colonel Kim, I can't express my real pleasure in the opportunity I've had to work with you."

"Colonel Meir, before you leave I feel there is a matter which should be brought to your attention," said Kim in a coldly formal voice, completely ignoring Meir's remark. "I know that were I in your position I would be most concerned, even though I were leaving as you are."

Meir's face was a combination now of astonishment at the coolness of his farewell treatment and perplexity as to what could possibly be of such importance to him in his last few hours, with perhaps a touch of anxiety at the clearly ominous tone of Kim's voice.

"Why of course, Colonel," he said vaguely, glancing at his watch. "If there is something you wish to discuss I am sure that I can spare the time," and as Colonel Kim seated himself behind his desk he reluctantly took a straight-backed chair, which Major Huc impassively placed squarely before the desk.

Here it comes, thought Scott, and I'm not at all sure that I want to be a witness. Even though Meir is basically a nasty little bastard, there is little joy in watching anyone suffer, especially when the suffering is as pointless as this was bound to be. Silently, Scott moved to a chair across the room from Kim's desk, away from Meir and Major Huc.

Colonel Kim unhurriedly took a finely made red-lacquered box from the drawer of his desk and carefully placed it before him, sliding it over the gleaming desk until it was slightly past center and nearer Meir. Gravely he looked at Meir for a long moment before he spoke, softly, but with a vehemence that was startling in its intensity.

"Colonel Meir, you well know that we are in a death struggle with Communist Hanoi, and that there can be no peace or even truce between Ho Chi Minh and Giap's agents, the Viet Cong, and us of the south. You also well know that these bandits are merciless to our people, and by murder, kidnapping, and all manner of violence and threats of violence, attempt by terrorism to gain some degree of cooperation from our people. We here in Ngo Tho have managed to protect our people from this terrorism far better than most of the other commands in our army, and one of our best defensive measures is our concentration on the denial of all information to the enemy. You are fully aware of the extreme measures which we take to conceal advance information of all movements of our troops, their destinations, objectives, strengths. anything at all that may be of value to the Viet Cong, and I am sure that you have been in full agreement with our concern for security. After all, this is one of the principles of war, as taught in your Command and General Staff College at Fort Leavenworth."

"Well, of course, I understand and agree to all this, but what . . ." began Meir in honest amazement, and was cut off by Kim.

"Please allow me to continue, Colonel Meir," he said in the same soft and increasingly ominous voice. "One of our continuing problems is the enemy subversion of some few of our more innocent and gullible people, and by promises and bribery, converting these misinformed dupes into spies or saboteurs. You will recall the time one month ago when we became suspicious of a young girl who was a clerk in the civil police office, and after extensive and prolonged questioning of this girl we uncovered a cell of some twenty-five of our civil police who had previously been considered to be of unquestionable loyalty. I recall that you were present when we executed these twenty-five traitors in the square in front of this building, and of course you know that the girl quite unfortunately died during the course of our interrogation."

"Please do not interrupt," Kim cautioned sharply as Meir squirmed in his chair in evident prelude to speaking.

Jesus, what a performance, thought Scott, this man is an academy-award candidate, sure as hell. And he must truly hate this poor miserable son of a bitch.

"You know all these things I have just told you," continued Kim, his voice even softer and quieter. The room was utterly silent but for his voice. No sound came from the outside, from the adjoining room of General Huu-Lac, or from Major Huc's office. No sound in the entire world except the relentlessly ominous softness of the voice of Colonel Kim.

"What you may not know is that we Vietnamese are realists enough to know that a single female spy can be more effective than an entire platoon of men, especially if this female combines an attractiveness of person with a willingness to use her body to gain her ends. Consequently our special attention is devoted to the observation of any female who is in a position to gather important information for the enemy. Last night, months of effort were rewarded, and we exposed such a female agent, most unfortunately operating within your MAAG compound, where she had comparative freedom of movement and where she had operated undetected for months."

"My God, not in my headquarters," Meir burst out. "Every one of the people there have been screened by your security people, and were in fact placed in their jobs by you goddam Vietnamese. I sure as hell didn't hire a one of them."

"True, as you say Colonel Meir, we goddam Vietnamese are responsible for each person allowed to work in your compound," said Kim, the softness gone from his voice, to be replaced by a rasping hardness. "We accept that responsibility and the fact that we have discovered this spy is evidence that we are serious in our efforts toward security. But you, too, have some responsibility in this, since it is from one of your soldiers that this agent has been getting information, and also much money."

"Who, who is it?" demanded Meir, fairly bouncing his plump rear end in the chair. "Who is it, and I'll have him out of here so fast you wouldn't believe it. Just give me his name."

"Unfortunately we do not know his name yet, for although we have questioned this agent all through the night, she refuses to reveal his name," said Kim in an almost apologetic voice. "She readily admits that she has worked for our enemy, and that she has a lover within your com-

84

pound with whom she is intimate almost every day, but she will not give us his name."

"This is an absolute outrage," shouted Meir. "To think that a soldier in the United States Army would lie around talking to some whore, blabbing off his mouth about our business. He'll be court-martialed immediately if you can just give me his name."

Scott, sitting with easy and relaxed alertness well outside the group, had by now lost any feeling of pity he may have had for Meir. For any bastard to have as much on his conscience as Meir must have on his, and still be able to develop a seemingly sincere rage over anyone else having done almost the same thing required an incredibly hypocritical twist in logic. Except that perhaps, remembering what Zeke had said, about Meir's quick and silent technique—"hardly breaking stride—" it could be that Meir could truly not relate his own action to that of someone who actually "talked" to a woman.

"Colonel Meir, believe me, we appreciate your concern and indignation," said Kim, with an almost overwhelming change in manner. Gone was the grave note, the ominous tone and the more recent harshness. Now all was warmth and friendliness. "I know that it would give you great satisfaction if we could provide you with the name of whichever of your men is involved with this Viet Cong agent. I know you would like the personal satisfaction of seeing to his punishment and professional disgrace, and knowing this we tried in every way to gain a confession last night. However this agent is truly brave and she would admit to very little except as I have already told you, and she has absolutely refused to reveal the name of her lover, or anything about him or their affair except to say that they always made love in his quarters and only in his quarters, and that he gave much money."

Meir was silent but Scott thought that there was just the slightest tensing of his shoulders, or perhaps his neck and head, as if suddenly he were aware of some menace, some danger ahead. Kim, too, must have sensed this, since he continued in an even more friendly tone.

"It would appear that you must go away from us today without knowing which of your men is involved, and that you must leave to Colonel Leonard the unpleasant task of dealing with this problem. However, I promise that I shall personally forward you a full report on the outcome of this to your address in the United States, so that you may know everything. And of course you can be sure that a similar report will go to your General Wesley for his personal attention."

Get it over with, get it over with, Scott silently urged, his distaste for the entire affair growing, in spite of his admiration for the flawless performance of Kim. A born actor, con man, with a real talent for sadistic humor. And now his role was that of a friendly brother-in-arms.

"Before you go, Colonel Meir, to lessen your disappointment, I have a gift for you which I think symbolizes both your intense hatred of our common enemy, and the relentless effort we devote to the detection and apprehension of spies."

Raising his eyes to Major Huc, who had all this time stood quietly and silently, with his whole attention fixed on Meir's face, Kim said a single word in Vietnamese. Immediately Huc stepped forward, and lifting the box from the center of the desk and carefully and ceremoniously holding it with both hands underneath, offered the box to Meir.

"This is awfully nice of you, Colonel Kim," said Meir, his apprehension gone, as he awkwardly placed the box on his knees and began fumbling with the catch. "This box is absolutely beautiful, how your people achieve this particular red color amazes me, and some of the primitive working conditions in the shops where they make . . ." His voice trailed off into a puzzled silence as he finally managed the catch and raised the lid.

Almost involuntarily Scott had arisen and moved forward to look over Meir's shoulder. On a bed of snowy crystal white salt, lay two livid things. Pouches of skin, each with a nipple, unrecognizable as either human or animal, but it was quite apparent that they had been only recently severed and the flesh removed from inside.

Slowly Meir's head raised from his horrified examination of the abomination he held, and his hands pushed and his knees spread in an instinctive desire to rid himself of contact and possession. Major Huc was waiting, and with effortless ease caught the box almost before it moved; caught it without the slightest disturbance of the artistic arrangement of two hog tits on a field of salt.

"These are the breasts of the agent Kei, who was employed as a maid in your compound," continued Kim, completely ignoring Meir's reaction, "and had we the time I would have had them properly tanned and made into tobacco pouches. However, I have arranged for this to be done for you in Saigon by a most competent workman who will contact you immediately upon your arrival and will have completed the work before you leave for your home."

It was quite obvious that Meir had not understood the reference to Kei, since his protest was, "But Colonel Kim, I don't smoke a pipe. I have no use for a tobacco pouch at all." That he was absolutely horrified at the thought of owning such a monstrous thing as a set of female breasts was painfully apparent.

Grandly ignoring Meir's total rejection of his gift, Kim continued with undiminished friendliness and mounting enthusiasm. "Perhaps you will not use these yourself, Colonel, but think of the marvelous gifts they will be for those of your friends who do smoke pipes, or of what a magnificent conversation piece they will be. After all, when we finally make a public disclosure of the activities of the spy Kei you can be sure that all your news correspondents will seize upon this story as unique and that it will be published all over the United States. The name of Kei will be known to all, and you will have her breasts as war trophies. What could be more remarkable?"

Now the name hit home. Incredulity gave way to an almost feral look of desperation on Meir's face, as he said wildly, "But that is impossible. Kei is only a housegirl and has no access to any information. She couldn't possibly be an agent. All she does is clean up our quarters and do laundry, and she is never allowed in our offices or working area. I tell you, goddamit, you've made a mistake. You've got the wrong girl."

"I hardly think that possible, Colonel," said Kim, his friendliness continuing. "After all she has told us quite a bit, and before we are finished she will tell us much more."

"My God, this is barbaric, to mutilate a girl like that. How can you place any faith in anything she says under torture. She might tell you anything, accuse anyone at all, just to get you to leave her alone." Meir was almost shouting now and the fear in his eyes was sickening.

"I think not, Colonel," said Kim. "She will tell the truth without fail. My men who are questioning her are most skilled, and one of their techniques, which almost never fails, is to give a complete description of what they intend to do. Kei knows now what is planned for her during the next questioning period, and the next, and the next, and that these, her breasts, are only the first step. As she rests now she will think long of the next period of questioning and of

87

what will happen if she does not answer truthfully. Our only failure is through death before we have finished our questioning."

"Is she in bad shape now?" asked Meir, with an eagerness that was sickening—as if some hope had been offered, some relief from the certain destruction that was engulfing him.

"Of course she is not in the best of health," answered Kim, and in deliberate misunderstanding of Meir, and with the same friendliness, the same air of comradeship, continued. "I understand your concern, Colonel Meir, and you may be sure that we will be most careful. She will have all possible care until we know all there is to know, and we will not repeat the mistake we made with the police clerk last month."

This is absolutely disgusting, Scott thought, a slow anger growing within him as he watched the three of them. Kim the personification of good will, but with a glint of hardness in his eyes. Huc, his face expressionless but with his eyes almost greedily fixed on Meir's face as if he must catch every slight change of expression, know every twinge of pain and guilt and fear, and record this scene indelibly in his memory.

"I would like to talk to General Huu-Lac, privately," Meir said suddenly, rising from his chair and turning toward the door of Huu-Lac's office. Kim quickly came to his feet and was between Meir and the door before Meir could take his first step, but it was Scott, his anger now complete and equally divided between Kim for his staging of this pointlessly cruel farce, and Meir for allowing himself to be so ridiculed, who assumed control.

"I would prefer that you did not see the General again, Colonel Meir," he said in a flat and toneless voice. "I'll handle this affair from now on." The three of them might have almost forgotten that he was in the room, he thought, as their surprise froze them in place. Letting the silence linger for just a moment longer, he said to Kim. "I'm sure that will meet with your approval, Colonel Kim?"

"As you wish, Colonel Leonard," answered Kim, his eyes still on Meir. "I assume that the regulations of your army have established you as commander of your troops upon your arrival here, and that you are now fully responsible."

"You are quite correct, Colonel," said Scott using the same expressionless voice. "And if you have completed your business with Colonel Meir, I think we should be on our way. We have a number of things to do before he leaves for Saigon."

Meir had stood motionless, arrested in his movement toward the door of Huu-Lac's office, but now he turned to Scott, "Look, Leonard. there are things about this you couldn't be expected to understand, and I insist on seeing . . ."

"I think not, Colonel," said Scott easily, and taking the red lacquered box from the silent Major Huc's hands, he laid it on the desk. "Colonel Kim, I'm sure that Colonel Meir will not possibly have time in Saigon to have these properly treated, so I ask that you have it done here, and then give them to me and I will mail them to Colonel Meir." Turning to Major Huc, he said coolly, "I'll see you at eight, I assume."

Meir was not yet to be silenced. "I must insist . . ." he began. Clamping his elbow, Scott moved him along toward the door, giving a calm "Good-bye, gentlemen," to Kim and Huc who stood unmoving.

Halfway through Huc's office Meir made a small effort to free himself, to be met with Scott's muttered, "Go out with some dignity, you little bastard, and don't disgrace the whole goddam U.S. Army." Major Huc, the ever-correct escort officer caught up to them at the top of the stairway and escorted them quickly and silently down the stairway, and as silently stood by as they stepped into their jeep. His farewell salute was of the same violence as his first one had been on the veranda at their meeting.

From the moment of unsuccessful attempt to break away from Scott in Huc's office Meir had been quiet, his face dead white under its sheen of sweat and his eyes staring almost sightlessly straight ahead. Now as Sergeant Hoan, his posture as straight and rigid as ever, slowly started the jeep, he sat perched in the back seat, still silent, still dazed. It's probably the first time in years anyone has called the little bastard a little bastard, thought Scott without regret. And it must have been the first time ever that anyone had implied that he, Colonel Meir, could possibly bring disgrace to his uniform. So let him sulk; if he wanted an explanation, he had only to ask.

The square was almost completely deserted now, he noted, as his mind began automatically to check the points of vulnerability, which were to him so evident, and as they moved through the narrow passage of the exit lane he again thought of what a target this early-morning massing of troops presented.

"You should not have interfered," Meir broke the silence with bitterness. "If I could have talked to Huu-Lac I could have gotten the whole thing quieted down. After all, the way he whores around he would have understood."

"Understood what," Scott asked laconically, "that someone in your compound has been screwing the maids? I'm sure he couldn't care less, and I'm also sure that he would in no way interfere with anything now in progress, for you or for anyone else." Turning in his seat so that he faced Meir he asked, "Why are you so concerned? Soldiers have been laying the natives since the beginning of time, and this is just one small incident. Admittedly it's pretty rough on the girl, but you know damned well that not much can happen to whichever of your men was getting in her pants. An official reprimand, maybe, but nothing more. You can't have a court-martial without a witness, and I doubt this girl will be in shape to testify. And besides, don't we have a Status of Forces agreement here which requires that we try all our general court-martial cases out of country, in Okinawa?"

This is your last chance, Meir, he thought. Your very last chance to be a man. Admit to me that you are involved and I'll let you leave here with a free mind. What I'll tell you I don't know—that I'll intercept all reports, that I'll persuade Huu-Lac to not make a report, or maybe even that this is obviously a Viet-style joke, but I'll reassure you some way, out of sheer goddam pity. Still turned in his seat he watched Meir, whose eyes remained fixed straight ahead, the look of a man condemned on his face.

The silence grew, and as Meir refused to meet his eyes or to speak, Scott turned forward again. It was useless, years of denying himself to himself, of fornicating only in the dark, of giving way to the pressures of his lust only with a sense of sin, had created a man who could never admit that he would stoop so low as to consort with a native. Already in his mind Meir had probably constructed his defense, his absolute denial of any semblance of guilt, together with an attack on the credibility of any confession gained through torture. This would shield him from any feeling of guilt over the supposed mutilation of the young girl. He would heal quickly. He had probably had much practice in quick healing in times past.

Silently they moved through the traffic, now markedly thinned after the first early-morning rush, and through the gate to the compound, where the four Viet guards, still trim and spotless in spite of the heat, alertly presented arms, and on across the square to where the same small group of officers stood waiting at the chopper pad. They seemed not to have moved since he had left, but a glance at his watch showed that some two hours, and this, plus the fact that a considerable quantity of boxes, footlockers, and packages were neatly stacked awaiting loading, seemed to establish that someone in Huu-Lac's headquarters must be friendly with someone here. At least friendly enough to call ahead with information that we had left Huu-Lac and were on our way back.

Meir seemed to have recovered. Recovered at least enough to count the pieces of his luggage and permit their loading to begin; enough to get a note of feeling in his voice as he made a short farewell speech to these, his loyal helpers; and almost enough, but not quite, to feign sincerity when he wished Scott the best of luck. Lieutenant Smith wound up, lifted off, and away they went. And there goes the second one, the second in less than forty-eight hours who I've managed to turn into a mortal enemy, thought Scott, as he turned away from watching the disappearing chopper. I'd better start making a few friends, just for the sake of having a few people on my side.

Turning to the group to find their eyes on him in the waiting and speculative look that must greet each new commander as he assumes a new command, he addressed Gerrard, "What's next?"

"Whatever you wish, Colonel," answered Gerrard somewhat hesitantly. "Colonel Meir has called a conference of all our advisors out with the units for tomorrow, thinking that he would have several days with you here, but his sudden recall has sort of left today unsettled."

"What I wish, Colonel Gerrard, is to be educated by you gentlemen," said Scott with a half smile,, "But what I want first is a shower and a clean uniform."

difficult if Meir had been taken out of action before his normal rotation date.

Stowkowski, Plans and Operations, was a damned fine young officer and in spite of the pressure that Meir must have put on him to pass on MAAG direction in letter-perfect manner, just as it had been received, he had evidently managed to do so and still remained on fairly decent terms with Colonel Trink, his opposite number in Huu-Lac's staff. He seemed to spend a great deal of his time with the Viets and was in with them well enough that he actually had a desk assigned to him in Colonel Trink's office. He was almost alone, except for Swann, in knowing of a great number of Viets—all of Trink's officers and men, down to the last sergeant. It seemed that most of the others knew only the most senior of the Vietnamese and had made no effort to establish any sort of a relationship with the majors and captains and lieutenants and sergeants. Stowkowski was basically sound, and his weaknesses were not entirely his own fault, the most glaring being his inadequate personal knowledge of the province, which was a direct result of Meir's policy of discouraging his officers from traveling except when absolutely necessary. Consequently, while Stowkowski had truly remarkable map knowledge of the province, he had never really been anywhere. One visit each to the 12th ARVN Division at Ghum Kong and to the 30th ARVN Division at Knan Ghe, and a few other sporadic and brief trips to a couple of the fortified villages, constituted the whole of his firsthand knowledge of the countryside outside of Ngo Tho. All this was easily correctable, of course, and there was no fear or reluctance on Stowkowski's part—he was eager to get out of Ngo Tho and to see what was going on. But it would take time, lots of time.

Lieutenant Colonel Storm, his physical condition not good, and most certainly his overweight was of no help in this regard, seemed quite professionally competent. Both during his formal briefing and again during Scott's long private talk with him he had had all the facts on instant recall. Nevertheless there was something about the man that aroused a sense of caution in Scott. Without completely defining the cause he felt an instinctive lack of trust in Storm; and while Storm professed to be on the best of terms with all the Viet intelligence types, several times a tone or inflection of his voice seemed to infer that he had little faith in their competence or veracity. Which was not at all bad, Scott thought upon reflection; it is proper for anyone in the intelligence business to decline to accept anything at face value. Still, although not clearly evident, Scott thought he could sense a certain contempt on Storm's part for the Viets as a group. Two things seemed to establish that Storm was operating on a fairly dependent basis, accepting information only from Huu-Lac's staff as given and not having developed his own independent sources. The first was his full belief in the fact of Huu-Lac's drinking and wenching activities, and the second was his complete ignorance of any aspect of the story of Kei, either the fiction that Colonel Kim had created, or the true situation. Scott asked him to ferret out what information he could on the Kei case for two reasons: to determine if he did have good Viet contacts, friendly enough to let him in on what must by now be a widespread joke among them; and to see what his reaction would be if the Viets gave him the standard, for-U.S.-consumption-only, story that Kei was truly a spy. To give Storm the benefit of any doubt, it might well be that his faintly evident distrust of the Viets and his half-expressed bias against them were direct results of contagion from Meir, and perhaps with time and another example to follow he could change.

His Headquarters Commandant, Supply and Maintenance Officer, responsible for God-knew-what other unassumed and unassigned duties, Lieutenant Colonel Swann, was a jewel. Solid as a rock, with an unflappable calmness, Scott had needed only a few minutes to establish a complete understanding and mutual admiration. They were both cut from the same cloth, with an ability to instantly discriminate between the unimportant and the critical, to make the necessary decisions, and to insure that their decisions were translated into proper direction and carried through to completed action. Swann considered Colonel Trac, Huu-Lac's G4, to be a close personal friend, both socially as well as professionally, and had evidently consistently risked Meir's disapproval by spending most of his evenings with the Viets, and he seemed to know them all, from Huu-Lac and Kim on down through the ranks of the entire staff. He was the only one to express a real admiration for Huu-Lac, and Scott was sure that Swann was completely aware of the true situation in regard to the Huu-Lac-Kim-Meir relationship, although Scott did not question him or explore several openings that occurred during their talk. Swann would be truly invaluable, especially since he had excellent contacts on the MAAG staff in Saigon and had casually assured Scott that anything that Scott wanted out of MAAG Saigon resources he could get, authorized or not. It was a damned shame that he had less than four months to go until the end of his tour.

Pickering was a hard one to figure. Any man who survived the army promotion system to the grade of Lieutenant Colonel, with its selective weeding out of ineffectives at each level, just had to have something on the ball, but this man sure as hell made no great display of his talents. While he knew the details of his job well enough, each fact had to be almost pried out of him, and the overall effect was of a plodder, one who thought only in terms of the minutiae of his own job, and never of the command as an entity. Still there were moments when a gleam of potential had shown through and at least Scott was sure that his day to day performance of duty would be a model of professional competence. His relationship with the Viets was open to question, since he himself was reluctant to give an opinion of Colonel Ngyen, his counterpart on Huu-Lac's staff, or of the status of his relationship with Ngyen.

Albright was a junior edition of his brother back in MAAG Headquarters. Open, frank, with a total dedication to his job, and an enthusiasm that was remarkably contagious, he was proud of the performance of his men and visibly disappointed when he could not persuade Scott to make an immediate inspection of his operation. To him the Vietnamese were the greatest and he evidently devoted much time and effort to assisting them in their training and operational problems. It was only with difficulty that Scott was able to shut the boy off, and then only by promising to spend at least a half day with him as soon as possible.

Those were his key staff people, and on the whole they were not half bad. Once he got to know them, and they understood him, things would work out. Later in the coming week he would get to know the rest of his staff here; he had counted some twenty officers and men that he had met so far, but these things could not and need not be rushed.

He had made two decisions during the afternoon, one so abruptly that his reasons might have been misunderstood. At the briefing in the war room, where all were assembled the discussion of the scheduled assembly of all the U.S. Advisors—Division, Regiment, Battalion, and Company, including the Special Forces types—had been abruptly terminated when Scott had canceled the meeting with a terse statement that it was entirely unnecessary and a waste of time, and that when he wanted to see them he would go where they were, not have them come to him. He was sure that his anger had been evident to everyone in the room, as it well should have been. To ask some forty-five men, who he hoped were very busy men, to travel the better part of a day through country that was in some cases downright dangerous just to meet him, was a stupid waste of their valuable time. Meir had probably had some fine program of farewell oratory in mind when he had ordered the assembly, but with Meir gone, so was the reason for the gathering.

His other decision had been a real earth-shaker. Hesitantly, reluctantly, and probably only because the rest of the officers had insisted that he ask, Pickering had mentioned that he had noticed Colonel Scott's two cases of Scotch, and could it be understood that Meir's long-standing prohibition against any sort of intoxicants was now lifted. Gravely Scott had assured him that he considered all soldiers to be fully adult and able to make their own choice as to drinking or not drinking, and as gravely offered one of his cases of Scotch to be shared by all until some arrangement for supply could be made.

Stubbing out his cigarette and swinging off the wide and soft bed, he went across the spacious room into the shower. The room was beautiful, furnished in heavy hand-carved teak, with a gleaming dark floor and beautifully draped windows. But the plumbing, French-made and very old, was a different matter, and instead of a forceful stream, the shower was a thin and almost intermittent trickle. And warm. His days of cold showers were over for a long, long while. As he soaped himself under the stream he checked his tentative schedule for the next day. The Aviation Battalion Commander, whose unit was at a temporary field on the far side of the city. Major King would certainly take up a half a day, and which half, morning or afternoon, and in fact his activities for many mornings and afternoons to come, would depend on what sort of a working situation with Huu-Lac and Kim developed out of tonight's dinner.

8

AT SEVEN-THIRTY Scott sat in his office, dressed somewhat against his better judgment in a freshly pressed tropical worsted blouse, all four rows of ribbons in place, and with a gleaming polish on his shoes. He had asked Gerrard what he considered to be the proper uniform for such an occasion but had been met by a plea of complete ignorance. Swann had likewise been of no help. No precedent existed; Huu-Lac had never invited an advisor to dinner before, at least not within the memory of any of those now present. Surely Meir had gone through such an operation upon arrival but no one had ever heard him speak of it, so deciding that he would much prefer to be overdressed than appear in a duty uniform and find all the rest in full regalia, Scott had gone all the way. He had even momentarily regretted the set of tropical whites in one of his footlockers in Saigon.

This decision made, he ceased to worry about it, but another problem did bother him. This was the remaining case of Scotch. Zeke had assured him that Huu-Lac truly appreciated good Scotch. but there was real danger that to rush in bearing gifts was likely to give the impression that he was trying to buy something rather than to arouse any feelings of gratitude. Surely, with the power and connections that Huu-Lac must have in Saigon, a steady supply of Scotch was the least of his worries. The real reason, in

Scott's mind, for the presentation of such a gift was in its symbolism—the ending of the tour of the teetotaler Meir and a new beginning with his own arrival.

Scott had just arrived at this conclusion, after giving much more serious thought to such a trivial matter than he would like to have admitted, when Gerrard knocked, opened the office door, and announced the arrival of Major Huc, now awaiting at the compound gate to escort Colonel Scott to the residence of General Huu-Lac.

It seems as though the young Major's extreme dislike of all of us prevents him from even setting foot in our camp, thought Scott. Now is just as good a time as any to begin the young man's education as to what we are really like, and maybe to begin to change his attitude. "Colonel, please ask Major Huc to come here to me, and while he's doing that have someone get the case of Ballantine's still up in my room and take it out to Huc's vehicle. Don't load it in the vehicle, just set it down nearby," he told Gerrard.

Huc came almost immediately, knocking on the half-opened door. "Come in, Major Huc," said Scott, arising from his desk and coming forward across the room to meet Huc. Ignoring Huc's stiffness and half-attempt to salute, Scott warmly shook his hand and led him to a chair beside the desk, and seating himself again behind the desk, leaned forward toward Huc. "Major, I have somewhat of a problem in good manners and taste and I'd like your advice. As you know, I am not familiar with the customs of your country, and so while my intentions are good, I want to avoid offense in the manner in which I do a specific thing. Simply, I'd like to present General Huu-Lac with a case of whiskey I have brought from Saigon, and I don't know whether it is best to bring it to the dinner tonight, to personally take it to his office tomorrow, or to have it sent to his office tomorrow. What should I do?"

If you have not disarmed this young man, if you have not begun to make a friend, at least you have confused him, thought Scott. Major Huc had at first sat stiffly, resentful and almost truculent, and his eyes had that same expressionless hardness and thinly disguised dislike as on their first meeting. But at least now the dominant impression had changed to one of a puzzled and hesitant young man.

"I would truly appreciate your advice," said Scott, as Huc remained silent, his eyes fixed upon Scott's.

"Tonight would be best, I think," he finally blurted reluctantly, almost embarrassedly, as if this answering of Scott's request was in some way a surrender of something on his part.

"Thank you very much, Major Huc," said Scott quietly. "I realize I have much to learn and I am grateful for your help." Rising he continued, "Shall we go now?"

It was almost fully dark outside as they silently crossed the compound to the gate where an aged but immaculate Mercedes limousine waited, its motor quietly idling. The driver, a Viet Sergeant, stood at rigid attention at the opened door. Two escort vehicles, one of civil police followed by a jeep-load of ARVN soldiers, were parked in front of the Mercedes, and three jeeps filled with soldiers were lined up at close intervals in the road behind. They were evidently to travel in style, Scott thought with some amusement, as he seated himself and the driver closed the door. The case of Sctoch was on the ground near the rear of the limousine and Huc, without prompting from Scott, barked an order in Vietnamese as he rounded the rear of the car to enter the left rear door, and two soldiers from the first following jeep quickly loaded it in the trunk.

The lead escort vehicles moved out, slowly at first and then at what seemed to be a truly dangerous speed, toward the center of the city. Remembering the traffic of early morning Scott almost flinched as they approached the intersection that Sergeant Hoan had had such difficulty in entering, only to find all traffic halted and a lane cleared by a covey of civil police. Almost without slackening speed the corner was made, and with the siren now turned on by the lead vehicle, clearing the streets ahead, they continued, past the turn-off to Huu-Lac's headquarters and through the city before turning down a narrow side street and through a wide gate, guarded by about twenty Viet soldiers, and into the grounds of Huu-Lac's villa. Throughout, Huc had sat silently on Scott's left, and only when the siren was silent as the lead escort vehicles dropped off at the gate and the headlights of the Mercedes picked up the white villa ahead in the driveway did he speak.

"The whiskey will be taken care of by the driver, Colonel Scott," he said in his usual tone, seemingly recovered from whatever penetration of the armor of dislike Scott's request for his advice may have made. As the vehicle came to a stop before the entrance to the many storied villa and guards sprang forward to open both rear doors, Huc said, "If you will please follow me."

Up the shallow and short flight of steps, across the veranda, through the wide-open double doors, and across the wide entrance hall they went swiftly, and without pause through a wide doorway hastily opened by a guard, into an immense and beautifully furnished room, and straight forward toward Huu-Lac who stood, resplendent in a high-collared dress uniform, foremost in a half-circle of some twenty or more people. There was none of the babble that would have existed in any pre-dinner gathering of Americans, no cocktail-party atmosphere, although Huu-Lac and a few others did hold glasses in their hands. There was instead a respectful silence, and a watchfulness as Scott and Huu-Lac met again.

"Good evening, General, I hope I'm not too very late," said Scott, stopping just in front of Huu-Lac, not extending his hand first but awaiting Huu-Lac's movement. Thank God he had had sense enough to wear the proper uniform, he thought.

"Not at all, Colonel Scott," said Huu-Lac quietly and firmly but briefly shaking Scott's hand. "We were just relaxing for a moment before going in to dinner. I'd like you to meet my staff, both the military and some of the key civilians."

Here it comes, thought Scott, nodding his assent. Here comes the gimlet-eyed examination of one Scott Leonard, of his every action, his every movement, his every response, and he faced the evening not as an ordeal, something to be endured, but merely as another of the many challenges that must be faced when one goes into a new command. There is always this thinly veiled speculation when a new number one man comes on the job, be the troops our own soldiers or those of a completely foreign culture and different background. It is always the same, and tonight was no more difficult or critical than many another time he had gone through in the past, he thought as the introductions began. First was Colonel Kim whose only reference to the events of the morning was a sly remark to the effect that he hoped that Colonel Meir had left in good health and had a pleasant journey, to which Scott replied, completely deadpan, that Colonel Meir had indeed been in the best of health upon his departure.

With a complete concentration on the business at hand, Scott met them all, striving to distinguish differences in appearance that would enable him to remember and recognize them again, and to associate the unfamiliar sounding names with appearance. With these people there was a sameness of

102

appearance to occidental eyes that he had encountered before in his associations with the Koreans and Japanese, which required a real and concentrated effort in order to distinguish individuality. Knowing that his score would be far less than perfect, he nevertheless tried in all the proven ways to fix each individual, his title, and his job in his mind. He gave special attention to the first four civilians in the line and Huu-Lac's four principal staff officers following.

Mr. Thieu, short and stocky, with the most direct, forthright, and friendly manner Scott had so far encountered, was the chief civilian dignitary of the province, insofar as he could understand from Huu-Lac's introduction, and in oversimplification he was Huu-Lac's deputy in all matters other than purely military ones. There was an evident close rapport between Thieu and Huu-Lac, and a complete, almost familiar, ease of manner as they spoke. In the short conversation possible, Scott thought that here, at least, was one who seemed without a watch-and-wait attitude, and who was quite prepared to accept Scott on the face-value basis of his title as Senior U.S. Advisor to Huu-Lac.

Mr. Thi, the equivalent of mayor of the city of Ngo Tho, was likewise openly cordial and insisted that Scott must allow him to provide for an escorted tour of the city at the earliest possible date. He, too, was somewhat shorter than the average Viet, but where Thieu was stocky and heavy, Thi was slender to the point of emaciation and fairly reeked of barely controlled nervous energy and drive.

The third man in line was a startling contrast to the others in the room by reason of his age. To Scott's unpracticed eye all the others, with the possible exception of Huu-Lac's, seemed to be either young men, or at most of middle age, but this man was old, truly old. His movements were slow and uncertain and he appeared almost senile until one looked into his eyes, which were as clear and penetrating as the eyes of a youth. He alone of the group was without at least some ability in speaking English, and as Scott carefully held his fragile and almost lifeless hand he stared steadily at Scott for a long while before saying something briefly in Vietnamese that Huu-Lac did not interpret as he introduced him as Chieu, Chief of all civil police in the province, and with obvious respect and affection for the old man, advised Scott not to be deceived by appearances, that Chieu was a most efficient policeman and a dedicated hater of all Viet Cong.

Mr. Khanh was introduced vaguely as Chief of Refugee

and Resettlement Programs and was not quite as friendly as Thieu and Thi had been, whether because in his duties he had been thrown in greater contact with Meir, or whether simply as a matter of his basic personality, Scott could only speculate, but his greeting verged on coolness.

The same distant though respectful coolness was even more evident in the manner of Huu-Lac's officers. There was the expected attitude of polite watchfulness, a calculating scrutiny of Scott that said as clearly as words that he was not to be accepted on trust and that he must prove himself worthy of their friendship. Colonel Trink, the G3, was as Stowkowski had described him, the only truly fat officer in the group, but with the hard fat and physical strength that belied any hint of sloth or softness. Colonel Yuan, the G2, quietly dignified, with an air of complete detachment, almost disinterest, and a habit of looking completely through and behind the person he was addressing, of never meeting their eyes directly. Colonel Trac, G4, and Colonel Ngyen, G1, could have been twins to Scott's eye, and his only hope in distinguishing between them would come from developing a close acquaintance. For tonight he could cope by noting the difference in uniform and decorations.

Officer followed officer, and Scott disciplined himself to giving as much time to the last as he had the first, never relaxing in his concentration and effort to establish the individuality of each. In fifteen minutes it was over, the last junior major introduced, and the room had taken on a considerably more relaxed atmosphere, as those who had first been introduced acquired drinks and gathered in small groupings. Scott had been brought a gin and tonic by a white-clad waiter and he and Huu-Lac stood somewhat apart.

"That was quite an effort on your part, Colonel Scott," said Huu-Lac casually as they stood facing the room, Scott still lost in the process of correlating names and faces as his eyes roved over the group. "How many do you suppose you remember?"

"Nine for sure, fourteen maybe," answered Scott absently, his eyes still on the crowd, and then as the significance of the question hit him, he turned to Huu-Lac and asked, curiously but without resentment, "Was my effort too obvious?"

"Perhaps not to all," answered Huu-Lac in the same casual voice, "But to me it was at least a demonstration of your interest in my officers as people." And as Scott remained silent he continued in the same casual, almost careless tone. "You realize, of course, that you are being very carefully watched and that your conduct will be discussed by my staff in an effort by them to evaluate your character?" Turning he met Scott's eyes, an amused challenge in his gaze.

"And you, General, do you also watch me for indications of my character?" asked Scott, directly but without challenge and in simple curiosity.

"Of course not," answered Huu-Lac, the amusement still in his eyes, "but then I have had two recommendations as to your personal worth." As Scott silently questioned him he turned to the room again, "The old one, Chieu, is a man of great wisdom. He is able to look into a man's eyes and know him as a man at first meeting. His remark upon meeting Colonel Meir was not favorable to Colonel Meir, and events proved him to be right. He is favorable in his comment on you, and I'm sure he will again be proven to be right. Additionally, today I received a letter from Colonel Minh in Saigon. You know him, of course?" He turned again to Scott with his last remark and there was again the amusement, the challenge in his eyes, but also the first trace of genuine friendliness.

"I have met Colonel Minh, General," Scott answered slowly and carefully. "But I do not know him well, and in fact I had only a short meeting with him."

"Sometimes such a short meeting is quite enough," said Huu-Lac and abruptly changing the subject he asked, "Shall we go in to dinner?" and without waiting for Scott's response, he began to move through the crowd toward the door at the far end of the room, stopping here and there for a word with one of his officers.

Kim fell in beside Scott as they trailed behind, and as they halted momentarily he asked, in obviously strained innocence, yet unable to conceal his glee, "What did Colonel Meir think of his souvenirs, Colonel Leonard? Did he comment on them after you both left this morning?"

"I hate to disappoint you, Colonel Kim," answered Scott quite seriously, "But his mind was not on the souvenirs. His only concern was that some one of his men would suffer unnecessarily through an innocent association with this enemy agent, and he appeared to be quite upset over this." Kim had gone to great trouble to stage his little drama and had acted his part so perfectly that he deserved some satisfaction.

"That is surprising," said Kim, barely suppressing his laughter. "I didn't realize Colonel Meir was so concerned over his men."

"That is not the only thing that is surprising," said Scott. It was apparent that Kim was having a hard time in keeping his secret and that eventually, either now, this moment, or later this evening, or tomorrow, or sometime soon he would tell Scott the entire story. Perhaps it would be better not to wait for this confidence, Scott thought, and dropping his air of seriousness, he smiled as he continued. "What is really surprising is that a man of Colonel Meir's age and experience should know so little of the bodies of young females that he would believe your souvenirs to be the breasts of a young woman. Of a young pig maybe, but not a young woman."

"Really, Colonel Leonard, is this what you think?" he asked in amazement.

"That is what I think," said Scott. "And I also think that Meir was very naïve to have been taken in by your act, although you are a very good actor." In sudden seriousness and mock confidentiality he continued, "Do you suppose that Colonel Meir himself could have been the one who was involved with Kei?"

With this Kim could no longer restrain himself, and his laughter was so loud and uncontrolled that even Huu-Lac, deep in conversation with Thieu, turned with a questioning look on his face.

"Colonel Leonard." Kim said finally, wiping his eyes with a handkerchief, "you are very shrewd to have seen through our little joke. Very shrewd indeed. I compliment you."

"That's not at all true, and I deserve no compliment," said Scott, realizing that this was his opportunity to establish an atmosphere of frankness and honesty between himself and Kim, which might end the problem of carrying the orders of the day as originated by Buckmeister and Wesley to Huu-Lac. "I knew that you had arranged a farewell ceremony for Colonel Meir before I arrived today. If I hadn't I would have been as taken in as Meir was, because you are a marvelous actor, Colonel Kim."

Huu-Lac and those in the immediate vicinity had listened intently to this exchange—Huu-Lac with a broad smile —and as Scott finished he gave a satisfied nod and turned to enter the dining room. Kim, still laughing, took Scott's arm in guidance and as the others followed, Scott could hear the ripple of amusement as the story was passed to those who had not been near enough to hear. The tenseness, the watchfulness, the air of wait-and-see, had almost entirely disappeared now; Colonel Trink was on his left asking if Colonel Leonard had ever eaten Vietnamese food and Kim on his right had not loosened his grip on Scott's arm, and even Major Huc, who now stood just inside the doorway of the dining room, gave a small smile as they moved past him. There is really nothing quite so fortunate as being the one to follow a son of a bitch, thought Scott. He remembered the first time he had been advised of this by Boyd just after he had been commissioned—when there is a choice of two units to command, take the one with the worst reputation, the lowest morale, and the worst record. "There is really only one way to go then," Boyd had said, "And that is up. You can't do worse, and any progress, any improvement at all, will be really noticed." Boyd had given him more advice than he cared to remember, a lot of it not worth listening to, but this one time he had really scored.

And so he profited from Meir's errors, and the pitiful bastard had created an atmosphere where even the actions of the most mediocre replacement would be initially hailed as extraordinarily fine, and where any semblance of human warmth and sincerity would be a noteworthy change. And tonight at least it seemed that he had achieved the beginning of an understanding and a friendship with these people. But only the beginning, and I could goof anytime, he thought. He had thus far only established his goodwill. His professional competence remained to be tested, and until that time he could not truly be effective and would not be earning his pay by contributing toward a more effective fight against the common enemy.

The dining room and the beautifully set table, as Huu-Lac's office and villa, spoke of a man possessed of a connoisseur's keen appreciation of beauty and taste. He was seated on Huu-Lac's right, Kim beside him, and Chieu, carefully and solicitously seated by Huu-Lac across from him, and Thieu on Chieu's left, the rest of the crowd taking seats down the table, not in order of rank, Scott noted with some surprise, but with a fine disregard for protocol that he was sure was unusual for any group of Asiatics. God knew the Koreans or Japanese would never be so careless of their prestige and prerogatives, and he was sure that in any other gathering of Vietnamese there would have been a proper regard for the proprieties. His respect for Huu-Lac as a man had grown since their first meeting and this was but an additional indication that the Viet General was a most unusual individual.

The room seemed to be filled with servants, not obtrusively, but moving with quiet efficiency, as the dinner began. First a clear soup with a trace of unidentifiable vegetables, and a beautifully delicate white wine, dry and chilled to a sparkling freshness; followed by a dish of mixed meat and vegetables, hot with small green peppers; then one of small whole fish; and finally a dish of rice and meat and vegetables. Scott ate with good appetite and small attention to the composition of the dishes, and with the rice dish he accepted without comment the clear amber-colored sauce passed by Colonel Kim and liberally doused it over his food as he had seen the others do. He knew well what this was; no soldier who had ever heard a war story out of Viet Nam was likely to be ignorant of the existence of *nuc mamh*, the fermented fish sauce the Viets loved, which was an abomination to all U.S. soldiers. The aroma was a little strong, he had to admit, but anyone who had mastered *kim-chi* with the Koreans should be able to partake of even this, and knowing that he was being unobtrusively watched, he ate with what he hoped was a properly casual manner and without flinching. The trick was to slowly exhale as he took each bite so that the taste was confused as little as possible with the smell, which as he ate progressed from being an absolute stench to the status of being merely vaguely offensive. The exhaling, combined with frequent sips of the excellent red wine and his concentration on the conversation carried him through, and although there was some uneasiness in his stomach, he finished his portion in concert with the others. He had supposed that the next test would be the *durian*, the spiny football-sized fruit loved throughout Asia, and which most Americans swore had a stench that made it impossible for any human to even consider it as food, and he was prepared to give it the same inwardly stoical and outwardly casual try. But fortunately dessert was a simple ice cream followed by exquisitely brewed coffee and forceful brandy.

All during dinner the talk had been in English, except when a remark was directed to Chieu or when he infrequently spoke, and Scott had followed closely as the subjects ranged from the prospects of a bumper crop of rice; the problem of protecting the harvesting and transportation to Ngo Tho and thence to Saigon; the most recent pattern of Viet Cong activity, which had resulted in the murder and decapitation of three village headmen during the past week and a complete lull in the heretofore periodic raids on ARVN outposts; the progress in the construction of the three fortified villages currently underway and the method to be used in resettlement of the surrounding rice farmers and refugees that would be necessary when construction was completed; and training and morale problems in the Self-Defense Forces that would defend the villages. Scott was sure that this was all directed at the beginning of his education and he did his best to absorb as much as possible, remaining silent for the most part and carefully phrasing his few questions to elicit additional information without disrupting the tenor of the conversation. The complexity of this war, for which he had had only an intellectual appreciation, slowly began to take on a very genuine reality, and his appreciation of the magnitude of the problem grew as he listened.

Conventional warfare, that of two military forces opposing in strength, had clearly defined objectives and a wealth of doctrine, both strategic and tactical, to support the management of forces. Even ordinary guerrilla war, where the warfare was limited to attacks on military forces and the pursuit of those guerrillas by the conventional force had some established precedent and was infinitely a simpler proposition than that which confronted Huu-Lac. Here there were purely military objectives, such as the defense of key cities and villages and the ARVN cantonments, and the offensive actions of searching out and destroying the Viet Con forces. But here also was the problem of the protection of the individual farmer, and not only protection in order to insure his personal safety in some guarded village, but to enable the continued productivity of the land. This produced a conflict not easily resolved, involving the deployment and constant movement of Huu-Lac's forces, where the necessary weakening of an ARVN strong point to provide harvest protection invited Viet Cong attack at the weakened point, and where, lacking the overwhelming superiority of force that would be required to deny the Viet Cong lucrative targets throughout the province, Huu-Lac was forced each day into the weighing of choices to find an action that would minimize his vulnerability. It was a game of finely balanced risk, where each move must have an unpredictable consequence and where the initiative and the freedom to choose time and place lay with the enemy.

Two things began to be apparent to Scott as the evening progressed; and they were perhaps the answer to the comparative stability of Huu-Lac's province. The first was the fact that Huu-Lac, although trained by the French and exposed to their doctrine of defense during his early and formative years, had not created a purely defensive posture within his command. True, the important key points—the cities, the larger villages, points along the routes of approach from the Gy Than hills to the north, the confluence of the more important waterways, and the fortified villages—did take the larger part of his forces, but even within this formidable commitment he had a program of aggressive patroling, including night patrols and ambushes, which had as their objective the finding, fixing, and destroying of the Viet Cong.

The second point was of even more significance to Scott in his evaluation both of Huu-Lac, the man, and of the capability of his command eventually to win the war in Ngo Tho. This was the concern over the morale and will to resist of the civilian population. Huu-Lac attached more importance to the murder of the three village headmen than to a number of ambushes that had resulted in the loss of one entire patrol and substantial losses in two other cases, and there was considerable analysis of each incident to determine exactly where the protection of the headmen had been inadequate. In addition to the unexpectedly elaborate measures taken to guard the governing elements of the villages, was Huu-Lac's evident concern with the government's image among the rank and file of the population. It seemed that Huu-Lac was not providing the central government with the taxes that they expected from his province, and to further complicate the problem, the General had placed quite extensive demands on Saigon for military supplies and for civil aid. He had also, it seemed, aroused the rage of some few absentee landlords, safe in Saigon, by recently issuing an edict that no rentals would be paid for any land until sometime in the future when hostilities had ended, and this proclamation had been so worded to imply that the central government in Saigon was the issuing authority rather than Huu-Lac himself.

During this phase of the evening, the real role of Thieu began to be apparent as the executive of Huu-Lac's civilian program and heir-apparent should Huu-Lac be killed or incapacitated. In a country that had for years existed solely through the force of the military with those few short-lived civilian regimes a mere façade for the continuing power of the army, any cooperation on an equal basis between civilian and military was truly surprising, but it seemed to exist here in a very real sense. Thieu showed respect and consideration for Huu-Lac as a peer, and was in no way subservient or motivated by fear. On occasion he differed with Huu-Lac in some small detail of interpretation of the significance of events or the proper action to be taken in the future, and he did this with complete freedom and confidence.

Finally the evening drew to an end. Huu-Lac rose and with a brief statement in Vietnamese to the rest of the group, drew Scott aside to say briefly, "There is a proverb in my language which fits you well, Colonel Scott Leonard, and it is that big ears make for great understanding. Take the next few days to become familiar with your command and then come and see me—or come sooner if you wish. My door will always be open. And thank you for the Scotch, it is my favorite brand."

Scott did not linger long, only for a farewell drink with Kim, who by now was well on the way to being smashed, all friendship and brotherly love, and then signaled Huc and they were on their way. In the big limousine Huc was silent as before, but now with a silence that Scott thought spoke of ease, if not liking, and Scott was quite content to relax on the soft cushions and half doze until they entered the MAAG compound. With a brief farewell to Huc, he went quickly up the stairway and along the hallway to his room, and directly into the bath and barely in time. There would need be some conditioning before he could eat *nuc mamh* with impunity.

tions. Here in Viet Nam the problem of providing adequate material at the right place and at the right time was further complicated by transportation problems, both in-country and in the long haul from the States, which made the precise calculation of requirements far in advance an absolute must.

The basic items were in fairly good condition—adequate small arms, machine-gun, and mortar ammo, adequate grenades, adequate number of rifles, although they were the old M-1, which was a hell of a load for a small Vietnamese to carry, and a plentiful supply of mortars, machine guns, and all the other of the equipment needed to make a shooting force. The replacement requirements for weapons were quite startling to Scott, although Swann assured him that the losses here were far lower than in any other ARVN force; it was evident that the Viet Cong were steadily acquiring a sizable arsenal through weapons lost or abandoned on the battlefield.

Aviation maintenance was in good shape with an adequate supply of parts and an overstrength of aircraft maintenance technicians and of pilots. His impression of Major King was of a hard-bitten, almost ruthless man, whose job was his life and who had an almost fanatic hatred for the Viet Cong. Scott's short but thorough visit to his base showed he ran a gung-ho outfit, twenty-five choppers, eight armed HU-1B models for suppressive fire and seventeen slick, or unarmed, except for a 50 caliber machine gun mounted in the cargo door, with four Mohawk fixed wing planes that would carry a bewildering load of electronic gear for battlefield surveillance now waiting in Saigon for the completion of the landing strip. All this was manned by a group of young officers and warrant officer pilots who treated King with a wary respect, and while walking softly in his presence, showed a real pride in their organization. The field was a model of a ready-round-the-clock organization, with every aircraft not on mission or in maintenance ready to scramble, and with a revetted parking area that made the likelihood of damage from sniper fire remote. The field defense provided by the two ARVN rifle companies also looked like a well-planned and adequately manned operation and it was evident that King was personally involved in this also and that he was not about to lose any aircraft on the ground through lack of alertness.

Scott had forced himself to deal with administrative and logistic matters first, taking a full day and a half, resisting the temptation to make a superficial first pass at these matters with the procrastinating intent to really dig deep later. Major King had consumed most of the afternoon of the second day and he had finished it off by spending the late afternoon and early evening with Captain Albright and his well-managed communications operation. He had tried, honestly tried, to be interested in Albright's presentation of records on circuit outages that showed they had never been out of contact with Saigon for more than a few minutes in any one day over the past five months, but his real reaction was that it was a damned shame to find a real honest-to-God competent communicator in a spot where an occasional prolonged breakdown might prove to be a true blessing. He was much more interested to find that the radio nets down to his advisors and the ARVN nets from Huu-Lac down to his subordinate commanders were almost equally efficient and that the air-ground and ground-air communications used in calling in Air Force support for ground operations were a going operation when required. Scott thought it quite significant that Albright had no confirmed record of the intercept of Viet Cong radio traffic and that although he had the capability to locate roughly the site of any Viet Cong radio station through triangulation he had never had occasion to use this capability. Evidently the Cong had other ways of passing the necessary information and orders down through their echelons of command.

On the morning of the third day he began with Stowkowski and Storm to review the battle situation in a state of pleasurable anticipation of dealing with those things he knew best and where the certainty of cause and effect, of force and counterforce, had always before seemed to be a thing of beauty and joy in the stark simplicity underlying the complex of circumstance and detail. His pleasure was short-lived. Stowkowski was unaware of any Viet battle plan directed toward the final clearing of the province of all Viet Cong and was convinced that there was no such ambition in Huu-Lac or his forces and that their whole concept of the war was a combination of static and mobile defense of the province in order to protect the economic base, and the long-term destruction of the Viet Cong through attrition. Sweep, clear, and hold. An area here and an area there, action always related to the rice harvest, and by reason of Huu-Lac's paucity of forces, without hope of ever permanently clearing any area. That it was an expedient and working operation within the limits of its objectives, Scott accepted; what he could not accept was the limited objective. There could be no end to this war until there was complete destruction of the Viet Cong, and any concept of war that relied on reaction, no matter how decisive and lethal the reaction, was doomed to either failure or to only a limited success, a success as lacking in finality as was the concept of the campaign developed by Huu-Lac's forces. But to fight this war for victory rather than a stand-off required some real intelligence on the enemy, and this Storm assured him was not easy to come by. Of course there were defectors, and Huu-Lac's policy of humane treatment of all such people assured a small but steady flow. Almost without exception these were Ngo Tho natives, recruited by the Viet Cong either through persuasion and promises, or through terrorism. Finding unkept promises did not compensate for the rough life of a Viet Cong soldier, or with a change in circumstances that made reprisal against their families unlikely, they either gave up during battle or came out of the jungle sick and alone, and almost worthless as a source of real information. Not within the memory of Storm, perhaps not for two years, had a real hard case North Vietnamese Viet Cong defected or been captured alive. Many had been killed, but none had come into Huu-Lac's hands for the kind of interrogation that could provide really worthwhile information.

To Scott's amazement, at first he was frankly disbelieving, there was absolutely no firm knowledge of any Viet Cong base of operations. No knowledge of where the main force was hidden, of the probable location of the Viet Cong commander's headquarters, no indication even of areas held in unusual strength by the Viet Cong. In fact the only significant contribution Storm could make to Scott's understanding of the situation was contained in his observation that almost never did the Viet Cong attack in those areas that Huu-Lac had reinforced for increased protection, but seemed to have a sure touch for assault on those points that had been most weakened by the redeployment of forces, and that there were two distinct types of Viet Cong operations insofar as composition of forces was concerned. One type, usually directed against targets of minor importance, utilized an attack force composed of locally recruited Viet Cong led by only one or two of the North Vietnamese. The other type of operation was an attacking force composed almost entirely of North Vietnamese in a major engagement against a critical point in Huu-Lac's defense. In either type of operation those who had defected were in agreement that they did not know where the leaders or the forces came from, that they would one night assemble, and that when the battle was ended they would disappear. Storm was quite insistent that none of Huu-Lac's staff had even a half-way good idea of the method or routes of infiltration of these forces and that opinion was almost equally divided between those who held that the Viet Cong refuge was to the north in the Gy Than hills, or even farther to the north in Sy Ghan Province, and those who were as convinced that they came from over the Cambodian border. Huu-Lac's forces had long-established outposts covering all likely routes of approach and an aggressive program of patrolling, which had thus far had indifferent success. At most they had flushed groups of two or three men infiltrating from the north in the operation of the Viet Cong replacement system; none had been worthwhile sources of information even when they chose to talk rather than face execution.

Stowkowski was of little more help in developing a sense of order in the situation. His evaluation of the worth of Huu-Lac's defensive concept was to the effect that it was working well in insuring the protection of the economic life of the province and of the key cities and defensive points, that the situation was much better here than in almost any other province, and that defense was truly the single option available to Huu-Lac, considering the strength of his forces and his inability to fix the Viet Cong in place for an attack.

It's all so goddam logical, thought Scott. When you can't do what truly needs to be done you do the best you can. The only thing wrong is it's not the way to win. Even if Huu-Lac had the best and most effective command in the Vietnamese Army, he was not on a winning course of action. Especially was this evident when after much research Pickering finally produced a rough estimate of Huu-Lac's losses for the past twelve months, which showed he had had a 15 per cent casualty rate with more than half killed in action or wounded so severely as to be unable to return to duty.

Finally, partly out of frustration and the desire for something, anything to do, and partly out of a vague conviction that somewhere there must be a pattern, an indication of some design behind the Viet Cong actions, he started Stowkowski and Storm on a tedious and time-consuming project, which he himself was not sure was worthwhile, and which he was sure they both considered to be an absolute waste of time. On a separate map in the war room he started the posting of all Viet Cong actions, going back through the files of operations reports and marking each action on the map, coded in red for a major attack in which North Vietnamese Viet Cong had participated—yellow for minor actions when few North Vietnamese were involved, and blue where the composition of forces was undetermined or unknown. This was no overnight project, Scott knew well; it would take weeks and he would end up with an acetate map overlay that was a blaze of meaningless color. But it was at least a start at something and it would provide Stowkowski and Storm and their sergeants with something to do in their spare time, and to hell with whether they liked it or not. The wasting of time to satisfy the whim of a commander was part of being a soldier.

Scott had kept Gerrard at his side throughout the whole of these three days, and was cautiously optimistic as to his ability and motivation. Between them they had developed a tentative working schedule of alternate days in the field, Scott out one day and Gerrard the next, with an evening conference to compare notes and coordinate with the others. Gerrard was openly delighted with this arrangement. "I've had six months here without seeing hardly a damned thing except Saigon and the inside of this compound," he said, "And I'd sort of resigned myself to leaving here six months from now knowing damned little more about this country than when I came. Which is a hell of a tour for a man to have to admit to."

Scott nipped his implied criticism of Meir before it could be expressed. "Different people have different ideas on how to run an operation like this, and Meir's way was his own, considerably different than my way, but that's in the past, so forget it. As I see our job we have got to be an auxiliary set of eyes and ears for Huu-Lac, covering his command as completely as possible, and providing him with an unbiased viewpoint of his strengths and weaknesses. By the nature of his duties and responsibilities he cannot spend as much time in visiting his troops as we can and the same is true of his staff. They must spend most of their time here in Ngo Tho where the decisions are to be made, while we can spend as little time here as we wish and, if we can establish an atmosphere of mutual trust and confidence with these people we can be of really great assistance. And I don't mean only with Huu-Lac and his people here in Ngo Tho, it's probably more important that his commanders in the field learn that we are not out to carry tales back to Huu-Lac and get their asses in a jam. And this requires that we be understood, which means that we can't depend upon all the Viets we meet to speak English, and that you need an interpreter. You got any ideas?"

"Well, all our advisors out with the ARVN units have interpreters of one kind or another, either junior ARVN officers or sergeants, and I suppose we could work through them. As far as that goes maybe our channel should be through our advisors and we should restrict our contact . . ."

"We'll deal with both, our advisors and the ARVN commander on the spot, and your idea is not good enough. What you need is an officer of experience and rank who will go with you on every trip. Someone you can get to know, whom you can trust, who will advise you on all matters of protocol and how to conduct yourself, and who will give you a true evaluation of the Viet's reaction to you personally. Go see Swann. He seems to know more Viets than anyone else around here. Get a name from him. Someone he thinks will work well with you, and I'll ask Huu-Lac to make him available." Scott paused thoughtfully. "For myself I think I'll ask for Major Huc."

"You're not serious, Colonel," said Gerrard. "That SOB will be of no use to you whatsoever. He's actually anti-American, and an arrogant bastard besides."

"Maybe that's why I want him," said Scott, still thoughtful. "Maybe that's why he'll be the best choice I could make."

10

HIS SECOND ENTRY into Huu-Lac's headquarters was far removed from his first with Meir. Late in the morning of his fourth day, without prior notification and casually, he rode again with Sergeant Hoan through the streets, carrying his battered dispatch case, and allowing Hoan to drive as he wished and realizing that his nerve was being tested during the careening ride. He left Hoan and went quickly across the veranda, returning the salute of the Viet guards, across the entrance hall and up the stairway and into Major Huc's office, empty and with the door to Kim's room ajar. Without pause he was across the room and through the doorway, stopping just inside the room where Huc and Kim were in consultation at Kim's desk. Kim was the first to become aware of Scott as he stood silently watching them. There was no hesitation, no slightest stinting in his cordiality as he came around the desk, hand outstretched.

"Colonel Leonard, how nice to see you again. The General had expected you would stop in to see us today and we can go right in."

Scott, returning the warmth of his greeting, locked eyes with Major Huc who had not moved from his position behind Kim's desk, and whose eyes reflected the same unconcealed hardness as on their first meeting. Evidently any softening of his feeling had been only temporary. We'll see about this, my friend, he thought, as he nodded a greeting to Huc and followed Kim into General Huu-Lac's office.

Where before the room had been a blaze of orange, yellow, and black, today it was almost empty of furniture and without color; only the massive carved teak desk and a few straight-backed chairs placed near it remained.

Huu-Lac slowly arose from his chair behind the desk and leaning across the gleaming surface grasped Scott's hand in firm friendliness. "Welcome, Colonel Scott Leonard. It is nice to see you again. I trust you have used your time well." Noting Scott's dispatch case he continued, "And I suppose you have come to tell me how to win our war."

"General, I am a solider as you are, and as such I must obey orders," answered Scott, with real gratitude toward this remarkable man. Here there was no evasion, no talking all around the problem, but rather a direct acknowledgment of the fact that a problem did exist and that it must be solved. And also that it would not be handled as in the past through the sham of Kim's game with Meir, but straightforwardly and honestly. This more than any show of friendliness was the true mark of Huu-Lac's acceptance, he thought, as he continued. "Each day and probably oftener I will be directed by my superiors in Saigon to bring certain matters to your attention and to urge you to take a recommended course of action. And as you well know, I will be required to report back on the results of our conversations. I realize this is distasteful to you but . . ."

"Please do not trouble yourself over this, Colonel Leonard. It is a matter of no importance and little trouble. I will admit that Colonel Kim and I played a little game with Colonel Meir, but that is past and we will at least go through the proper motions now, although you undoubtedly realize that I shall do almost nothing that your people in Saigon suggest. Shall we begin?"

As Huu-Lac returned to his chair Scott seated himself in the nearest chair, and opening the dispatch case, brought forth five pages of yellow teletype paper, the accumulated directions of Buckmeister and staff since his arrival. Beginning with the oldest, he read the first item. "Patrol in force from the village of Xien to vicinity of village on Bhan Me Han. Clear Bhan Me Han. Prepare ambush along road Bhan Me Han-Khan Ghe."

"Accomplished," said Huu-Lac, "Sometimes we too can see the obvious. Please continue."

One by one Scott went through the fifteen paragraphs of

accumulated orders, pausing without comment at the end of each and noting Huu-Lac's terse, "Not Approved," "Accomplished," or occasional "Impossible" appropriately on the margin of the paper. It was quickly completed. "Thank you very much, General," said Scott, returning the folded papers to his dispatch case.

"And having accomplished your job so quickly, what will you do for the rest of the day?" asked Huu-Lac in friendly sarcasm.

Man, you really provide all the openings, don't you, thought Scott. Meir must have really been an insufferable sonofabitch to have loused this up. The man seems to know all my problems as well as I do, and at least for the present, he is truly making it easy for me to discuss them, openly and without any discursive lead-in. For an oriental, Huu-Lac had a most un-oriental approach to the conduct of business. No trace of the ceremonial, ritual-ridden protocol of the Japanese and Koreans, which required thirty minutes of polite conversation and an intricate pattern of response upon response before the true subject of any conversation could be introduced. Grateful for such simplicity and honesty Scott said, "General, my duty here is to advise you and I can either be only a figurehead, in effect be here only to show the U.S. flag, or I can really try to be of some use to you. I'd prefer to be of use, and to do that I've got to understand the problem. I'd like your permission to spend some time in visiting all the U.S. Advisors and your units within the next few weeks, and the privilege of reporting to you whenever I observe anything which I may think is of importance. Otherwise I'd like not to take up your time or bother you except when absolutely necessary."

"Most commendable," said Huu-Lac, "Although do not fear bothering me. When will you begin?"

"Tomorrow, I think," answered Scott, and outlined the plan he and Gerrard had developed, a day in and a day out. Huu-Lac nodded in agreement, and as Scott paused momentarily he asked, "Is there something else, Colonel?"

"There is. If I am to make contact with your commanders on any basis of mutual understanding, I will need one of your officers with me, as an interpreter. But not only as an interpreter, more as an advisor to me on matters of protocol and custom. To explain the local situation and to help schedule my visits so that I arrive at an opportune time, not right in the middle of an operation or the planning for an operation, or while the commander is otherwise busy and can't easily spare time. Colonel Gerrard has the same need."

He stopped a moment. Huu-Lac had listened attentively, although he had half turned in his chair and was looking into space, his face expressionless. "Major Bhan of your G3 office has been suggested for Colonel Gerrard, and I thought that perhaps you might spare Major Huc to work with me on an every-other-day basis."

Huu-Lac did not move, did not react in any way, but Kim, who had remained unobtrusively quiet thus far was immediate in his "Oh, I'm afraid that is quite impossible, Colonel Leonard. We cannot spare Major Huc, and besides it would be most difficult to persuade . . ."

Huu-Lac had turned slowly to meet Scott's eyes, and with a single movement of his upraised hand cut off Kim's protest.

"Major Bhan will work with Colonel Gerrard," he said quietly. "But I am not sure that Major Huc is the best person to escort you, Colonel. There may be problems that you do not fully recognize. Why do you ask for him?"

"Because of the problem," Scott answered bluntly, and turning to Kim he continued, "It is fairly obvious that there is a problem, isn't it?"

"Perhaps. Perhaps, and with a reason that may have now lessened," answered Kim reluctantly, and looking at Huu-Lac's impassive face across the desk. "I don't know, General."

"Colonel Leonard, you may not know this, but Major Huc is a protégé of mine. I knew his family in the old days in Hanoi and his father was a boyhood friend of great closeness. He did not come south when the rest of us did, but stayed in Hanoi, and died there five or six years ago. Major Huc himself escaped from the north five years ago and has been with me ever since. He is a very good officer and I have seen that he has had the proper assignments, platoon leader, company commander, regimental and division staff, and for the past year here in my office." He stopped and thoughtfully looked down at his hands, folded and relaxed on the shining desk top. "You have quickly recognized the single weakness I have found in Major Huc, and that is his antipathy for all foreigners. Don't think that his feeling is for you alone or for all U.S. personnel—he is equally unable to like the French or the English or the Japanese."

Again there was silence, longer this time, until he raised his eyes to Kim and nodded thoughtfully. "We will try this.

At least it can do little harm, and if it does not work well we can change."

Kim nodded silently and at some imperceptible signal between them arose to his feet and left the room.

"Is there anything else, Colonel," asked Huu-Lac, still seated and with the faintest of smiles on his face.

"Nothing at all, General," answered Scott. "Unless you have something for me—advice, for example."

"I need not advise you, Colonel," said Huu-Lac rising from his seat. "You and I have an understanding, I think, and from your way of beginning I think that you will shortly have some advice for me."

"Thank you, General," answered Scott. "I will try my best to insure that nothing happens to disturb our understanding."

Again there was the brief handshake and Scott turned and left the room. Kim, behind his desk, rose and meeting Scott's eyes directly gave an oddly formal bow, his hands remaining at his sides. "I have just sent for Major Huc," he said gravely. "I shall explain his new duties and he will be available at your call, as will Major Bhan whenever Colonel Gerrard wishes. And good luck to you, Colonel. It is a very good beginning, the beginning of a soldier, which you have made."

"Thank you, Colonel Kim," said Scott with equal gravity. "I shall try to make the ending as good as the beginning."

Leaving as quickly as he had come, he was evidently well ahead of Sergeant Hoan's alarm system and had the satisfaction of seeing his disconcerted look and double-timed scramble to get the jeep out of the parking area as Scott stood waiting at the curb. Of course he paid dearly for such petty satisfaction, as the embarrassed Hoan made the return ride to MAAG a magnificent demonstration of his driving skill.

And so began the real work. The visits to the two Division Headquarters first, with Colonel Kim as a surprise and bonus escort, and his meetings with General Tran Thuy commanding the 12th Division at Ghum Kong and General Le Hue of the 30th Division at Khan Ghe. These meetings served as further confirmation of his belief in Huu-Lac's ability to select only the most outstanding of men to serve with him. Down through the regiments, the battalions, to the special units, the fortified villages with their U.S. Special Forces detachments, and the outposts along the key roadways and the main streams and rivers. At the end of thirty days Scott could look back on some ninety chopper landings in as many places, countless land miles by jeep and on foot, and a sheaf of annotated maps and notes to reinforce his memories of people and places. Gerrard had done equally well, and Stowkowski, Storm, and Swann, released from Meir's restriction on their movements, had also done a fair share of traveling. Scott could actually feel the change in his staff, the new authority in their voices when they spoke of plans, places, and events. Much more important to him, however, was the reaction of his advisors and the Special Forces detachments with the Viet units. He could see a slow, gradual, and steady change for the better in the *esprit* and morale of those on this often lonely and always isolated duty. As one captain, an Infantry Battalion advisor at Thran Bac, almost on the Cambodian border had said in more than a little awe, "I thought for a while I was the only U.S. soldier in the whole goddam country since the last chopper landed here three months ago, and now I've had three visits already this month—Colonel Swann, Colonel Storm, and now you. This makes the Viets think I'm a real VIP."

It was beginning to shape up, and the nightly staff meeting where those who had been out during the day and those next to travel compared notes were at last beginning to be productive. He had already taken up a number of matters with Huu-Lac, such as inadequate training at company and platoon level in airmobile operations, where the confusion in loading and unloading of personnel aboard the helicopter, the inability to organize quickly in the landing area, and a consequent reluctance to move out of the landing area on to the objective, had been a contributing factor in the lack of success of several recent attempts at closing with suspected Viet Cong concentrations. The training program that resulted, supervised jointly by Major King and Colonel Trink, utilized a reinforcement group of ten helicopters from Saigon, which Buckmeister had produced after considerable argument, and insured that over the next few weeks every ARVN rifle company would have at least one live exercise in the planning and execution of a helicopter operation. There would be no immediate and spectacular results, of course. But slowly and surely the reaction time for these operations, the time from the reporting of a band of Viet Cong to the arrival of ARVN soldiers on their backs, would be reduced, and even a few really successful operations would fully pay for the effort involved.

Huu-Lac and his staff had been a joy to work with, not agreeing with everything he suggested, of course, but even when they did not accept certain proposals they gave such patient and detailed reasons for the rejections that Scott often thought that he gained more understanding of the complexity of the political-economic-military factors involved in this war through his unacceptable ideas than he did in any other way. Colonel Trink had been a special fount of information. The man was absolutely fearless and proud of his reputation for bravery, and with a real sense of destiny, of the historical background of this war, and of the true objectives of the fight and his personal role. One thing he had said, late one night as they sat with his favorite drink, brandy and soda, after a grueling analysis of the defense of an outpost that had been completely overrun by the Viet Cong, brought a new awareness to Scott of the quality of the Vietnamese as soldiers.

"No offense meant, Scott," Trink had said, "but your country lacks a true perspective on war. Admittedly you have a terrific technology and have developed a sound doctrine in the employment of this technology on the battlefield, but it is your philosophical approach to war which shows your immaturity. Your experience has only been with short wars, wars settled in a short span of years and where there has been recognizable defeat of one force and victory for the other. This plus the fact that your country has existed as a culture for only a few hundred years gives you a short-sighted view of problems as they exist here in Viet Nam and an impatience to solve all these problems in a single masterful stroke. We Vietnamese on the other hand have a history and tradition of war of a thousand years or more, and throughout our existence as a people we have fought almost constantly for our right to exist. The Hindus in the first recording of our history, the Chams in the seventh century of your calendar, the Khmers, and the Chinese—always the Chinese for many centuries, from the Mongol invasion in the thirteenth century—and the French in the late 1800's, before World War II, the Japanese during the war, and the French again after the war. You Americans thirst for and must have victory. We Vietnamese, while we hope for eventual peace, recognize that it may be a long time in coming. We may have it sooner for your help, but even if you did not help us, if Ho Chi Minh should close in and force us from the cities, we would still fight on. We would then be the same stone around the neck of Ho Chi

127

Minh that this Viet Cong are to us. I have read in the writings of you of the west that the Vietnamese are Buddhists, and as such are not a warlike people. This may be true of the peasants, generally they keep their heads under the water of their rice paddies and only wish to be left alone, but we of the mandarin class have always known war, and we shall always know war until we have established ourselves as a sovereign nation, free of all foreign domination."

Scott had sat quietly, in contrast to Trink, whose wry and humorous beginning had quickly turned to an emotional intenseness. "How can you ever become a true nation if you of the upper class are the only ones who have a sense of nationalism," he asked in a nice balance of the humble seeker of knowledge and the sarcasm of a skeptic.

"We cannot, but if you look around you, and if you have the background to understand what you see, you will realize that here in Ngo Tho we are beginning to build the foundations of a nation. You spend too much time with soldiers, and you think only of soldiers and their problems. Spend some time with Mr. Thieu, and Mr. Thi, and the old one, Chieu. We soldiers only hold what is needed for them to build upon. Ask any worker, any rice farmer, who it is that represents the government in Ngo Tho and he will tell you not General Huu-Lac but Mr. Thieu. They know of the General, of course, but only as a General, and they give their loyalty not to him but to Thieu. The same is true throughout the province. We know that it is only our military strength which makes any government possible. Our design is to insure that the real life of the province is in the hands of those like Thieu who can some day in the future create a government which will depend upon the military only for protection from enemies outside the country. We are different here in Ngo Tho than in all the other provinces. We are trying not only to kill the Viet Cong but to build a fortress in the minds of our people which will prevent their return. Are you aware of the number of recruits the Viet Cong have gotten from among our people?"

"Of course I don't know," Scott had answered, "But I understand that is quite small compared to other areas. But that may be because of your good fortune in having a surplus of rice here. A full belly makes the recruiting of revolutionaries more difficult, I imagine."

"The number is indeed small," Trink had continued, completely ignoring Scott's observation. "We have practically none in comparison to other places, but this was not always the case. When General Huu-Lac came here eight years ago, Premier Diem who then ruled our country, would have given him any command in our army. He chose this province mainly because it combined the greatest potential with the worst actual situation. Then we only held the cities and a few larger villages. The countryside, the rice lands, were controlled by the Viet Cong, and many of those who gave their loyalty to our enemies then were our own people. It has taken a long time, and many of them died, together with many of our soldiers, but with the first weakening of the Viet Cong, when we could control enough of the land to feed our cities and still ship rice to Saigon, they defected in great numbers and now we no longer have a significant local element to deal with. It is only Ho Chi Minh's people who come from Cambodia and the north that plague us now, and someday perhaps we will have killed them all."

That evening ended as had so many others, with Scott returning to his deserted war room, and slouched in a chair, studying the day's maps and then turning to the results of the day's research into the files to show the accumulted actions of the past. As he had more or less expected, his first idea of plotting everything on a single map with color coding to show the size and kind of action had long since been abandoned. Now he had three maps, distinguished by the size of the enemy force involved, and showing only Viet Cong attacks or ambushes. These did not show actions where terrorism, the formal and ritualized murder of a village chief or someone of known pro-government loyalties was the apparent motive, or the rare confrontations where ARVN forces had stumbled upon a traveling band of Viet Cong. They pinpointed attacks and ambushes where the Viet Cong had deliberately created a situation. Somewhere in all this there had to be a pattern, some repetition of events, some relationship of actions to terrain or to routes of approach that would indicate the origin of the attack or the lines of retreat. Some key to the creation of a plan that would strike at the Viet Cong rather than wait for their strike, some indicator that would permit the change of initiative to Huu-Lac.

One of his first suggestions to Huu-Lac, and one of the few that Huu-Lac had received with a tired smile and a pitying look, had been the infiltration of agents into Cambodia and the Gy Than hills with the mission of finding and observing the Viet Cong bases there. Huu-Lac had referred him to Colonel Yuan who had explained in great detail his network of agents all through the area, and the scanty information produced by them because of the Viet Cong single-man infiltration techniques. Colonel Yuan talked with weary patience and always with his eyes somewhere aside from Scott, or in the distance behind him, never meeting his eyes openly.

Perhaps it was a reaction to his embarrassment at having made such an obvious suggestion, or perhaps it was based upon the sound logic that if adequate measures had been taken to counteract a threat from a given quarter without diminishing the effectiveness of enemy action, then it was probable that the threat did not exist in that quarter. But in any event and for whatever reasons, Scott became a lone and very secret dissenter. He knew that his denial of the consensus that the hard core of the Viet Cong was based either to the north or in Cambodia to the west, was presumptuous on his part, with his incountry lack of experience and his obvious need to learn the ways of this war. But his attempts to correlate Viet Cong past history with bases in either Cambodia or the Gy Than Hills fell upon the hard reef of the time and space factors involved, for in many of the actions it meant that an attack could have occurred only by an infiltration march of two or three days' duration. While this was not impossible, it presupposed a movement of large numbers of Viet Cong, either in groups or singly, through areas where the routes of approach were well-covered by Huu-Lac's outposts and when patrols were constantly active. And although Scott was willing to concede exceptional march discipline and camouflage technique to the enemy, he could not accept the notion that the Viet Cong were universally and invariably successful in such operations.

Night after night he brooded over this lack of clear intelligence of the enemy. Only one thing emerged from the pattern on the map, and that was the absence of an attack in force on the city of Ngo Tho, or an attack of any significance within a ten-mile radius of Ngo Tho. True, there were few remunerative targets in the area, east and north a complex of rice paddies without villages of any size; south only the river, and to the west a swamp of such impenetrability that it had never been tamed to rice production and remained a sea of tall, dense grass. Still it would seem that the usual pattern of Viet Cong violence would have brought forth some incident, if only an ambush of the ARVN forces who were in constant movement in the area. Without drawing a real conclusion from all this, Scott carried his half-formed and undefined thought, like a festering chancre in his mind—a conviction that there was some significance in the information presented to him by his maps that was completely beyond his power to comprehend.

Another source of vague irritation to Scott, and at times not so vague but truly acute in its intensity, was his lack of success in the conversion of Major Huc. Their first encounter after his request for Huc's services had set the pattern. He was unfailingly polite, quick to see that Scott's slightest expression of need was immediately satisfied, solicitous of Scott's safety, a competent and thoughtful advisor, an accurate and competent interpreter, and as unbendingly cool as on their original meeting. Scott had truly believed that treating Huc as an equal, not kissing his ass, not trying to be buddy-buddy, but just treating him as a brother-in-arms, a competent and trustworthy soldier, must eventually break down the barriers. But it hadn't worked. True, when just the two of them were out together there had been times when he had seemed about to unbend, when in the companionship of their pleasure in observing a truly effective unit in action or in their shared bone-deep fatigue at the end of a trying day, he thought he could sense some vague seeking of empathy, some true rapport between them, but it always passed with the moment. Scott had never mentioned the matter to either Kim or Huu-Lac, and they in turn had not opened the subject for discussion, and Scott could only hope that he was expecting results too quickly and the emotional patterns, the resistance to all people and things foreign would, with time, fade in intensity.

Scott was learning his job, his staff was becoming an effective unit, Huu-Lac was seemingly pleased, and his staff had shown an ever-increasing degree of cooperation—with the possible exception of Colonel Yuan, the unfathomable G2, who incidentally had never seen fit to explain the Kei incident to Storm. All was well, even with General Wesley and Buckmeister in Saigon. Either through Scott carrying the orders of the day to General Huu-Lac, or by Gerrard covering with Colonel Kim on those days when Scott was in the field, it had been possible to give a same-day response to MAAG Headquarters and there was a grudging admission from Buckmeister, not direct, of course, but relayed through his G3, Colonel Loveless, to Stowkowski, that things seemed to be much improved in Ngo Tho. No compliment to Scott, of course, since the improvement was clearly tied to the reformation of Huu-Lac's personal life.

All was well indeed, but Scott was not content. Today Huu-Lac exercised a reasonable degree of control over the battle area, but it was at best a sometime thing. At any time or any place the Viet Cong could temporarily wrest this control from Huu-Lac. Perhaps only for a short time and at a cost to their forces, but with a certainty that brought a real sense of unease to Scott. And always the ARVN casualties far exceeded those of the Viet Cong. The truth—if one were not blinded by complacency over the thriving economy, the popular support of the government by the majority of the people, and the fact that things were ever so much better than they had been before—the truth was that Huu-Lac was fighting a holding action. Purely and simply a holding action. His entire philosophy was that of the defense. All initiative was with the Viet Cong. And if they could do so well with the forces now in the province, what would happen if Hanoi should decide that Huu-Lac was making too much progress, that a blow should be struck to curb his plans and that the people once more should be impressed by the strength of the Viet Cong and with the certainty of the Viet Cong's eventual victory. The Viet Cong's present strength in the province was anywhere from the twelve hundred that Zeke had given him during the briefing in Saigon, to the three or four thousand that Colonel Yuan seemed to think were based in Cambodia and another thousand or so in the northern hills. In any case, and whatever their present numbers, should they roughly double their present activity, Huu-Lac would be in a desperate situation and this, the knowledge that there was no defeat of the Viet Cong in sight at even their present strength, was enough to raise nightmares behind the façade of complacency in Huu-Lac's present dominance of the situation.

All this—his reservations, his doubts, and his suspicions—he carefully kept to himself; partly out of a sense of propriety, a feeling that someone who had been incountry for so short a period should not begin a rash questioning of basic and long-held concepts; partly because he was truly unable to define his unease, to intelligently develop a rationale that would cast doubt on any previously held concepts; and compounding these two quite logical reasons, the completely illogical and irrational fact of superstition. Maybe that was not the right word to define his feeling, but in Scott's mind it was the only term to define his convictions that it would bring calamity to discuss his thoughts on this matter with anyone.

All this, of course, was only the smallest of worries, the most infinitesimal of clouds in an otherwise cloudless sky, and outside of this small doubt there was nothing to diminish the sense of well-being, of doing a difficult job under difficult circumstances, and doing it well.

atop the building on the left of the entrance street. There had been a change of guard at 0400 hours, so that those who had been on duty during the time the demolitions had been emplaced were still alive, and in spite of the most intense questioning, and Scott could imagine that intense was hardly the word to describe the kind of questioning they had undergone, they had denied knowledge of any unusual activity during the night. Those who had been on duty at the time of the attack were quite dead and so the method of how the Viet Cong had accomplished such a wholesale destruction of the vehicles of Huu-Lac's elite palace guard, some fifty jeeps and three-quarter tons, remained a mystery.

There was no mystery about how they had killed the two hundred dead or wounded the ninety-odd. It had been like shooting fish in a barrel. First the simultaneous detonation of all satchel charges, killing many and throwing the whole courtyard into confusion, and then the careful and deliberate sweep of automatic fire from the rooftops of the two buildings to the left and right of the entrance passageway. Those in the courtyard never had a chance, and those few that did escape did so by crawling under the demolished jeeps or by seeking refuge in Huu-Lac's headquarters building, the troop barracks, or in tight defilade against the walls of the two buildings housing the Viet Cong. There were five Viet Cong casualties, all killed by a three-man jeep patrol coming home late from night duty who had opened fire from the main street leading to the entrance passageway into the square. Five Viet Cong dead and no sign of any others, only five weapons had been found on the rooftops with the dead bodies and some three thousand rounds of unused ammo and a bushel of grenades. They had come prepared to make the operation pay, and the slaughter had taken less than thirty minutes. Half of the Ngo Tho garrison force wiped out in thirty short minutes.

Both Stowkowski and Storm had gone to the area as soon as they had heard of the massacre and assured Scott that it was a sight to behold. The massed dead, the smoking and mangled vehicles, and the search among the dead for those with a spark of life still remaining, led by Huu-Lac himself and with all his headquarters staff helping. And Trink, incoherent with rage and with heartbreak that so many of his beloved soldiers had died, raging impotently, vowing vengeance, and mutilating the Viet Cong bodies with unashamed tears streaming down his face. Even Yuan seemed to be in a state of shock, wandering vaguely through the havoc, occasionally turning over a dead body with a look of wondering recognition, or seeing to the comfort of one of the wounded with an uncharacteristic gentleness.

"They've been clearing the area all day today, Colonel, and tonight in about an hour there is to be a big conference which you and Huc have been specifically asked to attend by Huu-Lac," Stowkowski had said. "Storm and I are also going at the request of Trink."

"I'll go now, while there is still time to see the area before dark," said Scott. Huc had listened without comment or apparent reaction to Stowkowski and Storm's account and now started toward his own jeep, which always awaited him at the MAAG compound when he was out with Scott. "And I want you with me, Major Huc. Have your jeep follow us," Scott called sharply.

The ride was short and quick, through deserted streets where the contrast with the normal packed busyness spoke of the shock and fear of the people, and where the air of waiting, of expectation and dread of another attack was an almost tangible thing.

There was no longer a narrow alley-like passageway between two high buildings, only the smoldering ashes where the buildings had once stood, and the widened entrance to the square was now jammed with a bulldozer scraping the still hot ashes into the main street and four wreckers lined up behind waiting to tow away as many jeeps in the final stages of the clearing of the square. Scott went on foot, with Huc following closely, into the square where only a few twisted jeeps remained, and standing in the center of the area he tried to visualize the slaughter. The paved surface was no longer smooth but was pockmarked by the fire from the rooftops. The front of Huu-Lac's headquarters building had been extensively damaged, as had the exit passageway wall. If three thousand rounds of ammo had been found on the rooftops, and if Scott's quick guess that even more had been expended in the square, it was quite a load for five men to have smuggled to the top of the roof.

Scott walked slowly to where the small knot of ARVN soldiers stood waiting for the return of the wreckers and carefully examined the jeeps. Whoever had laid the charges had done a damned fine job. None of these jeeps would ever run again.

"Ask them if there were any charges that didn't go off,"

he directed Huc, and in the babble and head shaking that came with Huc's question he did not need the translated answer.

"All vehicles had demolition charges under the hoods, and all fifty charges fired," said Huc. "The firing was done from the top of the building and the equipment used was captured U.S. equipment, and with fresh U.S. batteries."

"Does anyone know what explosive was used," asked Scott, and again there was the exchange between Huc and the men.

"Dynamite, everyone seems to think, and for sure it was used in at least some of the jeeps, judging from the debris."

Turning, Scott made his way across the square and up the steps into Huu-Lac's headquarters. The crystal chandelier was gone, and a few glittering shards of glass still remaining on the splintered floor testified to the way of its passing. The glass was gone from all windows and wherever the thick stone walls had not stopped the fire, the walls were shattered and riddled. Picking his way up the still littered stairway with Huc following closely, Scott made his way to the top, and debating briefly, bypassed Huu-Lac's office in favor of Trink and the adjacent war room. Anything he could say to Huu-Lac now would be futile and he would see him at the meeting anyway, and he could better question Trink. At the open door of the office he dismissed Huc with an absently curt, "Thank you, Major Huc," and went into the deserted reception room, across the floor, and to the open doorway of Trink's private office.

Trink did not raise his eyes or cease his methodical destruction of the surface of his desk. With a monotonous regularity and a vicious force he drove the short dagger in his hand into the desk in front of him, and raising his arm high, drove it again, chipping chunks out of the polished surface and carefully choosing the spot for his next blow. He had evidently been at it for quite some time judging from the state of the desk.

Scott stood for a moment in silence watching, waiting for Trink to become aware of his presence, and then said quietly, "Trink, my friend." There was no acknowledgment, no break in the rhythm of his savage blows.

Scott tried again, more loudly, again without effect, and then walking around the desk to Trink's side he caught the upraised hand at the top of his swing. Trink's glare of animal rage as he raised his eyes to Scott was startling, as was his utter lack of recognition. He did not struggle in

Scott's grip, but neither did he relax. No wonder he sat alone in his office, Scott thought, probably all his staff were afraid to be near him.

"Trink, my friend, we must talk," Scott said gently, his eyes unwavering, not evading the rage in Trink's eyes. "We must know how this happened, and how we can have revenge."

There was no change, no softening of the viciousness in the eyes, no recognition of Scott, nor any movement, and as they stood in stillness, there was still no change, even as Huu-Lac spoke from the doorway.

"Leave him, Scott. Let go and step back quickly. He is beyond thinking now, and he will be of no use until he has slept. My doctor is on his way now, and he knows what to do. This happened once before many years ago when we first came here to Ngo Tho and had General Le Hue's 30th Division command post overrun at Khan Ghe. But tomorrow he will be completely recovered, and an even better and deadlier soldier."

With Scott's release of his hand, down came the dagger, as if there had been no interruption, and Trink's whole concentration returned to his self-imposed task of destruction.

Huu-Lac, too, seemed to have suffered an extreme shock, Scott thought. He seemed almost dreamlike and shuffled with the gait of an old man as Scott followed him out through the reception room and down the hall to the war room. As they entered the assembled group came to their feet, the subdued murmur dying as they walked in the stillness to the vacant seats in the front of the packed room.

Huu-Lac motioned Scott to a seat, and remained standing as the men sat down. "We are assembled here for an analysis of just what happened this morning, and how it was possible for it to have happened. We will speak in English insofar as possible for the benefit of Colonel Leonard, and there is to be a complete freedom of discussion. If anyone has any ideas, please feel free to speak. Colonel Yuan has been in charge of the investigation thus far and will speak first."

As Huu-Lac took his seat, Yuan stepped to a map board and mounted a city map of Ngo Tho and a blow-up of the neighborhood of the square. Gone was the vagueness, the detachment of manner, and he spoke with an authority and a decisiveness that brooked no argument.

"General Huu-Lac, these things we know positively. First, that only the five Viet Cong who were killed were involved in the attack. We have made a house to house interrogation of all people along the streets to the west and the north and no one has reported knowledge of any movement of people through the streets during the night. Second, that all their equipment was transported by one of our own trucks, stolen during the early evening from the detachment guarding the airfield. Third, that the guards on duty were all killed, three by crossbows and the rest by the knife, and their bodies concealed in the ground floor front room of one of the buildings, and that all the twelve families in the larger building and the seven in the smaller building were also killed as silently and presumably before the placing of the charges in our vehicles began. Our losses were two hundred dead on the spot, together with the sixty civilians in the two houses, and twenty-one of the ninety-three wounded have died during the day.

"The Viet Cong terrorists undoubtedly came from Cambodia, or the Gy Than hills, as they have all come, and in easy stages, moving only at night, took several days to move their equipment into some location here in town. Then when all was in readiness, they struck, and had it not been for one of our night patrols arriving late and taking them from the rear, at least some of them, perhaps all, would have escaped.

"There were no identification papers or other means of identifying the Viet Cong by origin, but it can be assumed that they were hard-core Northerners. We captured three Swedish K guns and one 50 caliber U.S. machine gun and one Thompson 45 caliber submachine gun, together with a quantity of unused ammunition and grenades."

Scott listened in silence, occasionally glancing at Huu-Lac's impassive profile. Yuan went on with a description of the preventative measures that must be taken in the future in order to prevent any reoccurrence of this disaster. And Scott's disbelief grew as he read on the faces of those surrounding him their acceptance of Yuan's explanation. No one thought to question the premise as to the strength of the force, and the sheer physical limitations on what five men could do in the time between the relief of the guard at 0400 hours and the attack at 0630. Two and one half hours to kill the guards and sixty civilians, to place charges in fifty vehicles, and to carry their ammunition to the rooftop and set up their firing positions. This was absolutely stupid. But even as he thought to begin to take Yuan apart in cross-examination, a look at Huu-Lac's face warned him off. Huu-

Lac was a believer, convinced that this was the way it was, and glancing back into the crowd, it was evident that this was a true consensus. Even Stowkowski and Storm seemed to be listening with an unquestioning intensity.

Scott ceased his squirming, his looking around to measure reaction, and concentrated on what Yuan was saying—a series of great and obvious platitudes: increased guards, dispersion of vehicles, staggered assembly of troops, all that must be done to forestall a repetition of today's events, and spoken in such a surprisingly forceful tone that it obscured the basic wrongness of his entire analysis. At least when he got charged up, when he came out of his shell, he had a terrific stage presence, thought Scott, and wondered which of his images was the true Yuan. In any case, he was either plain goddam stupid or he was deliberately raising a smokescreen against any effort to truly evaluate the situation.

Scott endured, acutely conscious that his increasing disgust and anger was a dangerous thing and must be controlled at all cost. When it was over, when Yuan had finished his briefing and the few questions had been asked and answered, he asked Yuan a single question, carefully controlling his voice to show only the most casual curiosity.

"Were there any other things found with your five Viet Cong dead other than the weapons and ammo?"

"What do you mean, Colonel Leonard?" asked Yuan. "Do you have anything specific in mind?"

"I only mean what I have asked, Colonel Yuan," answered Scott. "Was there anything at all that you have not mentioned found on the rooftops with the Viet Cong?"

"Nothing, and I closely inspected both rooftops myself before anything had been taken away," said Yuan, fading back into his usual manner of detached and far away vagueness.

Huu-Lac had not spoken at all during the briefing or during the questioning, and now he rose abruptly and with a curt word of thanks to Yuan left the room, and on his signal the others began to file slowly out. Scott, mingling with the group as they moved down the hallway to the stairs, found Stowkowski and Storm, one on each side, and said quietly to them, "I give you an hour to nose around here and talk to anyone who you think may have any information, and then I want you back in our war room. We have some thinking to do." Making no effort to seek out Huu-Lac, or to find Kim, whose absence from the meeting was most unusual, he moved to the ever-waiting Sergeant Hoan, who drove almost slowly back to Scott's compound.

Scott went directly to his maps, this time not with the attitude of one seeking inspiration, a revelation, a vision, but of one who looks for specific information to support a well-defined theory. No one in his right mind could accept the idea that only five men had set up that massacre, and if a search to the west and the north had not established the presence of additional Viet Cong, then the directions chosen were wrong. He was in a mood that he had experienced many times in the past, always triggered by someone's stupidly conceived plan or sloppy execution of an operation, where his half-rage lent fuel to a period of truly intense intellectual activity. He settled himself down in his chair with the full belief that before he left this room he would have a concept of what had happened and what should be done about it that would be a damned sight more satisfactory than anything he had heard so far this evening.

By the time Stowkowski and Storm arrived he had assembled the few others of his staff he wanted—Swann, Albright, and Major King from the Aviation Company. He had also had three radios brought in and placed against the walls and tuned on the loudest broadcast station Albright could find. Six chairs were assembled in a circle in the center of the room with a one to twenty-five thousand map of the Ngo Tho area spread on the floor in the center of the circle. He motioned them to sit down, and leaning forward and speaking just loudly enough for the group to hear him, said, "Storm, when was the last time there was an electronic sweep of this room?"

"Why, I don't believe there ever has been," Storm answered in slow amazement. "Our compound is so well guarded that we've never thought it necessary, but if you like I can send to Saigon for some technicians and . . ."

"Absolutely not, I don't want anyone outside this room to know I even asked the question." He stopped a moment, waiting and then with all the emphasis he could put in his voice, he continued. "And that goes for everything else that is said in this room. Not a single soul, U.S. or Viet, is to have any idea of what I have in mind. Is that clearly understood?" He met each man's eyes in the circle and received his nod of agreement, Stowkowski and Storm both with a wondering look as if to ask what could possibly have wound him up so tight, Swann with unquestioning and confident good humor, King impassive and waiting, and Albright with an awed amazement at Scott's hard voice.

"Storm, I asked you once to get a report on the maid Kei, and just what went on here which led the Viets to charge her with being a spy. I asked you only once, and have never reminded you of it, but now I'd like to know what you have found out, if anything."

There was a momentary look of fear in Storm's eyes and Scott could understand this reaction. His tone had not been gentle and Storm could probably envision a bad session coming. "I have tried repeatedly to discuss this with Colonel Yuan and others but they refuse to even acknowledge my questions, saying that you know all there is to know about the case," answered Storm, his voice even, but with the faintest trace of resentment.

"Isn't it rather unusual for Yuan and the others to treat you in such a manner?" probed Scott, not relaxing the demand in his voice.

Storm sat a long moment, his face flushed and what had been perhaps fear, perhaps small irritation, was gone from his voice. It was flat and hard and almost defiant as he said, "Colonel Leonard, I know your feeling on getting along with these people, and I know it is the only way for us to be effective, but cooperation is a two-way street, and in spite of all the best intentions in the world on my part, for the past three months I have been getting the freeze from Yuan. His people are still fairly friendly when he's not around, but let him come on the scene and all I get is cold politeness. Maybe you'd better get yourself another G2, Colonel," he finished with bitterness.

"I'll get myself another G2 when I decide I need another one, and I don't need any recommendations on the subject." Scott said in sharp reprimand. "You said Yuan has been this way only the past three months. What kind of a situation were you in before that—and what caused the change?"

"My first couple of months were fine," said Storm with the same anger in his voice, the same even flatness. "I kept quiet and listened and learned, and every door was open to me. But as soon as I got my feet on the ground and began asking questions Yuan began to freeze up. Not all at once, but no matter how diplomatic I was, every goddam time I got interested in something I got nothing but evasion."

"Give me me some examples of the things you were interested in," said Scott. He could see in the faces of the others their puzzlement at the course the conversation was taking, and their speculation as to what was coming next, when their turn would come in what was apparently going to be a group ass-chewing.

Storm thought a short moment, and when he spoke the hard anger was replaced by a serious and quiet attempt at remembrance and analysis. "Colonel, my first run-in with Yuan was when I asked to be present and ask some questions of a hard-core defector who had wandered out of the bush and given himself up right here in Ngo Tho. I thought that if we could get some idea of the location of the Cambodia and Gy Than base camps and their favorite routes in and out, we could lay a few ambushes ourselves. He wouldn't hear of me getting involved at the time, and when he came around to agreeing, the next day the Cong was dead. It seems the prisoner had changed his mind during the night and was shot while trying to escape. We didn't have an argument or anything like that—I wasn't really insistent enough to cause it to become an open issue—but nevertheless that was the beginning. A couple of other things have added to it, like me getting some really fine AF photo coverage all along the Cambodian border, which showed not a damned thing suspicious for at least fifteen miles inside the border, and presenting this to Yuan. He got mad as hell then, you know he can drop that air of aloof dignity instantly, and on the grounds that I shouldn't have done this on my own but should have consulted him first. I could never get him to talk about the facts of the matter, the intelligence value of the photos, and from then on he really wouldn't discuss very damn many things with me. That's why I quite sincerely feel I'm no damned good to you. Maybe someone else could work better with them."

"You couldn't be more wrong if you had tried, Colonel," said Scott without hesitation and with the harshness gone from his voice. "In fact if you had been deliberately trying to tell me what I wanted to hear you couldn't have done better. Captain Albright, tomorrow I want you to look over this entire building, starting with this room, to see if we've been bugged. Don't disturb a damned thing you find, and don't be obvious about your search. I don't want anyone to have any idea of what you are looking for, or even that you are looking, for that matter. Also, I want you to take a careful look at your comm center. Somehow the Viets knew the substance of Meir's reports on Huu-Lac's drinking and

144

sex life damned near as soon as they did in Saigon. Understood?"

"Yes, sir," answered Albright, the awed amazement still on his face.

"And now gentlemen, I'd like you to consider the military situation in Ngo Tho, based upon the assumption that someone is making a fool of someone, and that the Viet Cong are in our midst rather than spending all their time in forced marches in and out of Cambodia and the Gy Than hills."

Rising from his chair he went to the map board and lifted his plot of the attacks in force of the hard-core Viet Cong and laid it over the other map on the floor in the center of the group. Standing behind his chair, his eyes roving over their raised faces, he said, "Observe the previously untouched area of Ngo Tho and vicinity, and stop thinking of this singular fact of invulnerability in terms of days of march from any outside safe haven or the efficiency of the Vietnamese defense of this area. Start thinking of it in terms of not fouling one's own nest, and that until today the Viet Cong left this area alone because of the danger that any analysis of a major attack here might result in someone beginning to doubt Yuan's theories, and then think of two other things: where the Viet Cong base could be, and how they get in and out without detection."

Bent forward, their eyes fixed on the map, no one spoke. Scott continued in a light and humorous voice. "I've never completely accepted Yuan's idea on this, any more than you did Storm, and tonight was the clincher. It is almost impossible as a matter of time and sheer logistics for five men to have prepared such a slaughter. It must have taken over two hundred pounds of dynamite for the jeeps, another couple of hundred pounds for the ammo and the weapons, which is a hell of a load for five men to have carried any distance, and discounting the truck stolen from King's airfield guard which would have helped only within the city. It just isn't credible. And even if you could believe all that, tell me how five men could have done all the quiet killing of the guards and the civilians and then had time to wire up the jeep charges and set up their firing positions before Huu-Lac's troops began their usual early morning scramble in the courtyard. And even if it were possible to accept the fact that this little band were all ten feet tall and fast and strong, there is one single thing that louses up the entire picture, and I'll bet someone, somewhere, is being burned for oversight this minute, and that is the lack of any tools, not even a pair of wire cutters, which would have been absolutely necessary in wiring those jeeps for demolition. One doesn't crimp blasting caps or cut wire with one's teeth."

Again there was no sound from the group, no movement except for Swann who leaned back in his chair and raised his eyes to Scott in a slow and deliberate wink.

"So if you don't believe Yuan's story of a five-man attack, and there had been no trace of any movement to the west and north during the night, there must be another direction that points to home for the rather large group who prepared this show. So now we think about that for awhile." Lifting his map of previous Viet Cong actions, he uncovered the Ngo Tho map, and resuming his seat, leaned forward, pointing to the area to the south of the city, the grassy swampland lying along the Se Reo Kri for some ten miles to the west, unmarked by any sign of road or trail on the map, and labeled Ngo Tho.

"Major King, you've flown over this area countless times. What's in there?"

"Water, grass, and more grass, and not a living soul or a sign of anyone ever having been there, that I've ever seen," answered King. "I don't know how deep the water is but it stretches clear to the river and there is no open or high ground."

"Notice this, though," said Scott. "There are three well-defined streams running through the area, and this one on the west is actually a small river, the Ngo Kri, which comes from the Gy Than hills. Where there are such well-defined stream channels it might be a good assumption that the surrounding ground, at least in some places, is above water at least a few feet. With the grass covering everything uniformly it would be impossible to tell for certain from the air, but my bet is that here, where the Ngo Kri branches and doesn't rejoin for the remaining five miles to the Se Reo Kri, is at least one spot that is not under water."

"Could be, but what the hell does that mean?" asked King with his customary bluntness. "There hasn't been anyone in the area anyway. Any extensive movement would eventually show plain as hell in that grass. That stuff is six or eight feet high and a man would have a hell of a time moving through it, let alone move through it without leaving a trail of bent grass. That's one man I'm talking about, and when you talk about a number of men it's out of the question."

"Who said anything about walking through any grass?" asked Scott. "All I'm looking for now is possible high ground. Getting in and out without leaving any sign would be simple as hell in boats." His elbows braced on his knees and his head resting on both his hands, he continued his study of the map. "The damned trouble is that if anyone goes in there he has got to be right the first time. This is no place to be floundering around on a routine clearing action."

"How about infra-red photo?" asked Storm. "If there is a temperature gradient between the water and dry land it should show, but with all that damned grass as insulation I guess there really wouldn't be a detectable difference." His voice trailed off into silence.

Stowkowski and Swann had both been silent thus far, but now Stowkowski said thoughtfully. "How about bringing in some of Huu-Lac's river flotilla and making a search of the banks for a landing spot they've been using. All his boats are up-river now, but we could get a couple of the smaller ones back tomorrow or the next day."

"I don't really like that," said Scott, still preoccupied with the map. "We stand too much chance of not finding anything and only managing to alert them to the fact that we're suspicious." Suddenly he raised his head and turned to Storm. "Infra-red will do it though, but not because of the water-dry land temperature gradient, but because the bastards can't eat uncooked rice. They must be dug in with their whole base underground, and of course they don't cook in the open, but when they do cook there must be some real warm air coming out of their entrance and ventilation holes. In fact, it may well be that just about dawn when the ambient air is at its coolest this contrast might be reasonably apparent. And this would be much better than any rough indication of high ground, where we'd still have the problem of area search for the precise location of their entrances and exits."

"And think of this, Colonel," said Swann, speaking for the first time. "Their operation must involve most of their raiding parties getting home before first light in the morning, just at the time their cooking would be going on. So what we need is a couple of those Mohawk recon planes with both infra-red and side-looking radar going full blast, for say about one hour before dawn. No great show, a flight toward the Cambodian border and a return flight a half an hour later, both passes at a fairly high altitude so that we can hope they will be considered routine Viet Nam-Thailand traffic. I don't know for sure whether any canoes or whatever they are using would show up on radar, but it seems worth a try, even if our airstrip isn't completed and we have to talk Saigon into running the mission for us."

"Good thinking, old soldier," said Scott with appreciation in his voice, and then looking at Swann speculatively. "What did you tell me when I first got here about your contacts and your ability to scrounge a few unauthorized items out of the treasure houses in Saigon?"

"You name it, give me twenty-four hours back there, and I'll have it. Within reason of course, but you don't have to be too reasonable," answered Swann unperturbed and cool.

Scott nodded his acknowledgment and turned to King. "Those three Mohawks back there don't really belong to you yet, do they?"

"Not until they move up here," answered King. "And even then we'll have only part of their mission capability. MACV will still lay a hell of a lot of out-of-province stuff on them."

"You checked out on Mohawks?" asked Scott.

"I'm checked out on every frigging aircraft the army owns, and then some," answered King with a belligerent pride. "But if you're thinking what I think you're thinking, it isn't quite that simple. I could go back and take one out on a check flight, but it takes a crew to operate all the gadgets inside and it would look a little odd to them if first of all I wanted a night flight, and then if I wanted the flight to go full mission all of a sudden, it would look odder and odder. Besides you might not get the best registration if it were done on such a half-assed basis, and that's damned important to you, I think. When you look at any pictures taken of this area you want to know precisely which piece of ground it is." Looking at Scott with friendly frankness, he asked, "My God, don't you trust anybody today, Colonel?"

"There's a small possibility that I'm being a little psycho just now," answered Scott without resentment. "But you gentlemen will just have to bear with me, and I'll have your individual and collective asses if you don't. If I'm right, this is too ungodly big to expose to any single chance which isn't absolutely necessary.

"But you're right, of course, Major," he continued after a moment of thought. "Even if you made a good run over the area we'd have a real mess in getting the film and data processed in Saigon on a bootleg basis, and so we'll just have to arrange a legal mission. Which can be done by an old buddy of mine, and we'll go into that later. But now we've got to decide what we're going to do about the situation if our suspicions turn out to be fact. And what we need to do it with."

"We could lay on an Air Force strike," Stowkowski started, to be brought short by Scott's look.

"Please don't, Colonel," said Scott in mock pain, and then, seriously, "The Air Force are fine in close support against troops in the open, but all they would do here is let the Viet Cong know that we had found them, and this isn't a situation where we can either close in on them in a conventional manner after they have that alert, or set up blocking positions to catch them coming out. There is too damned much of that swamp and they know their way around in it much better than we do. So we'll have to do this the hard way, and a pretty goddam primitive way at that.

"First of all, we need a means of getting them out of their holes, which means a supply of smoke and tear-gas grenades, and give me no conversation about policy. Screw policy, U.S. policy that is. The Viets will be doing this, not U.S. Forces. Get this in grenades or cannisters, whatever you can scrounge, Swann. Second, we need some firepower and I can't see these Viets carrying M-1's damned near as big as they are, plus the ammo that is going to be needed, through that muck and grass and arriving in any condition to do their best. So what we need is about fifty ARfourteens, or Armalite's, or Swedish K weapons, something that doesn't weigh much and where the ammo weight is way below our standard thirty caliber, plus about five hundred rounds of ammo per weapon per man. Try to figure it on a basis of about forty or fifty pounds per man basic load of weapon and ammo, with grenades and rations additional. This is going to be a slow movement so a little overload isn't going to matter too much. Anything else you can steal that you think would be useful to a group of men who are going to crawl through some miles of swamp and flush out an underground redoubt and kill one hell of a number of Viet Cong will be welcome. Use your own judgment."

"Colonel, even if everything is as you think it is, and we do all the planning for the complete show, I still don't see how we're going to get this operation off the ground," began Storm. "The minute you go to Huu-Lac with this you're going to run head on into Yuan, and even after you've convinced Huu-Lac, it's going to take Colonel Trink quite some time to assemble a force to go in against them, and meanwhile . . ."

"I'm coming to that problem," said Scott. "And I think we may be able to take a few shortcuts. King, you and Swann head for Saigon as soon as you can get ready. Take at least two choppers, more if Swann's estimate of the load involved warrants it. Albright, when we have an approximate ETA in Saigon I want you to get a message to Colonel Dodds in MAAG Headquarters, for his eyes only, telling him to meet our people at the airfield. Nothing else, no reason, just that I want him to meet Colonel Swann and Major King."

Scott was truly happy at this moment. He knew what needed to be done and exactly how to do it, and this was what he had been trained for, had lived for, all his adult life. And he was completely honest with himself as he had been from the start, since the first beginning of the suspicion that he was on a hot trail. He was going on this operation himself, and while his basic reason for such tight security was his distrust of Huu-Lac's staff—Yuan and people— there was another quite valid reason for such extreme measures. He didn't want any interference, anyone involved, until he had completed all preparations and there could be no disapproval of his personal participation. He could imagine Buckmeister's reaction if he knew what Scott had in mind, and how quickly he would be able to persuade General Wesley to forbid Scott's participation or direct involvement on grounds of undue and unnecessary risk or some other specious reason. Which would play hell with the whole operation. Without analysis or even thought as to whether his certainty that only he personally could bring this off constituted arrogance or egoism, he knew it to be true. Trink of course had the leadership and the personal bravery, but his last sight of Trink and his condition did little to inspire any belief in his ability to plan and execute an operation as deliberate and delicate as this. And besides, Trink was, after all, a member of Huu-Lac's staff and absolutely could not be brought in on any planning now. The man he needed as the Vietnamese commander of the force, the only one who could both convince Huu-Lac in secrecy of the necessity for the action, and train and lead the troops was Zeke's friend Colonel Minh. Scott could only pray that he was still in Saigon and that Zeke would be able to contact him. And if this prayer were answered, Scott had not the slightest doubt that Minh would come. He well remembered the absolute sincerity in Minh's voice when he had said that if Scott ever had some real action in prospect he would "come running."

"You two can trust Colonel Dodds all the way with anything, and you're to tell him the entire story from beginning to end. Impress on him the fact that Yuan is either plain stupid or is deliberately misinforming and misleading Huu-Lac, and that right now we don't want a damned soul to know what we're thinking or what we are planning. Finally, tell him that we must have his friend Colonel Minh here to organize and command the Vietnamese force. In fact, I'd damned near say that unless you can bring Minh back with you, not to come at all. He's that damned important to us, and if he isn't available, every single idea I've got on how the attack is to be developed has got to be thrown out and we start all over. I hope to see you back here day after tomorrow, but I realize that is the soonest possible time, so don't sweat it." He rose to his feet. They had beat this around long enough, and all now depended on Swann and King and Zeke Dodd's efforts in Saigon.

"Has anyone thought of just why the Cong made such an attack, right here in Ngo Tho?" asked Stowkowski, as Scott started toward the door. "It is so out of their normal pattern, and it really was an unusual risk if their main base is actually in that damned swamp. It must mean something, and the only thing I can think is that Huu-Lac has been just a little too successful here in Ngo Tho, and that orders have come down from the north to break things up. If we're going to do anything at all, we'd better do something fast."

"I couldn't agree with anything more than that," answered Scott. "I'll bet the next week is going to be a real bad one for Ngo Tho."

12

THE NEXT DAY was the day of the big funeral, a state
funeral with speeches by Thieu as civilian Chief of the
Province, by Thi as mayor of Ngo Tho, and finally by Huu-
Lac as commander of the victims of the treacherous Viet
Cong. Speeches but no bodies, since each of the dead would
be disposed of by his family in accordance with their
custom, most by cremation, some few by Christian burial. It
was a solemn and a sad occasion, conducted with great
dignity in the main square of the city, and attended by
what must have been most of the population of Ngo Tho.
And there could be no doubt of the sincere grief both of the
speakers and of the crowd to which they poured out their la-
ment and benediction for the dead and their firm dedication
to revenge. Scott stood with his officers, a small knot in the
close-pressed ranks of the Viet military, at rigid attention.
His mind was not on the ceremony, but with Swann and
King in Saigon, and on his conviction that this was but the
beginning of the bad times for Huu-Lac and Ngo Tho.

He was right, of course, even when he would rather have
been wrong. He had stopped by Huu-Lac's headquarters
briefly before the ceremony, and returned with him from
the square, riding in the big Mercedes, with Huu-Lac completely silent and withdrawn, his grief for the dead so very
apparent. Their arrival at the headquarters, with the sentry
opening the door of the automobile while the remainder of

the guard stood at rigid attention, was marred in its military correctness by the frantic haste of a young Viet captain who came headlong out the door, across the veranda and down the steps, to stop rigidly, salute, and in rapid and voluble Vietnamese, tears streaming down his face, report something to Huu-Lac.

With a brief "Come" to Scott, Huu-Lac went up the steps at a half run, across the veranda and the main floor, and without pause up the steps and directly to the war room. Yuan was there, waiting with the first sketchy reports of a double tragedy. A force from General Le Hue's 30th Division at Khan Ghe, en route to reinforce Ngo Tho, had been ambushed with an estimated more than half of the force killed or wounded. Even worse, Khan Ghe itself had been attacked with great losses and with General Le Hue himself badly wounded. Basically the same kind of attack used in Ngo Tho, only this time the Viet Cong had entered the troop barracks just before dawn, and had at first killed silently with knives until the alarm had been sounded, and then with automatic weapons, killing many of the garrison before a stand could be organized, and then breaking out into the city to mow down hundreds of defenseless civilians. At least this time there was no question as to the size of the force; somewhere between three and four hundred Viet Cong regulars had been involved. Very few, a very, very, few had been killed, and by mid-morning the entire force had faded away.

Where yesterday Huu-Lac had seemed dazed, even somewhat enfeebled, by the Viet Cong attack, here he was completely himself. Gone was the air of preoccupation, the mantle of grief and sorrow, and in place was the forcefulness, the decisiveness of the commander. He barked questions at Yuan, and orders that sent junior officers scurrying off on errands and missions.

"Scott," he said finally, turning away from his grouped officers, "I know you will understand when I tell you that there are so many things that I must do today that I shall have little time to talk to you. I'd suggest that you leave Colonels Storm and Stowkowski here to work with my staff so that they may keep you informed of the plans we develop, but you must please excuse me. Trink is still not fully recovered, and to my great sorrow Kim was with the 30th Division force which was to come as reinforcement for our badly reduced garrison. You do understand."

"Of course I do, General," Scott answered. And he did.

He would have felt the same way under the circumstances. This was no time for visitors. As he left he thought that Huu-Lac must look years younger and if the Cong thought that stepping up the pressure on this man was going to be easy they were in great error.

Actually, Scott was more than happy to break away from Huu-Lac and his headquarters. There was much confusion, and in the pressure of this confusion all were speaking in Vietnamese and any request for interpretation would only have caused delay. And he had thoughts and plans of his own to occupy his mind. After a brief word with Stowkowski to the effect that whenever he felt that he was getting in the way he should come back to the MAAG compound, and a suggestion to Storm that he should stay until they kicked him out, that he should watch Yuan as best he was able, and come home with the latest Yuan-created theory accounting for the enemy's increased activity, Scott left.

Albright met him as Hoan pulled to a stop in front of the entrance, and waiting for Hoan to pull away, he said, "Colonel, you were absolutely right about us being bugged. We are, and not only in the war room and your office. Damned near every office and officer's quarters room is bugged, and it's a damned professional setup which was installed some time ago. This is strictly a wire job—no radio—and as far as I can tell, all the wire leads to an underground conduit laid in the sewer and at least on initial heading leads toward Ngo Tho."

"Surprises, surprises, surprises," said Scott, patting Albright on the shoulder. "I hope you didn't disturb anything, although it might be real interesting just to rip the whole thing out and wait for someone to come along to see what happened."

"It's all just as it was before I started looking," said Albright, "But I can put the whole system out of order by cutting the cable where it enters the conduit, and since it's right in the area where the gardeners have been cutting out a dead tree I could probably make it look like an accident."

"Good, but let's save it until we really need some privacy," said Scott, heading toward the entrance.

"Sir, there's one more thing," said Albright, and as Scott stopped and turned back to face him, he continued rather self-consciously, "I've been thinking that if the Cong are really out to spoil everything that Huu-Lac has built here in Ngo Tho, it would be a real prestigious thing for them to knock off a few U.S. types. What I thought is that we've got about twenty able-bodied soldiers here in this compound and maybe we shouldn't depend completely on the Viets protecting the place. I've worked out a tentative plan, and with your permission I'd like to go over it with a couple of the sergeants, and then, without the Viets knowing that we're doing it, put this place on a full alert basis. Since my duty keeps me pretty much here in the compound I thought . . ."

"You've been thinking a lot more clearly than I have, it appears," said Scott in sincere praise. "I really never gave it a thought, and I really don't even have much of an idea of just what the Viet's defense plan for this place is. You've been way ahead of me, so go to it. But give special attention to the point you made about not letting the Viets know that we're doing a little extra something about our own safety. It would be real nice if the Cong made a serious underestimate if and when they try to come in here. And now come and show me where the mikes are in the war room and my office and my quarters."

The day passed as slowly as any day had ever passed in all Scott's years, and he endured it in stoical restlessness only because he well knew there was nothing he personally could do to move things more quickly. He spent two hours with Smith, Stowkowski's operations sergeant, in a detailed calculation at the maps, which established that moving only at night and by water at an upstream rate of three miles per hour, a force could have moved in a single night to a point where only three hours of night march the next night would have enabled their strike on Khan Ghe. Further, that their breaking off of the action at Khan Ghe was timed to enable a return to their boats just after dusk and that they could have been back in the swamp, back to their home in Huu-Lac's back yard, in a very few hours. While he really didn't reveal all of what he had in his mind to Smith, it was evident from the first that Smith was reading him loud and clear, and so he had gone through the same routine with him that he had with the others in the war room last night—not a word to a living soul under any circumstances. But still, that made seven here in his group who knew what he had in mind, and with each one added, the chances of an inadvertent slip increased.

Stowkowski came back in the late afternoon with a report on Viet plans. All the usual things—more patrols, more night patrols, ambushes along all likely routes of approach but still oriented toward the west and the north, an increase in sentries, and during daylight an intensive search of all suspected or likely Viet Cong assembly areas. Huu-Lac had really shaken up his command—all leaves canceled, full alert status of all Self-Defense Forces and all civilian police, and a roundup of some few individuals who in the past had not exactly demonstrated their full support of the Government. He was in fine fettle, according to Stowkowski, and was as professionally competent as any general in any army in the world. It was truly unfortunate that the things he was doing, and the only things that he could do on the basis of his intelligence of the enemy, were all defensive in nature and left all initiative, all choosing of time and place of action, in the hands of the Viet Cong. One encouraging development that Stowkowski had was that Huu-Lac had called a conference with Yuan and Trink, who had shown up late in the afternoon, his old self again except, as Stowkowski put it, with a "totally visible meanness," and with the ancient Chieu. It was not a conference in the sense that there was a discussion or participation by all those present. Huu-Lac was the sole speaker except for some few questions by the others asked in clarification of his orders, which were that Chieu would send civilian agents into Cambodia to a minimum depth of fifty miles, and north into the Gy Than hills. These were to be the best of Chieu's agents, and they were not to return until they could bring word of the precise location of the Viet Cong base camps. Trink was to organize and begin the training of two units of two hundred men each, capable of a forced march of fifty miles in twenty-four hours with a full load of individual weapons, grenades, and ammunition, plus an 81mm mortar and forty-five rounds of mortar ammunition per five men. Yuan was to lend all possible assistance to both Chieu and Trink, and provide Chieu with full details on his existing network of agents along and in both areas. The problem of the violation of the national border of Cambodia was not the concern of anyone else in the province other than Huu-Lac and he would make any decision necessary, and assume full responsibility for each decision, when he felt he had the required data. At the close of the conference Yuan and Chieu had retained their normal impassiveness, while Trink had had a wild exultation and an impatience to begin the campaign, which was in itself enough to insure that the others would know nagging such as they had never known before until such time as they produced some targets for his forces.

Storm returned much later, just before Scott drifted off into sleep, lying on his bed fully clothed. Storm's gentle but insistent tap on the door brought him fully awake in an instant, and as he had done with Stowkowski, he led Storm out into the open air of the compound before hearing his report. What he was going to do about the bugging of his headquarters he was not then sure, but he knew well that any attempt to obscure conversation with loud music as he had done last night would only arouse suspicion if repeated too often. The best temporary solution was to remove all important conversation to the open air.

Storm had little to report in amplification of Stowkowski's information, except that after Huu-Lac had issued his direction, Yuan and Chieu had been in conference in Yuan's office for two hours. Storm knew nothing of what had been said, of course, but he was able to distinguish voices and almost the entire time had been taken by Yuan, in explanation, justification, or whatever, with Chieu speaking but seldom and then most briefly. Neither of them had looked too happy as their conference ended and they parted, but then neither of them normally gave any appearance of either happiness or unhappiness, so it was most difficult to tell just what had gone on. Storm's impression, based upon the emotional atmosphere rather than any factual data, was that this was the first time that Huu-Lac had brought Chieu and his civilian agents into the military intelligence picture, and that Yuan was quite resentful of this intrusion into his personal empire, and that he had spent quite some time in an unproductive attempt to convince Chieu that he had already done everything humanly possible to determine the location of the Viet Cong base camps.

By Scott's rough calculation, the Mohawk flight could not arrive before four in the morning, and with utter confidence in the precise functioning of his mental alarm, he lay down at midnight to await the hour and to sleep a troubled, restless sleep in which he dreamed that Minh could not be found and that he had gone to Huu-Lac with the infra-red photos showing the precise location of the Cong and his plan for a small force to go in and take them, only to have Huu-Lac call in Yuan who promptly convinced Huu-Lac that Scott was subject to hallucinations and that the Viet Cong were all in Cambodia.

He woke well before four, and shaking off the depression brought on by the vividness of his dream, and cautiously easing open his door, silently mounted the steep, ladderlike stairway to the roof. Stowkowski and Storm were both there before him, and after their quiet greeting Stowkowski said, "I could see a thunderstorm to the southwest about an hour ago, just about over the swamp, which should be all to the good, and should give us the best thermal contrast if there is actually warm air coming from any ventilation holes."

They sat in silence after that, each with his own thoughts and his own prayerful hope that all had gone well in Saigon and that the mission would come off as planned. And it did. Soon almost due east they could hear the motor of first one and then two planes, and could follow them as they passed over the swamp and faded away into the west, and then, perhaps a half hour later, one plane returned, followed within fifteen minutes by the other.

"That should do it, Colonel," said Storm. "And they must have gone clear to the border before they turned around to come back, so I can't imagine that their flight could have aroused anyone's suspicion. All we can do now is wait and hope."

Scott put in a brief appearance at Huu-Lac's office, to be met by a much sobered and saddened but unwounded Colonel Kim who had brought in three hundred new troops for the Ngo Tho garrison, out of a starting force of five hundred, and who was engaged with Trink in a review of the entire defensive plan for the city of Ngo Tho. Kim, Trink, and Huu-Lac were all friendly, all cordial, but so obviously occupied that Scott did not impose upon their time but returned to his compound and his office. And to waiting. He did use up two hours in reading Buckmeister's communications on the subject of the increased Viet Cong activity in Ngo Tho Province, and in composing suitable and largely fictitious replies to the orders and directions, and then went to his room.

He had slept a long, long while he knew, when he heard Albright's knock and soft call at his door. Without rising he called for him to come in, and from the look on his face as he came into the room, almost stumbling in his haste, he knew the news was good. "Colonel Swann will be in in about a half an hour, Colonel," Albright said, carefully casual and pointing to the picture on Scott's wall which hid the microphone he had shown Scott earlier, "And he reports that he was able to get everything you asked for." He was fairly beaming with happiness.

"How very nice," said Scott, "Am I to understand that everything means exactly that—that he was completely successful?"

"That is his report, sir," answered Albright, and making a chopping motion with his hand he asked, "Shall I prepare the war room for a conference, sir?"

"I would greatly appreciate that, if you would be so kind," answered Soctt, returning Albright's broad smile and shaking his head in admiration as Albright saluted smartly and fairly ran from the room. They could now be assured of a degree of privacy for some time, and he had faith that Albright's cable-cutting would be done with such finesse that its deliberateness would not be too obvious.

Forcing himself to remain calm and not to hope for too much, he slowly went down the stairway and into the courtyard. Sergeant Hoan was as usual attending Scott's jeep and he and the four guards at the gate would have a clear view of the landing pad, but there was no possible way of alleviating that. The equipment was no problem, it need not be unloaded here. But Minh—if Minh were indeed aboard—was a different matter, and Scott derided himself for not having thought to give Swann instructions that Minh should not appear in his Vietnamese uniform. Civilian clothes would be best—there was always an Information Service or USOM civilian hitching rides around the province, and Minh might go unremarked in that guise. But if he came in full regalia as an ARVN Colonel, Scott knew damned well that Hoan or someone would get the word to Yuan within the hour.

Stifling the impulse to do something, anything, such as send Hoan on an errand, which he had never done before and which might therefore arouse speculation, he waited, and soon he could see a flight of four helicopters, small dots in the distance close on the horizon, and coming in with wide-open speed. A few miles out, three veered off toward King's airstrip across town. and the fourth slowed, hovered briefly, and set down gently. As the motor died Swann came out the door, running in a half-crouch from under the shadow of the blades and then slowing to a brisk walk as he crossed the courtyard toward Scott. King followed close behind, with his co-pilot dismounting but remaining with the aircraft, and in the open doorway Scott could see the crew-chief and another soldier unlashing cargo.

No Minh, unless he was in one of the others, which must

now be landing at King's base—which was damned well unlikely. It was with keen disappointment that Scott watched Swann's approach, and then his disappointment faded instantly as King stopped halfway across the courtyard and shouted back to the group at the helicopter for Castro to bring something or other, and a small soldier, obviously of Philippine extraction, in glistening boots and an immaculate fatigue uniform, dropped to the ground and came on the double, bearing a large and bulging manila envelope. Minh had indeed arrived and as Scott saw him coming he turned and went up the stairway and straight to the war room, Swann close behind him.

Albright was there, waiting, and announced as Scott entered the room, "I'll stake my life on this room being electronically secure now, and they'll have one hell of a time fixing things without me knowing of it. It was a very bad accident." Scott nodded his appreciation as Albright added, "Colonel Storm is on his way now and Colonel Stowkowski will be here as soon as he gets my message."

Swann and King came through the doorway almost together with Swann's first remark being almost all that needed to be said. "You hit it on the head exactly, Colonel, even to the place, and we've got the whole package for you."

"He's right," echoed King, "And the infra-red came through so goddam well that it's almost unbelievable. Wait until you see."

Scott merely nodded as he grasped each by the hand in warm congratulation, his eyes fixed on the doorway awaiting the appearance of Minh, who he could hear coming up the steps and along the hallway.

"Major King, sir, here are the photos you wanted," said the short, slight soldier in the doorway, ignoring all others in the room, saluting King and extending the package. "Will there be anything else?"

The name CASTRO on the faded name tape, the flawless and unaccented English, and the casually correct military bearing gave Scott a moment of doubt. After all he had met Minh only the one time and under somewhat strange circumstances, but then the air of waiting, of barely controlled restraint on the part of Swann and King, and the sight of Minh's karate-scarred hands, gave Scott the recognition that he needed.

"Knock it off, you clowns," he said, and then striding forward he grasped Minh's hand and with sincere relief in his voice said, "Minh, I've never been so happy to see anyone in my life or needed anyone's help so badly."

"Scott, it's my pleasure." said Minh, relaxing from his role of the good soldier, and returning Scott's grasp with a strength that was amazing in one so small. "You've lived up to Zeke's expectations, and far exceeded anything I had hoped for, and from what I've seen and heard so far, we're onto the biggest thing that has been uncovered in years."

"Let me show you, Colonel," said King, ripping open the envelope and removing a handful of photos, which he began arranging on the conference table. "This alone is damned near worth all the R and D money that went into the development of the Mohawk. We've got coverage of the entire swamp area, but what you're looking at here is the only part that matters, the area we discussed where the Ngo Kri river branches before it runs into the Se Reo Kri."

King had nine large prints laid out in a square on the table and to Scott's practiced eye the sharpness of contrast and the wealth of detail in the photographs was almost incredible.

"You know how to read this infra-red, don't you, Colonel?" asked King, and in spite of Scott's nod of assent, he continued with unrestrained pride. "The light color indicates the warm areas and the dark the cooler. Here is the river, coming down from the north, and here is where it divides, with the high ground which we estimate is about ten feet above the level of the swamp and runs for about a half mile in the north-south axis with an average width of two to three hundred yards. The real thing to notice, and the thing which proves your guess that the Cong are in there, are these white dots, which the experts back in Saigon assure us are ventilation holes for the Cong hideout. There are six of them, laid out in a grid pattern, and when we converted the photo distance to scale we figured they are about seventy-five yards apart, which means that there is one hell of a lot of space inside their hole and room for maybe up to a thousand Viet Cong at one time. This is a wild guess in some ways, of course, but the man who gave us a reading on this is supposed to be the greatest living authority on the subject and went through a similar diggings up near Da Nang, where there were only four ventilation holes, and this is his best estimate.

"The entrance is right here about a half mile down on the left fork of the stream, and is shown by this light line along the river, where the warm air had dissipated and spread as it emerges. I guess they needed this large an area for concealment of their boats and it must represent one hell of an engineering effort, because it means they have excavated a considerable area up and down stream without disturbing the grass cover."

Scott and Minh were both totally engrossed in the photographs, so intent that they did not look up as Storm and Stowkowski came into the room and joined the others in looking over their shoulders.

"Beautiful, beautiful," murmured Scott, "But there is one thing I don't understand."

"It's there," said Minh, in complete rapport with Scott's thinking, "But it took the experts in Saigon to find it, and then after we insisted that it had to be. These very faint traces are the river watchers, two on the left fork; one right where it joins the Se Reo Kri and one upstream halfway to the fork, about two and a half miles, and the same thing on the right fork. They must change the guard at night and use boats to avoid disturbing the grass cover. There are none upstream—evidently their only fear is Huu-Lac's river flotilla."

"And that's everything?" Scott asked King, stepping back from the table.

"Not quite, sir," answered King removing more photos from the envelope. "Here is a look at the river upstream from the base camp area, actually about five miles upstream and taken from the Mohawk which flew south of the Se Reo Kri looking to the north. We can't be absolutely sure but we think these are boats or canoes on the river headed downstream. The experts won't say beyond that there is something warm on the river, but that it could be flocks of ducks or some kind of waterfowl. The radar showed nothing at all, but after all we don't need to know this for sure, do we, Colonel?"

"We know enough now," answered Scott tersely. "What we don't know yet is precisely what we're going to do about it, and when we're going to do it." Looking at Minh who stood in silence, still looking at the photos of the Viet Cong base camp, he asked sharply, "Would the good Colonel Minh care to hear some ideas on the subject?"

Minh turned slowly, still preoccupied, but with a broad smile. "He would, indeed. In fact considering the success of your ideas so far, he wouldn't dare have any ideas himself until after he had heard yours."

163

Motioning the group to be seated, Scott leaned against the table, and speaking directly to Minh, began. "First, I assume Swann and King have explained to you that I no longer trust Yuan and his assistants, and that that is why we went through the whole exercise in Saigon to get this information with the fewest people possible, U.S. or Viet, knowing of our interest."

"Add one more, Colonel," Storm interrupted. "Add your companion Huc. Today I came upon Huc and Yuan in the hallway, and while I don't understand much of this language, I know damned well they were talking about you, and that whatever it was couldn't have been good by the looks on their faces when they saw that I was listening."

"Good enough, he will be added," said Scott. "But that really doesn't matter too much. If some are suspect then we as U.S. Advisors must suspect everyone except Huu-Lac and Kim and Trink. We can't sort them out as you will be able to, Minh, and in all truth I don't think we have the time. We had a lull in Viet Cong activity but you can bet it is either because they wanted a rest or because they are now getting in place for another big attack tomorrow, and I think that it is a pretty safe prediction that the entire province is in for some very bad times unless we do something soon."

"And the something which you have in mind, Colonel Scott," asked Minh. "Is it to call in your Air Force, or surround the area with a regiment of Huu-Lac's troops?"

"Not likely, as you damned well know," answered Scott. "What I had in mind was for the two of us to go in with a few fighting troops and flush them out, along about midmorning when they would normally be resting, and kill the most and take a few prisoners. Do you know what supplies Colonel Swann brought back with him?"

"Generally, generally," answered Minh, neither approval nor disapvroval of Scott's concept in his voice. "And which of General Huu-Lac's fighting units do we take in with us, and how do we go in, and where do we stage this fighting force before we move into the swamp to close on the Viet Cong?"

"For a stranger in town, you're pretty damned smart," said Scott in friendly sarcasm, "And you can't know how I agonized over that little problem. The minute we take one of Huu-Lac's companies away from its presently assigned mission, everyone in the whole province will know that something is being planned, and any movement to any point in the province would be almost common knowledge. That's why you personally are so important to this operation. We can't take a unit, so we've got to take individuals, and since we cannot either spare the time or risk the notice involved in training we have got to have the best there is. Real dedicated Viet Cong haters whom we can assemble and move out on a moment's notice, and whose only training will be a short hour of weapon familiarization."

"I'm following you so far, Scott," said Minh, "And I agree so far. I suppose you have some idea on how we choose these men?"

"That is something that I haven't figured out completely," said Scott, "other than to develop a rather vague idea that after we have sold Huu-Lac on this operation you might be passed off as an inspector of some kind from ARVN Headquarters in Saigon and in the course of a whirl-wind inspection tour tag the men we need."

"That's one way to do it," agreed Minh, "We'll need to go over this with the General, though. He may have a quick solution that will not involve so much fuss." Glancing at his watch he continued, "It will be dark soon, and I must speak to Huu-Lac, alone I think the first time, and I'll not discuss our plan unless I feel he will be receptive. What I'll talk to him about will be a matter within my authority and which should be handled first anyway."

Minh had suddenly dropped the good-humored, half-bantering manner that he had so far maintained and his quiet tone and rapid speech were that of a man accustomed to taking charge, and of being obeyed. "Major King, will you please see that someone brings in my luggage, and Scott, I need to use a telephone, and with some degree of privacy. Do you have Vietnamese operators on your MAAG switchboard?"

"Yes sir, we do," volunteered Albright, "But there is only one operator on duty now and I can get him off the board for a short time and operate myself if you wish. Give me five minutes."

"Good," said Minh, "Where can I call from, Scott?"

"My quarters," answered Scott, leading the way out the door and along the hallway to his room.

Within minutes Scott's phone rang as Albright reported his control of the switchboard, and Scott silently handed the phone to Minh and left the room to speed along the delivery of Minh's luggage.

He allowed five minutes and then returned carrying the

light Viet-made suitcase he had appropriated from King. Minh was lying on his back on Scott's bed and it was evident from his manner that the call had been successful.

"I have just been speaking to the old one, Chieu," he said as Scott laid the suitcase on the bed at his feet, "And it is always such a pleasure to speak with one as wise as he. Although this time I suspect that you were suspicious long before anyone else even thought to question Yuan, and even now there is little more than suspicion to present to Huu-Lac." Sitting up he opened the suitcase and snatched out the two topmost garments, the pajama-like native dress common to all Vietnamese civilians, and a pair of canvas shoes, and quickly began to undress.

Scott sat across the room and watched as Minh underwent transformation from a trim and smartly-uniformed U.S. soldier to a Vietnamese peasant, a rice-paddy coolie who could walk along the road unremarked and unnoticed. First the fatigue top and the tee shirt to reveal a chest and shoulders where every muscle was clearly articulated, then the boots and the trousers and finally the GI issue shorts came off. Then standing naked, Minh mussed his hair and patted it down in a matted tangle, stepped into the pants, and pulled the loose-fitting top on over his head. Silently and quickly he groped inside the suitcase for the small black skull cap and the last two items of his dress. He strapped a leather-sheathed knife to the inside of his left forearm, and a 9mm Barretta automatic in a cross-body speed rig around his waist, the holster resting in front of his left hip and completely concealed by the tail of his shirt.

Scott watched in quiet admiration. Minh's body was that of an Atlas in miniature, a mass of snakelike coils of muscle without an ounce of excess weight, and with a grace and swift efficiency of movement that spoke of almost perfect coordination. He was badly scarred, especially his back and chest, with long welts that could only have come from a whip and a long and infectious healing. His left forearm was slightly crooked as if it had once been broken and badly set but it seemed completely usable. The aura of force that radiated from this small man was so intense as to make one forget his size entirely. Here, when the friendliness and casual banter had gone and the true man stood revealed, was a magnificently conditioned fighting machine, and a mind controling that machine motivated by an undying and unyielding hate.

"Scott, I know you'll understand and excuse me, but I

166

have little time now. I have many things to do during this night, and we will have time to talk later," said Minh, finally closing his bag and lifting it from the bed to set it beside the door. "How am I to get out of here without being seen by any Vietnamese?"

Without comment Scott stepped to the door and called for Storm and Albright, both still in the war room. His instructions were quick and terse. Albright was to insure that the back wall of the compound was clear of all observers and get Minh over the top and down the other side. Storm, on signal from Albright, was to go out the gate with a GI driving and pick Minh up as a hitchhiker and drop him wherever he wished in town.

"You'll need this, won't you," asked Storm indicating Minh's suitcase. "I can bring it in my jeep."

Minh stood a moment in thought and then turned to Scott. "I don't know exactly what is to happen tonight after I talk with Chieu, or where I must go, but I shall end up with the General sometime before morning. I'll need my uniform tomorrow morning but this will be a burden to me now, and perhaps it would be better for you to bring it when I call for you. I will undoubtedly be at the General's home at that time and I will have someone sent to bring you there."

"Not Major Huc, please," Storm interposed. "He shouldn't be given the slightest hint of anything unusual, and I think that he is already too damned nosey and thinking too much about us. He asked me today why you hadn't called for him to accompany you on any trips for the last two days, Colonel Leonard."

"Have no fear, Colonel Storm," said Minh. "I trust few people here now, and I'm not likely to do anything which upsets routine or arouses suspicion. What is this about Huc, Scott?"

Scott briefly explained the routine he had followed of every other day out in visits to units and Huc's role as interpreter and guide. "Maybe I have acted a little out of character from Huc's point of view. Perhaps I'd better set up a short trip tomorrow afternoon. We'll see how things look after we talk to General Huu-Lac, and if there is going to be any great delay facing us I'd better get back on schedule."

Minh nodded his agreement and with a quick handshake and a half smile with his, "Don't call me, I'll call you," was on his way, Albright trailing close behind.

13

THE CALL, when it came at six o'clock, was not from Minh but from Huu-Lac himself, and although there seemed nothing amiss in his voice, the mere fact of his calling rather than Minh seemed to indicate the General's realization that all was not well within his organization and that a certain cover must be in order until those not to be trusted had been identified.

The telephone beside his bed had rung stridently three times in the short seconds it took for Scott to reach it from where he stood, fully clothed and waiting before the open window. The Vietnamese operator, in heavily accented English and quite evident awe, informed Scott that General Huu-Lac personally wished to speak to Colonel Leonard, and after a short wait Huu-Lac came on the line.

"Colonel Leonard, I have some matters I'd like to discuss with you and since I have a full schedule later today I thought that you might have breakfast with me," he said quite formally, and with distinct coolness.

"Very well, General," answered Scott with equal formality, "I'll be on my way immediately. Is there anything I should bring with me?"

"It might be well if you brought the suitcase of photographs which you mentioned the last time we talked together," said Huu-Lac after a short pause. "And I do wish you would make all possible haste. I have little time this morning," he continued with the same stiff tone, and with even the urging for haste given more in the tone of a busy man with little time to spare than that of a man in need of assistance. Any telephone operator's report of the substance of the call would be most innocuous, thought Scott, as he threw the infra-red photos of the swamp into Minh's suitcase and went down the stairway to his jeep and the everalert Hoan who came running from his conversation with the gate guards.

Whatever Scott had expected—and in the fullness of his knowledge of the situation and his surety of the accuracy of his information, he had not thought of the shock to Huu-Lac that even the slightest suspicion of defection in his organization would bring—he was not prepared for his reception as he was ushered into the small breakfast room on the back veranda of the villa. The formality of Huu-Lac over the telephone had not been solely for the benefit of anyone listening. Here he was equally formal, almost hostile.

"Colonel Minh tells me you have come to some rather astounding conclusions regarding certain members of my command," he began without preface as Scott closed the door behind himself. There was no offer of hospitality, no invitation to join him and Minh at the table with its austere spread of bread, fruit, and tea. And there was absolutely no friendliness in the level gaze of his eyes.

Scott stood in momentary shock, shifting his eyes from Huu-Lac and Minh, still in his peasant garb, who returned his look impassively with only the slightest of apologetic shrugs to indicate his present helplessness. Carefully and slowly Scott said, "Astounding conclusions is not a precise description, General."

Huu-Lac waited in obvious impatience for Scott to continue, their eyes locked, and when the silence lengthened he snapped in irritation, "By whatever term you choose for definition, I would like to have you confirm what Colonel Minh told me earlier this morning, in your own words. Only then will I be able to believe that you have been quoted correctly."

Scott turned from Huu-Lac's implacable gaze, and setting down Minh's suitcase, quickly but carefully began an inventory of the room, the pictures on the wall, the furniture, the ceiling, the overhead light. Stepping quickly and as silently as possible to the wall he carefully looked behind a picture, a Chinese scroll, the back of a buffet, and on around the room to another picture, ignoring Huu-Lac's voice, angry now, as he said, "Colonel Leonard, I would appreciate your attention and an answer to my question."

"Yes, sir," Scott said easily as he continued his search for the microphone that he knew must be somewhere in the room, "I'd be most happy to tell you anything you want to know, except that I'm at somewhat of a disadvantage since I don't know this Colonel Minh you mention, and consequently I don't know just what I'm reported to have said." Rage and indignation made Huu-Lac momentarily speechless, and a dangerous reddish flush colored his otherwise pale complexion, as Scott paused for a moment, his fingers at his lips in a plea for silence, and again surveyed the room. Even Minh's composure seemed somewhat shaken as he looked questioningly at Scott, but then understanding came, and he too rose from his seat and with care and silence began his own check of the room.

"Frankly, General, about the only thing I have said to anyone recently which could have possibly offended you is that I think Colonel Trink has become a burden to you, and is no longer a useful member of your staff," lied Scott in the same easy manner, still searching the room with his eyes and briefly glancing at Huu-Lac, whose anger had run its full tide and was now tinged with puzzlement. "Although how my remarks ever got to you I can't imagine, since I discussed this with very few people, and in confidence. I fully intended to talk to you about this, but I didn't quite know how to open the subject without offending you, so in a way I'm glad you brought the matter up."

Minh, after his initial swift check of several pictures and the baseboard around the room had returned to the table standing behind his chair, his eyes slowly roving over the room. He then inspected the table itself and the centerpiece, a massive bowl of fruit. Gingerly he raised this to see if wires were attached, set it down in disgust, and then suddenly dropped out of sight behind the table to check underneath.

"Colonel Leonard, I am not a man easily confused, but your conduct here this morning is both confusing and outrageous," began Huu-Lac just as Minh's head raised above the edge of the table, triumph in his wide smile. "I fail to understand the purpose of your antics, nor do I understand your presumptuous attitude in making judgments concerning the competence of members of my staff." He broke off as Minh seized his arm and almost forcibly led him from his seat around the table, and lifting the cloth, showed him the small microphone attached to the main pedestal support of the table and the fine wire running to the hole bored in the floor.

Huu-Lac was a man for any emergency, thought Scott, squatting beside him as the three of them examined the apparatus. Without a break in the cadence of his speech or a wavering of his tone of rage, Huu-Lac continued, "In fact, Colonel Leonard, I feel that your conduct constitutes such an invasion of my prerogatives and is such an uncalled for interference in the functioning of my command that I should request General Wesley to provide me with a replacement."

"General, I certainly hope that you'll reconsider this," said Scott as all three of them rose from their crouched positions and Huu-Lac made directly for the doorway opening on the veranda. "You must understand what an action like that could do to my career."

"I have not yet made a decision to do this," said Huu-Lac as they crossed the veranda and descended the short steps to the garden path, "I have only said that I feel that it should be done."

"But General," began Scott, only to be silenced by Huu-Lac's weary "Quiet, please, Scott," in his old friendly voice. "Loyalty is truly a two-way street with me and I find it almost worse than death itself to find that I have trusted one who betrays me." He slumped wearily on a bench and raised his eyes to Minh, who had followed them, carrying his suitcase.

"Well, old friend Minh," he said in sad resignation, "I seem to have made a fool of myself in my protestations. It seems that you were right. My apologies to you, and to you, too, Scott. My defense of the traitor was emotional, not logical."

"General, I have not accused any of your people of treason," began Scott with a feeling of confusion. "I do think that there is almost a deliberate attempt to misdirect your attention and to lead you to some very wrong conclusions as to the location of the Viet Cong bases, but this could be solely because of misinformation and stupidity, and I really cannot charge any one of your staff, Yuan or anyone else, with being a traitor. My reason for calling Minh here to Ngo Tho was simply because I knew of no other way to mount this operation with the secrecy that is required, which could not be done working with your staff."

"Mind your own business, Scott," said Minh harshly.

"This is something entirely outside your area of knowledge or competence. I have spent the night with Chieu and between us we have established to our satisfaction that Yuan and several of his people are indeed of the Viet Cong, and I believe now that the General has seen that someone has invaded his privacy, he too is convinced. The only question now is whether these traitors are to be executed in public as an example to others, or whether the General wishes me to handle the matter in private."

Huu-Lac sat in absolute stillness, his head bowed, and only the whiteness of the knuckles of his interlocked hands showing his strain, until after a long moment he raised his eyes to Minh. "It must be in public. We must show that no one is immune to punishment, no matter how old a friend or how high his rank. I will convene a court this morning and we will have the execution this afternoon."

"Wait a goddam minute," said Scott in quick, incredulous anger. "You can't do a thing like that."

"Don't let your American ideas on justice and proper legal procedure interfere with your concept of the duties of a Senior Military Advisor, Colonel Scott," said Minh in anger and with heavy sarcasm. "This is our country and we do things somewhat differently, and very, very quickly. We have a tradition that the sun shall never set on one who is discovered to be a traitor."

"I couldn't care less about justice for Yuan or anyone else," said Scott, his anger growing. "For all of me you can cut them up in little pieces, but this is one time when you are going to have to forego the pleasure of immediate revenge. It is absolutely impossible and I'm surprised that you two would even think of such a thing."

"Scott, I've allowed you liberties which I never thought I would extend to any advisor, and I've even developed a certain feeling of friendship for you," said Huu-Lac in a tone of stern sorrow, "But don't presume to tell me what I will do and will not do. Minh is right, we do have a tradition, one we have never broken, and we will not break now."

"General, I thought you were a professional soldier, but I've just changed my mind," Scott said bluntly and in a tone that made no attempt to conceal his contempt. "If you and this blood-thirsty little bastard here think that the preservation of some lousy tradition is more important than wiping out the Viet Cong main force, then neither one of you is fit to run a war."

On his right Minh had dropped into a fighting crouch

facing Scott, his arms slightly out from his body and his karate-hardened hands raised and held slightly forward. "Your permission, General," he hissed.

Without looking away from Huu-Lac's eyes, and in an almost conversational tone of voice but with a lingering trace of contempt, Scott said, "If you give him your permission, General, you're going to have either a very badly hurt or a completely dead Vietnamese Colonel on your hands. And you realize, of course, that half of the people in your villa are undoubtedly watching this little show."

Huu-Lac did not move his eyes from Scott but they slowly lost focus so that he was not really seeing Scott, or anything or anyone. "The Viet Cong main force," he said almost absently, "Minh, you did speak of some plan for an attack on one of their bases, but I'm afraid that our discussion of other things led us away from the subject. Please explain your meaning, Colonel Leonard."

Scott turned to Minh, still poised for combat, but with a look of understanding on his face that denied his physical stance. "Minh, I'm sorry I called you a bloodthirsty little bastard," he said, the relief flooding through him at the signs of reasonableness on the part of Huu-Lac in no way lessening the irritation in his voice. "What I should have called you is a stupid bloodthirsty little bastard, and if you'd quiet down for even one minute I think you'd agree with me. I guess I'm to understand that all this pleasant little session is due to the fact that so far your discussion with the General has been exclusively concerned with whether he has or has not traitors in his midst and that you never progressed to the really important subject of how to use our information on the Viet Cong to best advantage." It was an almost reckless way to talk to a man of Minh's overdeveloped pride, but Scott was beyond caring. He had already said enough to hang himself and from now until he was either sent back to Saigon to the tender mercies of Buckmeister and General Wesley or had seen a proper force organized to go into the swamp, he would abandon any attempt to gain his ends by being polite. And he had a firm conviction that any apology to either Huu-Lac or Minh would be viewed as a lack of sureness on his part.

Gradually the tenseness went out of Minh and he straightened himself, an almost petulant resentment in his voice as he said defensively, "I guess I'm guilty, but the General is a hard man to get off a subject once he latches onto it, and although I tried several times, I just couldn't give him the full picture on what you've found."

Without comment Scott picked up the suitcase, set it on the bench, snapped the lock, and withdrew the photos.

"General, I don't know what you have scheduled for this morning, but I'd suggest you cancel whatever it is, at least for the next couple of hours. Nothing can be more important than this, because for the first time you have an opportunity to strike a truly mortal blow at the Viet Cong. And you can do it quickly and without any risk to your own forces. I sincerely believe that you cannot achieve any degree of success if you persist in your plan to make a public spectacle of Yuan, since if he truly is a traitor as you now seem to think, any move against him would alert the Viet Cong to danger and they would simply disappear."

"Colonel Scott, you have just told me that I am not fit to run a war," said Huu-Lac with a sarcastic weariness, "but I would appreciate a second chance to prove my competence. Why don't you just tell me what you propose without predicting my proper decision on the matter. And you do recognize the perhaps regrettable fact that it is my decision which counts, don't you?"

"I do, sir," answered Scott, "and I have no doubt as to what that decision will be after you hear me out."

And so he began, with his first vague discontent with the theory of a Viet Cong refuge in Cambodia or Gy Than, his absolute rejection of Yuan's reconstruction of the attack on Huu-Lac's headquarters, and the tortured logic and inspiration that had led to the return of Storm and Swann to Saigon to arrange for the photo mission.

Huu-Lac listened without question or comment, his eyes never leaving Scott's face and with complete concentration on Scott's words, broken only once for a nod of assent when Minh took the suitcase that still contained his uniform and requested permission to leave.

Finally Scott progressed to the actual photos, and with care spread them on the bench between them, explaining their significance, tracing the path of the river and the pinpointed location of the Viet Cong base. "And there it is, General. On any given day there are God knows how many Viet Cong resting underground right in your own back yard, and preparing for their next night's foray."

Huu-Lac raised his eyes from the photos, and there was no trace of any past anger, any irritation, any resentment at Scott's high-handed impatience. "This is truly an inspired effort on your part, Scott," he said softly, "And I can well understand your concern at the thought that we might throw all this away in seeking to punish a traitor. If Minh had only told me we might have been spared much unpleasantness this morning and the loss of valuable time." He paused in thought, his eyes idly wandering over the garden, the villa. "Not that I blame Minh. He couldn't have made me understand. The thought that Yuan whom I have known and trusted for so very long, had turned against me drove all else from my mind for a time. Now that you have explained all this to me, Scott, and I know what must be done, all that remains is to decide how we will do it," Huu-Lac continued, shufling the photos together and rising. "Come, we will go to my office and see what ideas Trink has."

"Please, General, have you forgotten the microphone under the table?" Scott asked quickly. "If your villa is bugged then surely your office must be. And besides I have already developed a plan for the entire operation which requires only your approval and the designation of Minh as commander. No one else in your headquarters need be brought in on this at all, neither Trink nor anyone else."

"Scott, do I understand that you also suspect Trink?" asked Huu-Lac, the calmness gone, and rage and a trace of real fear in his eyes, a dread that one more of his loyal band was a defector.

"Never, damn it, never, General," Scott said hastily. "I'd trust Trink with my life, but I just think that the fewer people who know of this the better chance we have of carrying it off with the utter secrecy that is necessary. And I don't think I need to go into the necessity for surprise. We both know that if we don't get it absolutely right the first time we'll get no second chance. The bastards will just disappear into the swamp and all we'll have is an empty hole in the ground."

"We can afford to withdraw a full half of my forces for something like this," said Huu-Lac, still on the verge of anger, "And we will surround the entire area, and I'll be damned if any will escape. Within twenty-four hours I can . . ."

"General, with due respect for the fact that you are the commander here and I'm just an advisor, I wish you'd listen to me before you even begin to think about what forces you would use and where you would use them. I've thought of almost nothing else than the best and surest way to run this operation for a long time now, while you've only had a few short minutes," Scott said, his impatience plainly evident and the fear that even now Huu-Lac or Trink could louse up the whole operation giving more harshness to his tone than he had meant. But he met Huu-Lac's eyes in challenge and waited.

"I agree, Scott," Huu-Lac said finally, his irritation fading, and with a trace of a smile. "This seems to be my day for impetuous anger. But understand one thing. Whatever plan you have developed must include Trink. There can be no question of this, and you must understand that Trink would be dishonored when Yuan is finally disclosed to the world as a traitor if he did not participate in this operation. It would be as if we did not trust him, as if we thought that he was in league with Yuan."

"I understand this, General," said Scott thoughtfully, "and I have no doubt of Trink's loyalty or his value on any operation, if we can just restrain his enthusiasm until the right moment. Because, General, this will require a great deal of cold-blooded patience and split-second timing if we are to have complete success. And anything else would be a criminal waste of an opportunity that may never come our way again."

"I will worry about restraining Trink's enthusiasm, Scott," said Huu-Lac, "But he will command the entire operation and be fully responsible to me. If that is understood I will send for him. And Scott," he said with great sincerity, "you have done a great thing for both our countries in this. I will never forget it and you can be sure that all in your army, clear up to the top, will know of your part in our victory."

"Thank you, but let me hope that my part is not yet finished, General," said Scott, and at Huu-Lac's questioning look he thought that he would never have a better time to lay it on the line. "As one solder to another, you can surely understand that I can't just drop this affair in Trink's lap and stand aside. I want to be in on this to the end, and as I've said before, I've got a detailed concept of what must be done and just exactly how to do it. I can either go over it with you now, or if you wish I will work it out with Trink and we will give you a completed plan with all the details worked out."

He knew that there was a note of anxiety in his voice, but he made no effort to conceal it. It was important to him that he be allowed to see this through to the very end, and Huu-

Lac must understand this and agree, for it was within his power to shut Scott out completely, either directly and openly or merely by not fully informing him of events as they took place over the next few days.

"Have no fear, Scott," said Huu-Lac, with full understanding and sympathy in his voice. "This could never have happened without you and you will not be excluded in any way." Rising from his seat and handing the photos to Scott he walked slowly toward the villa. "I think we need a quiet conference in complete privacy, and I can think of no better place than the house of Chieu."

THEIR PASSAGE WAS SILENT, as silent as the quiet flow of the broad Se Reo Kri itself, as they drifted in the total darkness of the night. For Scott it was a journey into nothingness, without a reference point or a landmark since they had boarded the converted LMC of the river flotilla at midnight and swung away from the village in a single short burst of power from the chattering engines. All one could do was trust Thrau, the simian-faced, bow-legged, and incredibly ugly captain of the vessel, and the fact that Thrau had made the same run in rehearsal for the past two nights, once accompanied by Trink himself, when they had put a pathfinder team ashore. Trust also in the fact that Trink was fully confident that they would arrive at the right place at the right time. All one could do was trust in many things, Scott had found in the last few days as his role had necessarily changed from that of the creator and director to that of a spectator. And an admiring spectator, he admitted. Trink was a true professional and a commander by any terms of reference in any army in the world.

Scott lay on his back on the deck, Minh beside him on his left and Huc on the right. Eyes closed to preserve his night vision against the star shine, Scott forced himself to relax, taking each muscle in turn, and in a long-ago-learned ritual, moving from his feet and legs up his body to his arms and neck until his entire body was in repose and almost as at rest as if he were alseep. Not that he intended to sleep during these last few hours. The adrenalin of anticipation would prevent that.

The last few days had been spent in the village of Bac Lu, a village consisting of seven thatched huts on the swampy banks of the Se Reo Kri long miles upstream from Ngo Tho, almost on the Cambodian border. Trink had selected it for the base camp because of its extreme isolation from and resemblance to the Ngo Tho swamp and because Thrai, the village headman, an ancient pygmy of a man, was reputed to hate everyone, government and Viet Cong alike. But not Trink. At one time or another Trink had saved the old man and his eldest son from some difficult situation and was now held in awe and veneration. No villager would so much as stir from the village to spread the word of their activities for fear of the certain vengeance of Thrai that would follow them.

And they had needed a base camp, much as Scott had been reluctant to admit it at first. He had first thought in terms of a quick assembly of individuals selected for their proven dedication and fighting ability, a short briefing on the plan of the operation and a period of weapon familiarization, and then a night movement from some near point of embarkation, either up or down the river, to a landing area between the two forks of the Ngo Kri, and then a slow and deliberate daylight movement of perhaps four hours into position to cover all exits and vent holes, with an attack by midday that would leave at least six hours of daylight for clean-up. He had expected argument from Huu-Lac, who he had thought would want a conventional attack using units of both the 12th Division from Ghum Kong and the 30th Division from Khan Ghe, moving units into blocking positions well before his assault force went in on foot or by helicopter, and he had expected even greater trouble with Trink, who he was sure would agree with the General's concept of the operation and would urge such haste to mount the attack as to be only half-prepared and lose any chance of surprise.

Both had surprised him. They agreed to his concept of the use of individuals quietly withdrawn from ARVN units, and had shown an awareness of the fact that a single leak of even the smallest bit of information could result in a complete loss of the whole catch. Trink immediately grasped Scott's plan, and after close examination of the photos and a detailed cross-examination of Scott and Storm and a transfer of the information to a conventional one to twenty-five-thousand map, had taken over the development of the details of the plan with a single-minded intensity and a ferocious urgency coupled with a surprising caution in his design for choosing his men. Which really had made the base camp necessary. Eighty of the best, the elite of the province, could not be assembled openly but must be withdrawn from their units, ostensibly for duty in Ngo Tho, and then moved in single chopper loads to the base camp.

Scott never knew Trink's criteria for selection. How brave was brave, what hate of the Viet Cong was hate enough, or what demonstration of fearlessness and devotion to duty had counted, but however Trink had chosen them he had chosen well. All were either lieutenants or sergeants and all had the poise and calm confidence and quiet acceptance of conditions that establishes a professional. All had been trained on the AR-16 and had fired at least a thousand rounds in familiarization, with Scott and Minh training the first group of six and they in turn training those who had followed. All had had long hours of drill in navigation through the barrier of the swamp grass, finding target stakes a mile, two miles, through the grass with only a compass heading for guidance. They were as ready as any fighting force Scott had ever seen. Not boisterously, loudly, gung-ho ready, but ready with a quiet deadliness and sureness of purpose unusual in any group of soldiers—explained perhaps by the fact that each one of the group had had a father, a grandfather, or in some cases his entire family killed by Viet Cong terrorists.

They would not fail in this mission because of the quality of the tools, Scott had thought in the last hours as they had waited for Trink's arrival and final prepartions before loading. They would fail only if the tools were not properly used, if the plan was defective, or if there was some unknown and unsuspected betrayal to the enemy.

As if on cue with Scott's thought of possible betrayal, Huc stirred at his side, raised himself to a half-sitting position, and slowly swiveled his head from side to side in an apparent effort to penetrate the darkness. For a long moment he remained an almost invisible silhouette until a faint stir from Minh as he changed position seemed to signal his relaxation. Huc's faint sigh as he again lay down might have meant anything—fatigue, disgust, frustration—just as his slump back to the deck at Minh's movement might indicate that he knew he was being watched or might have been only coincidence.

In any case he was a problem. From the very first there had been long debate on what to do with Huc. Minh was sure that he was an agent of Yuan, but when Trink and Scott had suggested that Scott might fake a trip to Saigon as a reason for dispensing with Huc's daily escort service, Minh had vetoed the idea. He had wanted Huc under his own eyes during the operation. He wanted to give Huc a chance to prove that he, Minh, was wrong in his suspicion, and he really wanted to be wrong, Scott was sure. They all knew how Huu-Lac would feel if Huc were guilty of treason. The treachery of the protégé whom he had treated almost as a son would be even worse than that of Yuan, and so Huc had been brought along.

He had been told nothing of the plan, but had gone through the same training as the other men, and as far as Scott could tell there was nothing in his actions that could confirm Minh's suspicions. Perhaps he was rather more curious about what was going on than were the others, none of whom seemed to display the slightest curiosity, as if the fact that they were there because of Trink was enough. But this wanting to know the why and the when and the how could be a very natural thing in a staff major, who until now had been in on everything. He certainly had not skirted or complained but had borne the three days and two nights of rather uncomfortable existence with the same careless indifference to discomfort as the others. But Minh's vigilance had not quieted. Huc was watched constantly, not obtrusively or openly, but nevertheless Minh was aware of his every move, his every conversation with the other men or with the villagers, and he was treated with cool correctness, not friendliness. In all his conversations with Huc, Minh was every inch the Colonel of the Army of the Republic of Viet Nam speaking to a lowly major. Which may have been from quite ordinary dislike, or from an effort to heighten Huc's nervousness if he were truly a Viet Cong agent.

Scott was sure that Yuan had not operated alone and that when Huu-Lac chose to expose him, the tender questioning of the ancient Chieu would lead to further tender questioning of others, until the entire apparatus of treachery was exposed, but meanwhile, for so long as Huc remained in their company he could do little to harm the operation. Nor could Scott see any possibility of Huc exposing himself if he were actually a Viet Cong agent. It was inconceivable that he would try to cross over to the Viet Cong side once the shooting started.

From Trink's reports there had been nothing thus far to arouse Yuan's suspicions that all was not as it appeared to be on the surface. Huu-Lac, by the exercise of great self-control, treated Yuan as he had before and gave a convincing performance in accepting Yuan's thesis of the Viet Cong refuge in Cambodia, even going so far as to direct the preparation of a plan to move a sizable force into Cambodia with the mission of seeking out and destroying the Viet Cong bases supposedly there. According to Trink it was quite incredible. Huu-Lac in his grief and rage at the betrayal of his old comrade had yet thoroughly convinced everyone of his sincere intent to move over the border and to hell with the international consequences.

From necessity Trink had been able to spend but little time at Bac Lu. He had accompanied Scott and Minh and the initial group as was necessary, since only he had the prestige to pacify and gain the cooperation of the headman Thrai. He had come once more in the late afternoon of that first night to run the river with Captain Thrau of the LCM and had come for the last, the final time, just at dusk on this night of embarkation and movement to the objective. He had had to keep his normal duty hours in the headquarters to allay any suspicion by Yuan, and he had had to be in close contact with Huu-Lac and sustain him during these agonizingly suspenseful days. But this in no way had prevented him from developing the plan with Scott and establishing himself as the leader and commander of the force. He dominated the men like some reincarnation of their god of war and he knew exactly and precisely what he wanted from each man and the exact time he wanted it. He had given two briefings today, one in the late afternoon immediately after his arrival to the six five-man teams that would cover the six ventilation holes and to the two two-man teams who were to secure the river-watcher posts. He had gone over and over again with each team the exact sequence of their action. Each of the men had a compass and knew how to use it and each member of the team had the proper compass heading. A five-way check should bring them to their objective with reasonable accuracy and thereafter it should be simple for them. Take out the sentries, if any, and begin the cutting of grass to clear their field of fire, working in from a firing point at least fifteen yards away from the vent hole and carefully oriented by Trink so that the teams would not fire on one another or on the far larger group that would be covering the main river entrance. The five-man teams on the vent-hole mission had only two radio reports to make, one when they found their objective and one when their preparations were completed; they were to be on radio silence except for these reports. They were to receive only one command—to execute—after all had reported their preparations completed, upon which they were to drop two gas grenades and one violet smoke grenade down each venthole and quickly spread a heavy plastic sheet over the hole and stake it down. And then all would wait, those at the vent holes and those at the main river entrance, for the gas to seep through the tunnels and into the rooms and for the frenzied exit to begin—and for the killing to begin. Scott had no illusion that Trink would take many prisoners.

The two-man river-watcher teams were instructed only to observe the actions of the Viet Cong outpost, and to take no action until they had determined just exactly how these posts reported back to the main Viet Cong force. They were to be left alone until the attack began, unless it was evident that they were sounding an alarm, in which case they were to be taken out at once and an immediate radio report given to Trink.

While Trink's briefing of his carefully selected five-and two-man teams had been long and in great and patiently repeated detail, his briefing of the full force just before dusk had been surprisingly brief. His voice had been harsh and just loud enough for the tightly packed group to hear, and his normally smiling and friendly manner had entirely disappeared. He had been the legendary Trink of old that Huu-Lac had described to Scott. Not the man who had demolished his desk in his grief and rage and helplessness and whose very depth of emotion had almost broken his mind. Here he had been the leader who knew exactly where he was going and how he was to get there, and what the end would be.

He had spoken and he had waited, and at each pause there was assent from his men, at first almost whispered and perfunctory in tone but with a growing enthusiasm and fierceness until the final cry was an almost frantic straining toward Trink and whatever goal he promised them. For a long moment he had stood in silence and without motion, a solid and rock-hard man of implacable fierceness, and then he had slowly walked to where Scott and Minh and Huc waited apart and to the rear of the group.

"There are still only the three of us who know precisely where we are going, Scott," he said, ignoring Huc who had stood transfixed and intent during Trink's talk but who now moved somewhat aside, "But they now know why they are here and they know that they have been specially honored in being chosen to avenge all their comrades, those killed in the attack on our headquarters and all those killed before, and they are as ready as any soldiers who ever lived. They know that they will be heroes when this is over and that it is the greatest honor to have been selected for this operation. They will not fail." Trink was satisfied. Trink was happy and Trink had no problems except his regret that he probably would not be present when Yuan was finally exposed.

Scott had several problems, one of which was causing him no little pain.

Trink had been most concerned that Thrai, the headman of Bac Lu village, accept Scott as a fighter against the Viet Cong and as an honored guest and he had made a long and elaborate introduction, telling all manner of unknown lies, to make this possible. Scott, of course, had had no idea of what was being said as the four of them—Trink, Thrai, Scott, and Minh—had squatted in the largest of the thatched huts following their arrival, but after Trink's departure he realized that whatever Trink had said had been most effective and that Thrai was giving him the most VIP of VIP treatments. With the training of the first few men on the AR-16, Scott's real work had been done, and outside of a few trial runs at navigation through the grass, he had had nothing to do except watch the training of the new arrivals. Active supervision was Minh's responsibility, assisted in carefully prescribed areas by Huc, and so while everyone else was busy, Scott had been idle. Idle except for the necessity of responding to the attentions of Thrai.

In the evening of the first day Thrai had begun, when he appeared at the hut he had vacated for the use of Scott and Minh and Huc with a small procession behind him—his wife and three daughters bearing a variety of dishes. He had been the most solemn and attentive of hosts, squatting on his heels in front of Scott and carefully directing the mixing of the basic rice with the other ingredients and watching as Scott ate with as good a show of appetite as he could muster. Minh and Huc were also fed, of course, but it was evident that they were there merely as Scott's companions and that Thrai's entire concern was for Scott.

The food had not been at all bad, rice and vegetables and other things concerning which Scott had not the slightest curiosity, on the basis that ignorance is bliss. But almost within the hour after Thrai and his women had left, as solemnly as they had come, Scott knew he was in trouble. Faint and then acute nausea had forced him out of the hut into the darkness and then at dawn the most excruciatingly painful diarrhea he had ever had left him weak and shaken, crouched in the tall and wet grass at what he hoped was a decent distance from the hut. All the second day and night in camp and into the third day he had fasted and evaded all of Thrai's offerings and today when he did finally take food again he had had only plain rice and strong tea. Still he had not been able to shake either the nausea or the diarrhea. Thankfully, while the nausea was with him constantly, the diarrhea seemed to come only in early morning. At least thus far. Neither Minh or Huc had been affected, a testimony to the immunity of lifelong conditioning.

Minh had been no help at all. He had been hugely amused by the ceremonious serving of Scott on the first evening, and although he had restrained himself and not marred the solemnity of the occasion and had been as dignified and correct as Thrai himself in serving as interpreter, he had broken loose when the three of them were alone. Both his knowledge of the effort required by Scott to eat with a satisfactory show of relish and Scott's response to Thrai's offer of his youngest daughter, a sloe-eyed and childlike creature of painful shyness and incredibly, dirty feet, for Scott's pleasure during his stay in Bac Lu—which Scott had refused on the ground that no soldier going into battle should consort with a woman beforehand—seemed to brighten Minh's entire existence, And when the ill effects of the food had begun to show, Minh had been even more entertained. He had assured Scott from the first onslaught of the nausea that his condition was caused solely by the fact that he had not accepted the whole offer, the girl as well as the food. And several times during the day he had left his training of Trink's chosen warriors to come to where Scott sat watching from the doorway of their hut or lay in a marvelously unyielding hammock he had spent three laborious hours weaving together out of bamboo, grass, and commo wire, and inquire with mock concern as to how Scott felt and whether it was not now time to bring the girl for Scott's embrace and the sure cure to follow. Minh had managed, however, to prevail upon Thrai to lessen the frequency of his offers of additional delicacies, so that Scott had had to go through the ritual of refusal of some choice dish no more than seven or eight times a day.

All this could have been avoided, Scott thought, if he had stayed in Ngo Tho with Trink until embarkation, which he conceivably could have done even though he had had to be in Bac Lu for the initial training on the AR-16. Complicated as it would have been, he could have evaded Huc's escort services by some stratagem for that period and returned and put on the same show of normality as had Trink during the past two days, and at this late date he could see that that was what he should have done. His reasons for not playing it that way were really pretty damned childish—partly his wanting to be in on every phase of the operation and a quite unreasonable fear of being left behind if he were not in the action every minute, and partly his increasing irritation with Buckmeister and General Wesley and their endless communiqués and directives. That, more than anything else, had caused him to turn over to Swann the task of quieting their petulant demands for information and imperious directives as to how to retaliate for the attack on Ngo Tho and accept the semi-isolation of Bac Lu. It was goofing off, pure and simple, on his part, since no one in Saigon had any idea that he was not in his compound in Ngo Tho and Swann was preparing all messages to Saigon as if Scott himself were the writer, but things had gone well enough so far. King, who had taken it upon himself personally to bring in each load of reinforcements, had kept him informed of the tenor of the Saigon messages and of Swann's replies and it seemed that the tone of near hysteria, which had prevailed just after the massacre of Huu-Lac's Ngo Tho headquarters troops, was beginning to diminish. In any case, whatever he should have done or not done, it made little difference now, and if everything went well in the next few hours there would be an action to report to Saigon that should warm even their bastardly hearts.

Time had run on and on, Scott realized with a start as he came fully awake. He must have dozed off, or at least been so occupied with his musings that he had lost the sense of the passage of time, for a look at his watch showed two-thirty and the movement of the LCM under his back had changed from passive drifting to an almost imperceptible struggle against the flow of the river in an effort to leave the main current and edge closer to the left shore. As he sat up, the thinnest sliver of a new moon provided enough light now for him to see the still and resting bodies on the deck, and as he turned shoreward, to distinguish the blurred mass of the river bank. Now their speed was diminishing and the darkness of the bank was nearer and nearer. Two deck hands padded forward, without spoken command and without sound as they maneuvered through the sprawled bodies, and shortly the muffled anchor chain began its slow unwinding. The first barely audible squeak of the chain brought movement to Trink's soldiers, the quiet awakening of those who had slept and the stretching of cramped and lax muscles of those who had lain awake in waiting, and soon the entire deck was in movement, silent and unreal in the half light, and with the discipline that made each man guard his weapon against the slightest clink and his voice against the slightest sound. At last all forward motion had ceased and they lay motionless, anchored fore, aft, and broadside to the shore.

For a long moment there was petrified stillness as all eyes strained toward the shoreline, and then came a single wink of blue light from the pathfinder team Trink had moved into position the previous night during his rehearsal with Thrau, and almost simultaneously with the sighting, two of Thrau's sailors went over the side, one at the bow and one at the stern with the guide ropes, and half swimming and half wading made for the shore.

Scott felt a firm touch on his arm and turning saw Trink beside him, and the monkey-like figure of Thrau, his features unreadable, but his very bearing reeking of his triumph in having brought their passage to this point without a hitch. As agreed, Scott moved toward the stern where one of Thrau's sailors carefully tended and paid out the slowly moving guideline and waited for the jerk that would signal arrival on shore. As it came and he went over the side into the chest-deep and faintly cool water, he could see Trink at the bow line, carefully silent in his entry into the water, followed by a file of ghostly figures.

The footing was firm and the current gentle as he followed the guide line. For him the passage was easy, and although from the spasmodic jerking of the line he sensed that some of those smaller ones behind must have found the

188

water deep, there was no break in the noise discipline. Not a murmur as heads went momentarily under, and as he reached the shore almost simultaneously with and twenty yards upstream from Trink, there was still no sound behind him.

Trink halted, dripping, and standing for a moment with Thrau's man and the two men of the pathfinder team, and then, as the signal came along his guideline that the last man had gone over the side and the line had been cut free, Trink moved inland with one, as the other came to Scott, and peering momentarily into his face in an unnecessary but instinctive search for recognition, turned and led the way into the grass. Scott waited a moment for his signal, which came both as a jerk and as a slackening in the tautness of the rope as those behind him closed in, and then, stepping past Thrau's silent river man and carrying the rope, he followed the guide.

The grass was thicker and taller and stronger than it had been in Bac Lu and in the half light it was impossible to protect himself from the cutting edges as he had in his practice navigation runs, but he followed closely on the guide, carefully counting his paces in estimation of distance. There were forty-odd men behind him in single file along the guide rope and they were to be moved inland so that the last man cleared the river bank and was at least ten yards inside the screen of grass. Here the footing seemed worse than in the river, with the mud sucking at his feet and the gnarled clumps of grass roots making each step a gamble or a turned ankle. Ahead the guide stopped and Scott in turn waited for the signal to come along the rope signifying that the last man was well within the screen and out of sight of any travelers on the river. As it came, Minh moved up beside him and sank down into the soft and moist ground and there was the soft rustle all among the line of men as they attempted to rearrange any crushed stalks of grass as best they were able in the darkness.

Now came the long wait until the light had improved enough for the next phase of operation, and now also came the end of Scott's active role, which had really been purely honorary in sharing the leadership ashore with Trink. From here Minh was in command of this column and would dispatch his teams on schedule, as Trink was doing for the other column some twenty to thirty yards away to the right, unseen and unheard in the all-covering grass.

The light was steadily increasing, Scott noted, as he

lowered himself beside Minh, and he could distinguish a number of the men as they made themselves cautiously comfortable. Huc, the nearest, could be seen quite clearly; his face was expressionless as he made a place for himself, and he was alertly watching Scott and Trink. Whether out of natural soldierly alertness and in anticipation of an order from Minh, or from suspicion, Scott could not say and refused to speculate. His defection or loyalty was a problem for Minh, Trink and Huu-Lac, a Vietnamese problem, and not for Scott Leonard or the U.S. Army. In any case, if Huc were one of the Viet Cong he must now know their ultimate destination and if he were going to break he now had a real reason.

Here, close to the ground, with the grass to muffle and smother any sound, it was possible to talk in a low and guarded voice, and Minh spoke his first words since their loading at Bac Lu many hours past.

"It goes well, Scott. Unless they have night watchers on the river that we know nothing about—which is extremely unlikely—we have done what may be the hardest part without detection. We have only to wait for a little while now until we have more light and we can begin."

"It does go well, Minh. I've never known troops with better discipline, or who performed so well," Scott said in agreement. "From here on all we must do is be slow and careful, and if we are that, we've got it made. Just follow the plan."

Minh nodded, and for a long while they lay in the mud without moving as the light steadily increased. Soon, Scott knew, the light of the moon would be replaced by dawn, sudden, with the almost breathtaking quickness of the tropics.

Minh was growing restless beside him, not in any excessive movement, but the rapport that existed between them made Scott know that Minh was not at ease.

"What is it, Minh," he asked softly. "What's bugging you now?"

Minh did not answer until he had inched himself closer to Scott with his lips almost touching Scott's ear. "I have a feeling Huc is about to try to leave us, and I need your help in watching him. And don't nod your goddamned head in such ready agreement. I know you think this is none of your concern and maybe even that we are wrong, but regardless of what you really believe, from now on I can't give him the attention that is needed and I really need your help. I mean it to the extent that if you see one damned thing out of line, you kill him. If he puts a round in the chamber of that AR-16 he's carrying before he is told to do so, you must assume he's going to fire in warning to the Cong, and you slam him in the head with your rifle butt without asking any questions. Or anything else he does that doesn't seem right to you. I'm sorry that we brought him along but it's too late now, and all we can do is make sure he doesn't get a chance to cause trouble. Do you understand and can I count on you?"

"You can," said Scott tersely, thinking that if Minh were now convinced of Huc's treason after these past few days of observation it was not his place to question how the guilt had been determined. At least he knew that Huc had been given a fair chance to prove himself and that Minh had wanted him to come out clean of any involvement with Yuan, if only for Huu-Lac's sake. What act, what conversation with the other men later reported to Minh, or what other indication had finally ended the debate as far as Minh was concerned he would probably never know or understand, but Minh's seriousness was enough for Scott. Huc would be his concern from now on, and of course the indication that Minh had mentioned, the loading of his AR-16, would be quite enough. There wasn't a loaded weapon in the whole force, as insurance against accidental discharge, and the force would load only according to plan and on Trink's order.

"With that understood, I've got to talk to Trink for a minute," said Minh, and was off through the grass to the right to where he knew Trink was waiting for the first light and the beginning, no more than twenty or thirty yards away.

Huc never moved the whole time, perhaps thirty minutes, that Minh was gone and in fact he appeared so unconcerned, so calm, so like the rest of the Vietnamese strung out behind him, that Scott wondered, even while believing and trusting in Minh. Not relaxing his vigilance, he nevertheless questioned the need for it.

Minh returned just as true dawn began to light the eastern sky and at once began. First the river-watcher teams, the two men immediately behind Huc, were called forward for a soft-toned repeat of their instructions and a check of their compasses and heading and then were off, a mere rustle of the grass, quickly fading, marking their progress.

Five minutes' wait and then the first of the vent-hole teams came forward for the same final checkout with Minh and went on into the grass, and each five minutes thereafter, team two and team three and team four went through the same routine. And then began the real wait, with Minh's radioman glued to his receiver, awaiting the reports. Unless one of the teams ran into trouble he would receive only four one-word reports, the arrival on objective of the teams. Until he did, no one would move from the spot.

Scott was not the most comfortable man in the world as he lay beside Minh in the mud of the swamp. Before the teams had moved out he had had two trips out into the grass as demanded by the wrenching of his gut, and shortly after they had gone he had had a third session. Which was quite remarkable, he thought, when you considered how long it had been since he had eaten anything to speak of. He knew that he was weakening, probably due to dehydration, although he had acquired three canteens and was drinking frequently, but he also knew that they really did not have far to go and that the whole show would be over soon. He would make it, but he wasn't enjoying it very much and he would be damned glad when it was all over and he could get his grass cuts and insect bites cleaned up and get some relief from his nausea and diarrhea. Not that he wanted out now, for in spite of his physical discomfort, his whole being was concerned on the success of their effort and his physical weakness and progressing illness in no way lessened the alertness of his mind. This whole thing could never have happened without him and he would stay with it until the end.

Forty-five minutes after their departure the river-watcher teams reported arrival on their objective. Nothing else, just that they were where they were supposed to be. What they would do or not do, how they would handle the situation, was entirely up to them, and there was no worry. Trink had selected four of the best men he knew for assignment to these two teams, four lieutenants, any one of whom, in his estimation, could command a Division, and there would be no mistake in judgment. If the Viet Cong river-watchers could and should be killed, they would be killed; if it were better to leave them alone, they would be left alone. Almost simultaneously with the report of the arrival of Minh's team came the report of Trink's team. One phase, one step toward success had been completed.

The vent-hole teams had much farther to go and it was a full hour later before the first of them reported—one of Trink's teams that had the greatest distance to travel and what had been considered to be the most difficult assignment. Navigation, luck, or something, they had gone the whole way without incident and landed right on top of their objective.

They were the first and it was long minutes before the next reported, again one of Trink's teams, but thereafter the reports came with speed and in relative sequence and with the report of the fourth of the six teams dispatched, Minh began the movement of his column to cover the main river entrance. This was the agreement, part of the plan, that when four out of six of these teams had reported, all forces—Minh's and Trink's—would move out to cover the main river entrance, and to get in place for the big kill. For even should a few of the vent holes remain open as exits, no major part of the Viet Cong in the lair under the swamp could use them as exits, and the killing had to occur at the main river entrance. The vent holes, loaded with tear gas and smoke grenades and then sealed with the plastic sheets, would function as rams to force the Viet Cong out their front door.

Trink's column had the easier task and route. Being on the right they were to move up to cover the downstream end of the entrance, deploying as the situation dictated, and keeping their fire down to avoid firing into Minh's force upstream.

While Trink had a simple straight line movement into his position, Minh and Scott had a more complicated maneuver to execute. Straight upstream but inland until they were well past the entrance, then a movement to the right to the riverbank, and then downstream along the river until their fires too would cover the entrance. The same restriction on angle of fire applied for the protection of Trink's men.

On Minh's command they moved out, still carrying the guide rope, bunched somewhat more closely together, and with Huc now just behind Minh and with Scott following. There was no hurry and they moved slowly and carefully and as quietly as possible. Within an hour they were passing the entrance and forty-five minutes later they made the turn to the right and came to the river.

He followed Huc and Minh right to the water's edge and the three of them stood together for a moment while the rest of the men, still holding the guide rope, closed up behind them. With a hand signal Minh caused them all to drop, and then edging close to Huc and Scott he said, "I'm going on a little look down the line by myself, just to see what we're getting into. Scott, you wait here, and Huc, I want you to have our men move back upstream a little way, maybe twenty-five yards. I'll be back in thirty minutes at the outside."

With a brief nod of understanding Huc was on his way; the men turned and soon were swallowed by the grass. Minh waited a moment longer in watching and then nodded in satisfaction and with a half wave of his hand and a smile was off himself.

The sound of both movements, faint at best, so effectively did the tall denseness of the grass serve to absorb and muffle their passage, were soon lost, and Scott was alone and in an almost complete silence. Only the occasional faint chuckle of the slow turgid water and the dim background of insect hum or the wind ruffle of the grass around him could be heard as he divided his attention between the two paths of disappearance with a sometime glance at the river and the heavily overgrown bank opposite. Of the two, Minh downstream and Huc upstream, he was much more concerned with Huc, whom he expected to see reappear at any moment. And he was also concerned with the curiosity of Minh's behavior in allowing Huc such freedom of movement, unless, of course, he had alerted some of the men in the column to also keep him under surveillance. Which must be the case; Minh could never be guilty of allowing his eagerness for personal reconnaissance to result in relaxation of his careful watch of Huc.

Ten minutes passed, with each minute increasing Scott's tension and uneasiness. Then, just as he had reached the end of his patience and was rising to his feet to go in search of Huc, he heard the sound he had been half expecting; the almost sub-aural sense of someone moving through the grass off to his right. Sure as God, Huc had finally broken and was on his way in warning to his friends. It was impossible to establish true direction or distance, it might be five yards or fifteen yards away, and as he came fully to his feet the sound ceased. Either whoever it was had stopped or had moved on past and out of hearing range.

He stood for a long moment with held breath, listening with all his being and then moved a few cautious steps into the grass on a diagonal and what he hoped would be an intercepting course, pausing to listen after each few steps and with his empty AR-16 at port arms. The stalking of Huc must be done with care, even at the sacrifice of speed, he thought, since once Huc knew that he had been detected he would abandon all effort toward caution and sound his alarm as best he could, by shouting or by a long series of bursts of automatic fire—and firing in his direction, Scott was sure, which would be one hell of a way to end his own part of the act. For the moment, with his excitement, with the pump of adrenalin into his system, he almost felt well, his nausea forgotten and his whole body tensely alert.

Suddenly Huc rose out of the grass to the right and behind him and drove his rifle butt into the side of his head.

It glanced high on the top of his head, and was not the solid killing blow at the neck and base of his skull that Huc had intended, but nevertheless it drove him to his hands and knees, and Huc could have had him then in the fraction of a second it would have taken for a second blow across the exposed back of his neck. But he was gone, half jumping over Scott and moving without caution now and with surprising speed.

In the second it took for Scott to shake his head clear and come erect, Huc had disappeared, but this time the sound of his passage clearly marked his route and Scott was after him in a floundering lunge through the mud and grass without regard to his head or the cutting edge of the grass or his illness or anything except the knowledge that Huc must be caught and caught soon, before he could give the alarm that would wreck the entire operation and turn it from the closing of a trap into a dangerous and nasty business.

The trail of trampled grass was clear, and Scott put all the driving force of his legs into a half falling run, his AR-16 still at port arms in front of his body, still his only weapon and still unloaded. To fire a shot now would be as bad as Huc himself giving the warning and if he could once get his hands on the little bastard that would be quite enough. And he would catch him, by God, he thought, as he went in a full length sprawl and almost without stopping his forward progress scrambled half erect again, lunged forward, and almost stepped on Huc's headless body.

"Slow down, Scott," said Minh, almost conversationally, as Scott slid to a kneeling halt astride Huc's body and raised his eyes, half blinded by mud and sweat and his own blood. Minh stood completely casual, Huc's head held carelessly by the hair in his left hand and a knife still dripping blood in his right. "You didn't think that unspeakable filth could outsmart me, did you?"

Now his head hurt. Now he knew of every burning cut on his face and hands and arms, and of his grinding bowels and his roiling stomach and of his gasping lungs. He also knew anger, quickly blazing with the thought that he had been used as a decoy, a sacrificial goat, and as quickly dying as he realized that Huc had not been after him at all and that if he had not almost stumbled over him he would have by-passed him completely, as he said with what he hoped was the equal of Minh's casualness, "Never doubted you at all, my dear Colonel. Just thought I'd flush the game and save a little time."

He thought he saw a look of concern and maybe even sympathy on Minh's face, fleeting and not evident in his manner as he leaned over and wiped his knife in two quick strokes on Huc's inert back and stepped around them, Huc's body with Scott still astride, and without a backward glance made off through the grass toward their original position, Huc's head still in hand. Scott slowly followed, the sight of the flaccid and still oozing stump of Huc's neck and the splash of his gushed blood slowly sinking into the swamp mud bringing his nausea to a full and spasmodic but dry heave. You must look like hell, he thought, and you didn't exactly cover yourself with glory on that one. If Minh hadn't been there on the spot and ready and waiting it wouldn't really have mattered. He would have gotten Huc himself in the next few yards, maybe not as neatly and quickly and finally, but still he would have gotten him. But why did they take such a chance in the first place? Whenever Minh had become convinced of Huc's guilt it had surely been before they had come ashore, and he could have been left as a prisoner of the LCM Captain, or Thrau, or even the Bac Lu headman Thrai. He could appreciate Minh's reasons, however—the loyalty and devotion to Huu-Lac that had forced him to give Huc every possible chance before passing final sentence. Even so, he had cut it mighty thin, thinner than was really safe.

The men were in place where Huc had left them, so quiet and unmoving that they were in among them almost before either Minh or Scott realized it. Without a word, and with only a hand signal of his right hand, empty now with the knife again concealed somewhere on his person, Minh brought those who could be seen, perhaps seven, to their feet, and all along the line back in the grass the others could be heard rustling as the column came to ready for move-ment. Huc's head, still held carelessly, almost negligently in his left hand, had stained his left leg from his knee down over his boot with a dark and clotted smear.

When all were erect and the silence back along the way gave assurance that all were ready, the seen and the unseen, he quietly raised what remained of Huc, the mouth twisted in what must have been a terror-inspired effort at a last scream and with wide open and horror-staring eyes, and said some few words in Vietnamese, and then stood in waiting as his words were repeated in a guttural muttering back along the line. "I told them that we had already gotten our first Viet Cong," he said, stepping around Scott and still carrying the head and moving back along their original route.

They went more quickly now, even carelessly, and with minimum regard for noise, since Trink must have long been in position and perhaps wondering at the time they were taking. The entrapment of Huc had added many minutes to their time en route, but even so it was only twenty minutes before Minh signaled a halt and calling his radio operator forward from his position just behind Scott, disappeared with him into the grass in what this time was a true reconnaissance and not a repeat of the deadly ruse staged for Huc. He was back in minutes that seemed like seconds, but were long enough for Scott to sense the tension building up in the line of men behind him. It was strange, he thought, how up until now his impression of these men had been of a body of troops marked by their extreme quietness and rigid discipline, and how the change began as they arrived on their objective with the knowledge that soon they would begin the kill. Not that discipline faltered, nor that there were signs of nervousness in these blooded veterans, but without any specific indication of the change, it was nevertheless there. All before this moment had been only in preparation, hardship endured for the sake of this, the end.

On Minh's signal the final maneuver began with a precision that would have been creditable on a clean and swept drill field with early-morning fresh troops. Each man first loaded his weapon, gently and quietly easing the bolt forward, and then each stepped off to his right obliquely, maintaining a two-yard interval from the man on his left. They were still quiet, without a word spoken, and with coiled alertness of hunters on the final yards of stalk, and as Scott looked back along the line while the first few began to move, he knew the pride of belonging that comes to a professional in doing a difficult task in the company of others of equal competence. He knew none of these men well and actually could distinguish between only a small few, but they had done something that would always be remembered by each man here, and of such a thing is comradeship made. As he turned and moved in proper interval, to the right of Minh and his radio operator, and with an unknown and unnamed man on his own right, he was truly a proud man, satisfied with life and the time and the place, and with his only concern his ability to control his own body and its weaknesses well enough to bring him through the next few hours with honor. For the moment at least he was free of all symptoms of his illness and was strong.

Fifty yards forward, the last twenty inched painfully along, flat on their stomachs, and the main entrance lay before them.

was brilliant and the fact that its true dimensions had survived definition by the infra-red photography proved the soundness of their work. The original screen of grass along the water's edge had been undisturbed and from the river there would appear only a carefully preserved and unbroken screen of grass.

The upper shore line of the cove, curving to the main tunnel, was perhaps fifty yards long, and here Minh's men were strung out almost shoulder to shoulder with a completely clear field of fire. Downstream, on the opposite side, Trink must by now have long been in place with an equally good position and even more densely massed in consequence of a much shorter shore line. The angles of fire were perfect; the entire mooring area must be clearly visible to every man in their small force.

The man pumping his bicycle was less than forty yards from Minh and Scott in their position at the extreme left and most distant point in the line, and must have been almost within knife-killing distance of Minh's closest man, away to the right and nearest the entrance. The second guard, who was inspecting the overhead, evidently to insure the adequacy of the irrigation, was only slightly farther away. The tunnel entrance itself was some ten to fifteen feet wide and pointed directly toward Scott and Minh. Their fire would be directly down the mouth of the tunnel while the troops nearest the entrance would have a true crossing fire, as would Trink's force on the opposite side of the cove. From the dispositon of the two forces there was, in fact, some danger that those of Minh's men nearest the tunnel and Trink's force opposite might fire into one another, and Scott was on the verge of suggesting that Minh withdraw some of his men and move them either into reserve of leftward and away from the entrance when he thought the better of it. All had been warned of this foreseen danger and with the discipline of this force all could be counted upon to obey the order to keep their fire down. The AR-16 muzzle didn't actually climb that much anyway, even when on full automatic, and these men had had plenty of practice on the weapon back in Bac Lu.

The guard on the bank under the canopy of shore earth and grass had apparently completed his inspection of the irrigation operation to his satisfaction and he barked a short command to his companion, who immediately stopped pedaling his bicycle-driven pump, and swinging his leg over the seat, moved a little into deeper water, lay down full length and then sloshed ashore. Half-squatting, half sitting on the gunwale of one of the canoes, he retrieved his canvas shoes, and wiping his feet free of mud and water, put on first one and then the other. Water and sweat streaming down over his brown, slim, well-muscled body, he then sank down on a straw mat to the left of the tunnel entrance. He had evidently been at his task for a long time from his heavy breathing and the tired slump of his body as he lay back, still naked and without bothering to dry himself. His companion, in the regulation black pajama dress of both the Vietnamese peasant and the Viet Cong, took an identical mat on the other side of the tunnel and he too lay down. Since neither had a visible weapon it must be that they were more concerned with the continual irrigation of the grass overhead than with guarding the entrance against intrusion. The long unmolested isolation of their sanctuary had given them a real sense of security.

Scott turned from his examination of this camouflaged marvel of engineering just as Minh placed his hand on the radioman's shoulder and nodded and the operator immediately slid back a few yards, and lying on his back spoke the few words that would inform Trink of their arrival on the objective and their readiness, and almost before he had finished a green smoke flare was fired from well in the rear of Trink's position across the cove. Now the vent-hole teams would begin their work and now Huu-Lac, some miles across the swamp in the city, would for the first time know that all had gone well and that the revenge of his slaughtered Ngo Tho garrison was underway. Somewhere now, in one of the regular units, troops who had been briefed on the planned border crossing into Cambodia in search of the non-existent Viet Cong base camps would be given a last-minute change in objective and battle plan and Major King's pilots would get their instructions on the new landing zone for their helicopters. And now a Colonel in the Army of the Republic of Viet Nam would change from a respected and trusted advisor to his commander, happily leading him astray into Cambodia, into a traitor to his cause, to be tortured with the most exquisite cruelty for the names of his accomplices, and to die before sundown and in the most degrading manner that the minds of those he had betrayed could devise.

Nothing happened and nothing happened and nothing happened. And time went on and on. And then the pajama-clad guard sat up suddenly and listened for a moment and swiveled round on his hands and knees looking into the tunnel. What he had heard, Minh and Scott soon also heard in their position directly opposite the tunnel mouth. The keening, choking, coughing, strangled cries of many voices, melding into a roar of panic and coming closer and closer from its origin far back in the tunnel.

The guard seemed frozen in his awkward position, widespread on his hands and knees, until he realized his danger of being trampled and flung himself aside and out of the way just as the retching, blinded, and completely helpless Viet Cong came boiling out of the tunnel mouth, blinded by their tears and trailing wisps of the violet smoke that had been inserted with the tear gas to mark any unsuspected exits. Just to prove to Scott that this force of Vietnamese, good as they might be, was not perfect in its discipline, one of Minh's men goofed. Down the line near the tunnel entrance someone fired a full automatic burst in clear violation of orders and killed the first seven or eight of the Viet Cong almost before they had cleared the tunnel entrance. The word had been clearly given: don't block the exit with dead bodies, let them come well out and away from the exit before firing, and don't waste ammunition by firing full automatic. Just one man goofed though, and the rest held their fire for the few minutes it took for the steady outpour of stumbling, moaning, screaming, coughing men, almost all without weapons and all completely helpless, to begin. They waited until the first reached the canoes and with fumbling and unseeing hands tried to untie the mooring ropes and escape from the all-pervading gas, and then they fired in cool deliberation to kill. Those that followed, more desperate from longer exposure to the gas, and without any thought other than to get out of the concentration of agonizing pain and running straight forward into the water, they killed in the river, and the water quickly changed from a thick and dusty brown to a raw cherry red. And still the Viet Cong came from the tunnel mouth in an unending, unswerving, and unbroken stream.

Scott did not fire a single round himself. There was no need, there was no need for half the men in their force, and five or ten good marksmen could have covered the whole operation.

Perhaps fifty of them poured out in a fighting, stumbling, clawing mass in the first minute, each in such agonized and retching pain from the tear gas that he was entirely oblivious of the death to which he escaped. And still they came in an unbroken flow. Those back in the tunnel must have been able to hear the constant firing and in some far corner of their panicked minds must have known that their destination would bring more than the fresh air their eyes and throat and lungs so desperately and screamingly demanded, but there was no slowing of the outpour. And in spite of the care of the killers to keep the exit free, the bodies began to pile up, first at the water's edge and in among the canoes, and then as the bodies heaped higher and higher, the men waited a little longer and let the Viet Cong scramble over their dead comrades before firing. And they began to fall into the river itself, with the water turning into a brownish pink and sickening froth.

This was not war, Scott thought; this was a mass execution. And it was sickening. Even Minh felt it, the revulsion for the task at hand, for as their eyes met he gave a slow shake of his head and a shrug of resignation and left off firing. At least a hundred dead lay in torn and mangled and naked and somehow obscene death, and still the flow from the tunnel mouth continued unabated, with these, the men farthest back in the maze of tunnels and exposed far longer to the deadly combination of smoke and gas much more enfeebled than those who had come out first, and even more frantically desperate for escape and the relief of fresh and clean air.

It was Trink who finally called a halt to the now senseless butchery. The radioman, his ear all the while glued to his receiver, tugged at Minh's arm, shook his head, and spoke some few words in Vietnamese. Minh immediately arose and went down along the line, tapping each man on the back and shouting and soon the firing died away to a spasmodic burst here and there and then ceased altogether. Across the cove Trink's men too had stopped and the silence was startling; until the deafening din of the firing faded from their ears to be replaced by the sound of the Viet Cong and their agonized retching, coughing, wheezing breath as they fought their way into free air. And the moaning of the few unkilled wounded.

Trink's men began to pour out of the grass now, moving the few yards to the canoe landing area and the tunnel entrance, and forming a barrier to turn the blinded and stumbling Viet Cong to their right as they continued to claw their way out of the tunnel, and Minh's men moved in a semi circle to receive them as they came into the clear air, taking the weapons of the unseeing, unknowing few who were armed, and then forcing them to lie down side by side in the mud to gasp with streaming eyes and noses for fresh air. There was no resistance, they were docile as only the thoroughly defeated can be, and Minh's men were surprisingly gentle, guiding rather than pushing and forcing them down into prone ranks with an almost tender care. These men were Viet Cong and they were the enemy, but just now for this moment they were almost pitiful. Each must have been convinced that he was to die of suffocation and drowning in his own liquids and each must have been ready to trade his whole world and being for a single breath of uncontaminated fresh air, and even now as they breathed with slightly more ease, it would be a long time before all were completely recovered. Few would die, only those with bad hearts or defective lungs, but all would swear that they had never been nearer to death. Scott would understand, remembering his experiences in gas training where his exposure had been only a matter of seconds or at most minutes and of how the panicky fear that he might not ever get clear of the gas had welled up in him, even when he knew it was just a training exercise. While for these men it had been so very real, so agonizingly real that all would have run to their certain death in exchange for a moment's relief from the gas.

The flow of men had dwindled now to an intermittent and widely spaced crawling few, as Scott turned from the captives, well-guarded by Minh's men now reinforced by a part of Trink's, to the sound of incoming helicopters. Six of them, badly overloaded with fuel sacrificed for added troop lift capacity for the short hop from Ngo Tho, landed a short fifty yards downstream and were off again in the second as the troops came off in a rush, and with a Major leading came on the double to report to Trink where he stood now in front of the tunnel. It was all over now, Scott thought; King and his choppers would pour the troops into the area as fast as they could make the turn around and soon the entire area would be packed with Huu-Lac's soldiers and the careful exploration of the underground maze would begin. Soon, also, Captain Thrau would come up the narrow stream to receive the Viet Cong in his steaming hold where they would know a suffocation of a different kind for the short trip out of the swamp. The work was all done and the battle was over, the battle that was not a battle but a triumph of maneuver, and Scott's entire body knew the pain and fatigue he had so long refused to recognize. He placed his hand on Minh's shoulder and said, "I think I'll bug out on the next chopper that comes in. I'm feeling a little puny all of a sudden, and I could stand a couple of shots of booze and a bath." Even to his own ears his voice sounded cracked and strained as he ignored Minh's look of questioning concern, and walking carefully in his mud- and God-knew-what-else-caked fatigues, started toward Trink and his Major, just as the officer and his men moved out inland. Trink was going to start his tunnel clearing operation, first opening the covered vent holes and then working from these points inward.

There was a movement in the crumpled mass of bodies to the right of the tunnel mouth and even before Scott knew what he was really seeing, he lunged the last few paces just in time to shove the startled Trink roughly aside and out of the sweep of the knife and to meet a black-pajama-clad figure. He missed the knife with his left hand but his backhand right-handed judo chop caught the Viet Cong cleanly below the ear and the shock along his arm told him more clearly than the sight of the lolling head as the man fell that the part-time gardener, part-time guard was dead. Which he should have been a long time ago, Scott thought, as he watched him fall.

Things got a little hazy for Scott after that, and he could but vaguely remember being loaded in a helicopter with Minh for the trip back to the MAAG compound, being met by Albright and his garbled explanation that while he and his brother back in Saigon had effectively faked a complete breakdown of all communications for the last few days as per Scott's instructions, it had not resulted in their being left alone but had brought both General Wesley and Colonel Buckmeister in person here to Ngo Tho. Everyone was now at General Huu-Lac's headquarters where General Wesley was confronting Huu-Lac with the ultimatum to either call off his Cambodian border crossing or face dire consequences back in Saigon. He remembered even less well being half-carried by Albright and Minh to his room and his filthy clothing being cut with precise skill from his shaking body by Minh, using the same razor-sharp knife that had taken Huc's head, and his wondering what Minh had finally done with the head. And he remembered Kei and another housegirl carefully washing his racked body and Kei applying the crude bandage to the long but shallow cut on his ribs and his confusion as to how he had acquired it and Minh explaining that the pajama-clad guard had presented it to him in the act of dying. Most clearly he remembered the horrible cold and the teeth-chattering shivering of his body as he submitted to the ministrations of the two girls who cleaned his body while he was held in obviously naked erectness by Minh and Albright. And how the shivering had gone on and on even after he had been given a fearful slug of bourbon by Albright and put to bed and covered by a weight of blankets. And how Minh had finally ordered the two girls into bed with him, to press their warm bodies against him under the layers of blankets. Later he remembered Albright placing whiskey bottles filled with warm water along his feet and legs, and then he must have drifted off into sleep just as Minh was saying something to Albright about Huu-Lac and a doctor and other things to which he was too tired, too sick, to give his attention.

How long he slept he did not know but when he came awake it was instantly and from the sensual womb-like warmth of the bed to the chill of fresh air as the blankets were suddenly jerked off the bed. Sick as he was, there was no delay in the transition between sleep and awakening. Damned few colonels had a Major General forcibly remove the covering from their bed to find them naked and accompanied in the sack by two scantily clad young females and a collection of whiskey bottles. It was enough to bring anyone instantly and fully awake.

Wesley was rabid. No other word could describe his livid rage, so frothingly intense as he stood at the foot of the bed, that he was completely unintelligible. Only the constantly interspersed son of a bitch and drunken bastard and court-martial, and the less frequent disgrace to the uniform and not fit to be an officer came through to Scott coherently, but the idea was clear. He, Scott, had been drunk for days, had avoided contact with his General, and was a disgrace to the United States Army.

Scott's first reaction was one of vicious anger at the outrage of being so contemptuously exposed and subjected to such vilification and he lay for a moment with his eyes locked on Wesley and with his body struggling to catch up with his fully awakened mind. The two girls had left the bed almost with the movement of the thrown-back blankets and crouched in terror on the far side of the room behind Wesley.

Finally and when he felt capable of movement, he raised himself slowly and sat on the edge of his bed and with an expressionless face and a stony anger in his eyes turned his attention to the rest of the crowd in the room and in the doorway and the hallway outside. Buckmeister, viciously smug and with a we've-got-you-now-you-son of a bitch look of satisfaction on his face. Swann and Storm and Stowkowski with looks of apologetic horror on their faces. Albright almost in tears with rage and self-blame for allowing Wesley or anyone into the room. And dimly in the hallway some others, strained forward in unbelieving awe. A wave of dizziness overwhelmed him and he lowered his head for the seconds it took for it to pass and then, entirely ignoring Wesley and his uninterrupted flow of screaming invective and moving past Buckmeister, he took a pair of shorts from a drawer, and leaning unsteadily against the wall, got first one foot and then the other through the legs and drew them on. Albright was beside him in support when he stood erect and Swann handed him a fresh set of fatigues from his closet, and Scott began to dress, neither looking at or listening to General Wesley. He was still sick, very sick, and only his blind and unthinking rage kept him moving as he fumbled with the buttons of his jacket and unsteadily, still supported by Albright, drew on the trousers and finally went back to the bed to sit while he put on his socks and boots—his anger and his stubborn resolve that he would see both Wesley and Buckmeister in hell before he would say a single goddam word in defense or explanation carrying him on.

The housegirls broke Wesley's tirade as their terror finally gave way to their desire to escape this scene of mad and insane foreigners and they wiggled eel-like through the others to flee through the doorway. The silence was now broken only by Wesley's gasping breath as he paused for a moment and then said in a quiet voice, brutal and somehow more deadly than his shouting had been, "Swann, I thought you said this drunken bastard was on an operation somewhere?"

"He was, sir," Swann said calmly, with no fear in his voice and with no deference to rank, no sign that he was in any way intimidated by the brutality of Wesley's tone. "He must have just returned, and I think Colonel Leonard is sick, not drunk."

"You've got a badly misplaced sense of loyalty, young man," said Wesley with the same brutality and contemptuous deadliness, "And I didn't ask you for your opinion as to anyone's condition. Buckmeister, clear this room," he snapped, overriding Swann's attempt to speak further.

This was an angry Major General speaking now, not a hysterical madman, and everyone obediently turned toward the door. Even Albright, who had kneeled to help Scott with his boot laces, left half-finished and Buckmeister closed the door behind him with needless force and turned with almost greedy anticipation of what he hoped was to come.

"You, too, Colonel," Wesley said, without the brutality or contempt, but with the rage still in his voice although not directed toward Buckmeister. "Stand down the corridor and let no one in."

It was almost worth it, Scott thought, just to see the look of disappointment on Buckmeister's face as he reluctantly and slowly opened the door and softly closed it behind him. Although he would have bet on the bastard listening at the door. This was probably the juiciest morsel of his career and beyond his wildest hope of revenge. It was almost funny in a way, and Scott could feel the waning of his own rage with the thought of what a barracks story this would make when Wesley finally knew the truth and realized his mistake.

"I don't want to hear any sniveling explanation for this, Colonel Leonard," Wesley began as the door closed after Buckmeister, and Scott knew from his voice, almost shaking as he fought to hold on to some degree of calmness, that it was not going to be funny at all and that Wesley would never know the whole story. He would never listen. For the first time Scott began to realize the true seriousness of his situation and that he was not now dealing with a rational man. Progressing from rage at the manner of his awakening to half-hope that everything could be explained, Scott's mind now assumed an implacable and bleakly cold anger and with it a resolve to give no sign of a request for quarter or to offer any explanation or apology for anything. This was not a masochistic acceptance and urge for punishment; it was the deep-rooted stubborn fortitude of a man who would accept any outrageous accusation without reply, out of his certainty that there could be no justice now.

"I don't need any alibi for what I have seen for myself," Wesley continued, gaining control of his voice as he spoke, "and I absolutely promise you that I'm going to break you for this. I trusted you and fought Hankins to get you for this assignment and you let yourself fall as low as that drunken bum Huu-Lac and even falsified your reports to me so that I began to believe that Meir had been wrong and things were improving here. You repay me like this for all I've done, so here's what is going to happen to you, and I want you to know about it now so that you can think about it while you're waiting for the end."

Scott started to tell him not to bother, that he couldn't care less what he intended to do, and then as Wesley paused, he thought the better of it. So far he had not done a goddam thing wrong, as an even superficial investigation would prove, and there was no sense in blowing this position and opening himself to charges of insubordination by telling Wesley to shove it. Besides he was just too tired. He could feel some of the erectness go out of his spine as he sat on the edge of the bed with his half-laced boots, and no matter how hard he fought, a slow swelling tide of fatigue and pain began to creep over his body and a fuzzy veil came down over his mind. He knew what was going on, what was being said in Wesley's cruel savoring of his own words, and he didn't give an utter goddam.

"You know damned well our status of forces agreement with the Viets prevents me from holding a general court-martial in this country, and I don't choose to have it in Okinawa because your brother is there, so I'm going to ship you back to the States on a slow boat and arrange a proper reception for you there. You're going to be busted right out of the Army and you're going to lose everything you have worked for all your lousy life. I personally am going . . "

There was the faintest sound of a scuffle in the hallway and the door opened with an explosive force and banged hard against the wall. Scott's slow and tired gaze met Minh's as he stood in the doorway, still in his mud-caked fatigues, without a hat and looking like something out of a rice paddy. "General Wesley," he said courteously and quietly and in his surprising English, "I'd appreciate it very much if you'd instruct your people in a more mannerly approach to their duties. I didn't hurt that man in the hallway very much this time but I can't promise what will happen if he ever tries to lay a hand on me again."

"Who in the hell are you, and what in the hell do you think you're doing here?" barked Wesley in pugnacious amazement, as behind Minh in the hallway Buckmeister scrambled to his feet with an "I'm sorry General, but this man got by me by accident," and giving Minh a wide berth sidled into the room to stand beside Wesley. Accident, my ass, thought Scott, noting how Buckmeister avoided any contact with Minh and ironically wondering if he stood by Wesley to protect the General or for protection for himself.

Minh stood quietly as Buckmeister passed him, his slight

body so relaxed as almost to invite Buckmeister's renewal of whatever had gone on in the hallway, and then he spoke in the same quiet and polite voice, "I am Colonel Minh of the Army of the Republic of Viet Nam and I am here to announce the arrival of General Huu-Lac within the next few minutes. He wishes to visit your heroic Colonel Scott Leonard and to speak to you, General."

"Isn't that nice," said Wesley with heavy sarcasm. "I don't think we are interested in seeing your General again today." Clapping Buckmeister on the shoulder as he went toward the door, he said, "Get Leonard packed and out to my helicopter in five minutes. I'll go check the pilots and see if they are ready."

Minh stood aside in silence as Wesley went by him and down the hall, fast and almost stomping in his anger, and then turned from watching Wesley with a puzzled look on his face. "What's wrong with him, Scott, and what's this about you leaving here now? The General is on his way to see you and I have a doctor due here any minute. We will have a big celebration tonight with you as guest of honor if you feel well enough . . ."

"Colonel Scott, you heard the General," Buckmeister interrupted. "Get your gear packed and let's get out of here on the double." He was at his most pompous and officious best, only marred slightly by his uneasy glance at Minh.

Scott ignored him completely. "Minh," he said, "Things have gotten a little mixed up here, and I must go back to Saigon with my General. I can't explain, but I must ask that none of you, you or General Huu-Lac or anyone else, get into this." Above all, he did not want this to become an international incident, with a consequent loss of face on both sides when the truth came out, and he knew that that was exactly what would happen from any encounter between Wesley and Huu-Lac now. Wesley had passed the bounds of reason and in his anger he would reject any attempt at explanation with cutting rudeness, and Huu-Lac would not accept rudeness from any man. Any quarrel between them could not possibly help his situation, and could only seriously hurt the entire advisory effort in Viet Nam.

"But, Scott," Minh began, only to be cut off by Scott's urgent "I'm asking you a favor, Minh. Don't argue with me, but just accept what I say and get down to the gate and stop Huu-Lac from coming inside the compound. Keep him away from Wesley and don't ask me why now. Maybe I can explain later." Which was not exactly a lie, he thought, if for "later" one accepted "much, much later." He doubted that he would be in Saigon long enough to see Minh there and once on the way back to the States it would be a long, long time, if ever, before he returned to Viet Nam.

Minh hesitated only momentarily, starting once to speak, and then turned and was gone. Evidently I got through to him, Scott thought; Minh was one of those rarest of rare men who when a friend asked him to do something in a tone of voice that meant do-it-now, reacted to the urgency without question. A true friend.

"We're wasting time, Colonel Leonard," Buckmeister said nervously. "The General said five minutes and when he says that he means it. You'd better start packing."

Wearily and completely ignoring Buckmeister, Scott finished lacing his boots, and raising himself painfully and unsteadily from the edge of the bed, went to the table where his money and his cigarette lighter and the contents of his pockets lay, and opening a drawer, took out a fresh pack of cigarettes and his check book, and still ignoring Buckmeister, went straight out the door. He did not break his weary stride as Buckmeister called to him frantically to come back and pack; let the miserable bastard do it himself if he thought it important to appear with luggage as Wesley had ordered. For himself, he was beyond caring. He was clean now and when he got dirty he could buy something new, and it didn't look as if he would need uniforms much longer anyway. He could hear a flurry behind him as Buckmeister began opening drawers in random and frantic haste.

Minh met him at the top of the steps holding a cup of steaming liquid in his hand and accompanied by a tiny old Vietnamese dressed in a heavy black western-style suit. "This is the doctor, Scott," he said hastily, "Drink this now and take one of these packets in hot water every three or four hours for the next couple of days. Huu-Lac hasn't come yet. I'll get back to the gate."

Scott accepted the warm cup in his right hand and the handful of small rice-paper packets in his left as Minh turned and ran, and nodding a toast to the tiny doctor, drank it down in one continuous series of swallows. He was pleasantly surprised at the faintly citric, faintly mint, taste. He expected little or no effect and drank only as a courtesy to Minh and to this small doctor who had responded so quickly to Minh's request for help but as he shook the offered hand and allowed the man to turn back each of his eyelids in turn, and then again shook hands in farewell, he began to feel some faint sense of ease come to his body.

He had heard the chopper motor start as he left his room, and as he came into the bright glare of the sunshine to where Swann and Storm and Stowkowski and Albright were grouped around the doorway, he saw Wesley in stamping impatience at the edge of the landing pad. He also saw Huu-Lac's limousine, half-in, half-out of the gate, and Minh in animated explanation to General Huu-Lac and Kim as they got out and stood for a moment listening. Huu-Lac shook his head violently, and ignoring Minh's further protests, headed directly toward Wesley, walking quickly and with determination.

Scott shook Swann's hand from his arm, and with a quiet but hasty, "Take care of yourselves, gentlemen, and stay to hell out of this," he walked as quickly as he could, not to intercept Huu-Lac, who he knew would not listen to him any more than he had to Minh, but straight toward the helicopter, knowing that the best way to avoid trouble was to insure the fastest departure possible. His best speed was not very good speed at all, he realized, as Huu-Lac arrived where Wesley stood hands on hips and with his feet spread apart in an unyielding stance, but he did not slacken and bore straight past them to the doorway of the chopper and loaded himself painfully and slowly aboard. Huu-Lac had been shouting to make himself heard above the flapping roar of the helicopter and Wesley had been staring in unanswering and tight-lipped silence, and as Scott fastened his seat belt and Buckmeister came on the double carrying a lightly packed duffel bag and passed the two of them, Wesley turned with studiedly rude abruptness and came aboard himself without a backward glance.

They lifted off instantly and Scott watched as Huu-Lac stood alone, straight and motionless, with Swann and the others still grouped around the doorway and Minh and Kim still by the limousine in the gateway, and then the compound wall blocked his view and they began their hell-for-leather, tree-top-level flight back. He glanced straight ahead and then slept all the way to Saigon.

it is at that, Scott," he said tiredly and with a rueful smile. "All the time you were talking I was thinking of a kid I knew once who was deathly afraid of snakes, so afraid that once a little girl ran him all over the neighborhood and sent him into hysterics with a little old dead garter snake. Were there any snakes in all that swamp, Scott?"

"Millions of them, Boyd," answered Scott with the slightest of involuntary shudders, and with an answering smile. "And that little boy hasn't changed much over the years, but I knew they were there long before we ever went in. They were all around Bac Lu too."

"Yeah, I guess you did, Scott," Boyd said with a resigned sadness. "Well, you don't need to worry about me and my promise. You can play it your own way from here on in." He went on across the room to the door and out with a "I'll be back in a little while," as he closed the door.

The air conditioner created a fearful din in the silence that lingered after Boyd's departure, a silence that neither Scott nor Allan seemed in any hurry to break. Scott's health had improved amazingly, due in part to the packets of whatever it had been that Minh and the little Viet doctor had given him, and in part to the surgeon, Colonel Lang, who had come and gone during the telling of his story. Come in surly bad temper that he, the ranking surgeon in the command should be compelled by the sheer force of Boyd's rank and personality to make a house call, and left long after he had completed his work on Scott, cursing the fact of a surgery appointment and swearing that all he had heard was privileged information, doctor-patient, but that Boyd must tell him the ending. And taking the last of the packets Scott had been given for analysis, he left.

It was hard to imagine how absolutely lousy he had felt during the past few days and as recently as twenty-four hours ago, Scott thought, standing and stretching his arm for the ceiling in sheer animal pleasure. Not that he felt too damned good in his mind though, he admitted to himself as he padded across to his footlockers, which through some miracle wrought by Captain Thompson had been retrieved out of a warehouse in Saigon and flown here and delivered to him an hour ago, along with the rest of his clothing, which by an even greater miracle had come all the way from Ngo Tho. There was something awe-inspiring in the things that your subordinates could do for you, once you convinced them you were worthy of their best efforts.

He was as depressed as he had ever been or was likely to

get. Although he had faith in the system and believed that when the entire story was known he would be vindicated, it was still a messy business—all courts-martial were, no matter what the charge, what the circumstances, or whether the man was judged guilty or innocent. And with always a cloud hanging over a man even when he was exonerated, since there were always some who would believe that no matter what the verdict, where there had been smoke there must have been fire. No man goes through life without acquiring a few enemies, and all these would pounce on his misfortune as on a treasure, to be fondled and savored and passed on and on and back and forth, until in the repeated telling and retelling there would be only a coincidental resemblance to the truth. While he was as impervious to the opinion of the damnable crowd as any man, still, no one is completely invulnerable. So even with acquittal he would not come off free, and he had no assurance at all of actually gaining such a verdict. General Wesley was an opponent he would not choose if he had any say in the matter, for he would be absolutely implacable. Silently he added up the charges, dredging the far depths of memory for the details he once knew in the days when he had been a captain and a major and had served as both Trial Judge Advocate and Defense Counsel in the many courts-martial that were once a part of the training of young officers. Drunk on duty, conduct unbecoming to an officer and gentleman, failure to report, gross dereliction of duty—all the sonorous and majestic and somehow guilt-establishing phrases ran in wild cacophony through his mind. And along this line lies the way to the psycho ward, he thought. Sufficient to the day is the evil thereof, and his court-martial might never come to pass.

"What's your best estimate of what is going to happen to you now, Scott?" Allan asked, as if reading Scott's mind. "Surely you're not really worried about Wesley. While he may file an initial report with the Department of Army based on his present rage, sure as hell someone is finally going to give the true story. Maybe your friend Colonel Dodds, or maybe through Huu-Lac going up through Vietnamese channels and the story coming down through Hankins' headquarters."

"Of course I'm worried, Allan. I'd be an idiot not to be. Justice is a fine concept, like the idea that virtue is its own reward, but still things don't always work out the way they should. True, I don't worry about being convicted, but that's the worst thing that could happen, and it's still bad enough to have to stand trial in the first place. You know that as well as I do, don't you?"

"I know," said Allan. "I also know that Jim Young of AP is in Saigon, and all I'd have to do is give him the bare outline of what you've told us this morning and he'd dig the rest out and have a story on the wires that would make any accusation of you by Wesley completely ridiculous."

"Absolutely, no," said Scott, without heat or in the tone he had used with Boyd. He feared no change of mind in Allan. Once he had given his word he would keep it, even though he might bitterly regret his commitment. There was no threat in Allan the way there had been in Boyd; he was merely exploring Scott's determination to play the game by the rules laid down, unfair as they were.

"You're really not very smart, Scott," he said mildly. "If you were in battle you'd use every weapon at hand and every advantage of terrain and maneuver. Above all things you wouldn't fight by any rules laid down by the enemy. But now, when you're in a fight of a different kind but almost equally serious, you allow yourself to be hamstrung without real protest."

"So I'm not smart, Allan, but I am a soldier and I have written orders which cannot be misunderstood, and soldiers obey orders whether they like them or not. I'll be damned and double-damned before I'll let either you or Boyd get mixed up in this. and that's the way it's going to be, so there is no sense in even talking about it any more. Besides, while Boyd is gone I feel I owe you some sort of explanation about Cindy, and our troubles."

"You owe me exactly nothing, Scott," Allan said evenly. "She's my sister and I love her very much but she's your wife first of all, and while I hate to see that you two have drifted so far apart, it's probably none of my business."

"Probably it isn't," Scott said thoughtfully, "But it might make it a little easier on Cindy and your relationship with her if you understood things a little better. Just in case you are ever inclined to take sides, because I have a feeling that most of our troubles are my fault. There's not going to be a divorce, neither one of us wants that, and I believe that when I finally retire, which may be a lot sooner than I had planned after Wesley gets done, we'll go back to living together. I'm the one who moved out in the first place and I've always known she's waiting for me to come back."

Slowly he began the polishing of his uniform insignia,

using the dregs of a can of "Brasso" and a torn and blackened undershirt, and carefully fastening each gleaming piece to the lapels of his tropical worsted blouse, only slightly wrinkled from shipment. Allan sat in silence, without any expression of encouragement and perhaps with an air of reluctance.

"You're allowed a few questions, you know, as long as you ask them before Boyd gets back. I don't want him involved in any way. He thinks so much of Cindy that he's liable to get a little emotional and there is no sense in getting him all upset in the little while left before I go aboard the *Buckner*."

"No questions, Scott," Allan said with a wry smile. "And no advice, lectures, or philosophical observations, or anything else except to say that I knew you had been having trouble before today, and that I hope things work out. And don't underestimate Boyd or the extent of his knowledge. What I know he also knows and that's a damned sight more than you may suspect. And don't get indignant; after all Boyd and I have common relatives and when we run out of high level military and diplomatic subjects, which doesn't take long, we talk about these relatives, which is a perfectly natural thing to do. Just because Boyd doesn't mention the subject to you doesn't mean that he isn't concerned and worried.

"That's quite surprising, that you two can't find something better to talk about than my personal life," Scott said in quick anger and resentment. "Almost as surprising as the fact that Boyd hasn't given me the word on how we make everything all wine and roses again, although he probably will when he gets back."

"Bite your tongue, you ungrateful bastard," Allan said, only slightly raising his voice but with an incisiveness that showed his irritation. "You've built up such an unreasoning complex about Boyd's older brother protectiveness over the years that you don't even realize that he stopped it long ago. It may make you a better army officer, this idea of taking no help from anyone, but this constant needling and belligerence around Boyd makes for a damned dull and uncomfortable time as far as I'm concerned. Really, you ought to consider that almost anyone could come here and tell a story about Wesley as you have and Boyd would feel that he should do something. It's a damned miracle to me that he doesn't tell you to go to hell and do what he thinks is right and forget this silly business of giving his word to you."

Scott was thunderstruck. Allan had always been the uncritical and silent observer, with never a word of advice or direction for his family or personal friends. No one ever really knew what Allan thought on any subject except from his writing, and never before had he spoken to Scott in such a tone of irritation, certainly never with contempt.

Shamed, silent, Scott finished polishing his brass and slowly began to dress. Allan was right, he knew, but still, old emotions and old prejudices die hard, just like old dreams. A man could make all his decisions on the basis of pure logic and fact in his professional life, but when it came to family and personal relations all was shaded by love, or hate, or resentment, or envy, or a formless amalgamation of all these. Even an understanding of himself, a knowing that the jealous guarding of his independence against Boyd was a prejudice from his childhood and a flouting of logic, didn't really change things much. He was still himself and about the best he could hope for was to live within his own code, and still avoid hurting too much those he loved.

Allan said no more, nor would he, if he knew Allan. He never spoke thoughtlessly, and he almost never spoke harshly or passed judgment. But when he did it was done, and there was no retreating, no apology. He thought that Scott was unreasonable in his fight for independence from Boyd and his refusal of all assistance, and although it wouldn't affect his friendship, he would go on thinking it. Just as he probably thought that his attitude toward Cindy was unreasonable. But what the hell, you can't have the good opinion of everybody, all the time.

Boyd came through the door, the air conditioner having obscured the sound of the arrival of his staff car. "Well, Scott, I guess it's about time to get you down to the pier," he said, with only friendliness and maybe a trace of sorrow in his voice. "It will take us about twenty minutes to get you there and they like to have everyone on board well ahead of sailing, so let's get moving. Unless you want to change your mind. It would be very simple for me to countermand Wesley's orders and detail you to some special duty here in Oki for the next ten or fifteen days, maybe time enough for things to get sifted out in Saigon."

"No thanks, Boyd," Scott said gently, mindful of Allan's outburst about his attitude toward Boyd. "All the sifting out in the world will never change Wesley and I might as well get on my way. What I think I'll do, in all seriousness, is put in for retirement the minute I step off the boat in San Francisco, and get a job with some research outfit in Washington and become a real elder-statesman-type thinker."

"So be it, Scott," said Boyd with the same friendliness. "I just thought I'd ask on the off chance you'd acquired some instinct for self-preservation while I've been gone."

Together they knelt and closed the footlockers and the houseboys loaded them and the rest of Scott's gear in the trunk of Boyd's car, and they were off—Scott and Boyd in the back seat and Allan beside the driver. Silently. Everything to be said had been said.

Scott rode unseeing, lost in his thoughts and entirely oblivious of the country, the people, the traffic. He really wished that he could be different, that he could take the easy way out in accepting either Boyd's help or Allan's offer to alert the press in Saigon, but he couldn't change without losing something of himself, some sacrifice of the principles he had lived by all these years and some real loss of his self-respect. And that's about all you're going to have left, he thought, so you'd better hang onto it with all you've got. That and Cindy. And somehow he felt differently about her now than he had in years. He was beginning to see that it was Scott Leonard who was wrong in it all, not Cindy. Intead of cherishing her in her fear he had insisted that she not be afraid, that she be cured and without flaw, and when it proved to be impossible to banish the nightmare that she had lived with for so many years he had rejected her. Maybe it was not too late.

"There's your home for the next twenty-odd days," said Boyd, breaking the silence as the road straightened out of the series of switchbacks coming down into the port area. The pier lay straight ahead with the MSTS *Simon Buckner* alongside. There was the usual confusion of sailing, people mounting the gangway, people already aboard lining the rail, and those on the pier waving and shouting unheard farewells, and the din of an Army band only occasionally rising above the hubbub. And incredibly, completely out of place in this scene, a giant in filthy fatigues and a grimly worried look on his red and flushed face stepped forward to open the car door. Zeke Dodds, in the sweating flesh.

"Jesus, I'm glad I found you," he said to Scott, relief in his voice. "I just got off the plane and came straight here. I didn't know the sailing time for sure and I couldn't afford to waste time looking all over the island for you."

"Did you come all the way from Saigon just to kiss this chowderhead good-bye?" asked Boyd in a gratingly amused voice. "They must have a damned liberal leave policy down there to allow something like this."

"Excuse me, General," Zeke said, acknowledging Boyd's presence for the first time. "But I'm not on leave. I'm here by direction of some high brass in Saigon, including General Hankins, with instructions to return with one each Colonel Scott Leonard as soon as possible. Scott, I commandeered an MP jeep and you can either ride with me, or you can follow me back to the field. The crew should be refueled by now and we've got to get going."

"What about Wesley . . ." Scott began, to be interrupted by Boyd. "Allan get in the back seat with us so that monster can get in the car. And you, Dodds, get in here and tell us what's going on. If you think you and Scott are going merrily down the road in that jeep and get on a plane and go off into the wild blue yonder without me knowing what's going on you're out of your mind."

Allan was out in the instant and squeezed himself in beside Scott. Zeke carefully and laboriously lowered himself into the front seat, and half turned so that he faced the three of them. The car sagged noticeably.

"What about Wesley?" asked Scott again. "Did he change his mind?"

"He hasn't got a mind to change now," answered Zeke squirming to get comfortable as the driver put the car in gear and turned in a slow half-circle through the milling gala crowd. "Last night as he and Buckmeister and Captain Thompson were in his office, working on his statement of charges against you, he had some kind of stroke. Thompson got a medic there in record time but they couldn't bring him back to consciouness, and after working on him in Saigon they decided it was best to evacuate him to Clark Air Force Base in the Philippines and then probably on back to the States. None of the medics held out much hope of his recovery and I'm not sure that they even expect him to live." Zeke spoke with the casual, almost calloused, tone of a man who had seen so many come and go, through death in combat, from disease, from accident, that personal disaster was a familiar and constant, though unlovely companion. Beneath his words, however, there rang a note of regret and sadness, which had its response in Scott, and in Boyd, and even Allan who had known Wesley but slightly.

"Once he was a great soldier," said Scott thoughtfully, without thinking of what this might mean to him personally. "I think he must have been on the verge of something like this for a long time."

"He was indeed a soldier, gentlemen," said Boyd, "and at one time, back in World War II, I would have bet anything I owned on his becoming Chief of Staff of the Army one day—he was that much better than the rest of us. Let's hope he isn't going to die, but if I know him he'd rather be dead than half alive."

Allan broke the short silence, his reporter's mind passing from the fact of Wesley's collapse as an incidental and probably unimportant item of information, to the main story.

"That's not the reason you're here after Scott, is it Colonel Dodds?" he asked.

Zeke's face cleared of its momentary solemnity as he smiled his wide and joyful smile. "You can bet it isn't. There's a countrywide search on for Scott, conducted mostly by Vietnamese who seem to think fairly highly of his ability, and assisted by a number of U.S. types, like the top brass, who have more than a passing interest in maintaining some accord with the Government of the Republic of Viet Nam. Even with everyone searching we might not have found out where Scott was so soon if Wesley had not had his stroke and Captain Thompson had not then felt free to tell how you had been bootlegged here to Okinawa, but we would have eventually found you and even if it had meant turning the *Buckner* around, I think it would have been done."

"What makes Scott so much in demand all of a sudden?" asked Boyd gruffly, with maybe just a trace of pleasure in his voice.

"Well, while it isn't exactly a true statement of the situation, he is credited with being the astute mind that uncovered the first link in a Viet Cong spy chain that ran clear from Colonel Yuan in Ngo Tho to the top of the Department of Defense in Saigon. In the last several hours there have been heads rolling like cabbages throughout the country, and in Saigon especially. Huu-Lac has moved in from Ngo Tho and he and Minh and Minh's uncle, the General, seem to be conducting a combination of investigation and purge. It's going to be brutal for a little while, but what is going to come out of it is an army that is clean and completely loyal. It's far from a democratic process, but these people must do things their own way."

221

For the first time since seeing Zeke, Scott truly realized that he was out of the woods and in no danger, and relief came flooding through him. Relief and curiosity and a thousand details he wanted to know. "What happened in Ngo Tho? Did Yuan actually talk?"

"Minh tells me he talked quite freely and at length after a three-hour private interview with an old man named Chieu, during which time Yuan seemingly had a defective eyeball removed by some sort of slow surgical process. He is alive and well now, and is in Saigon and still talking almost constantly."

"Jesus," said Scott with horror. He knew that the customs of the country must be respected and that their rules of the game must prevail, but he thought of how reluctant he would be himself to be questioned by the old man.

"And Gaston, you remember my friend the Frenchman, the one with the marvelous food. He was one of them too, and Minh assures me that he is still alive, and is providing a great deal of worthwhile information. I think Minh personally gelded him. After all, he fooled Minh as well as me and a number of others, and Minh doesn't exactly take to being fooled."

"So who will I be working with in Ngo Tho now? Will Trink take command or do you know yet?" asked Scott with eagerness. He was suddenly, wildly, impatient to be on his way back, to get on the job again, and to see the rewards of their killing in the swamp in the quiet and order restored to the province, and in the increased rice productivity, and maybe even the reopening of some of the rubber plantations.

They had entered the airfield and shot across a runway to pull up beside a C-130, and with their arrival the pilots and the crew who had been resting in the shade of a wing scrambled to their feet and went aboard on the double. When Zeke said they were going back without delay he meant it.

Zeke sat for a moment, still turned in the seat to face them, and with his eyes on Scott, said with a pitying shake of his head, "You either don't listen very well or you don't think about what you're hearing. Huu-Lac is almost bound to end up as Chief of State; you know how well he has run his province and made it a model of how the whole country should be administered. And I understand from General Hankins that Huu-Lac thinks you'd be a mighty fine replacement for Wesley, in charge of all advisory effort in the country. They may even pin a star on you, boy."

"Come on, Scott," Boyd said opening his door. "Let's get aboard and out of here. Right now you're AWOL from your unit and I want no part of harboring any fugitives."

The plane motors came to life with a deafening stuttering roar, and they began to taxi forward toward the runway, almost before the crew chief could help Scott and Zeke aboard.